Sue Ellen Learns To Dance

And Other Stories

by

Judy Alter

Panther  Creek Press
Spring, Texas

Cover design by Adam Murphy
Houston, Texas
Photo by Dorothea Lange © 1936
For the US Office of War Information
To the Library of Congress
Now in public domain

Printed and bound at
Houston Datum, Inc.
8888 Monroe Road
Houston, Texas

Library of Congress Cataloging-in-Publication Data

Alter, Judy.
    Sue ellen learns to dance and other stories/ by Judy Alter

0-9771797-3-7

I. Title   II. Author   III Texas Short fiction

ISBN   0-9771797-3-7

For Maddie, Edie, Sawyer, and Morgan

Contents

Sue Ellen Learns to Dance

"Sue Ellen!" He cut the engine on the clattering Model A truck, in 1934 some ten years old and threatening always to fall apart. When he raised his voice again, impatience rang in it. "Sue Ellen!" He stayed in the car and waited.

She came to the door carrying a child on her hip, though the child was plainly old enough to walk on his own. Still, his arms encircled his mother's neck with a tenacity that indicated he would not easily be put down. Sue Ellen Flett was a lean woman with lank hair, faded to the pale yellow of corn silk. She wore a shapeless cotton dress and over it, an apron that clearly said "Burrus Flour Mills" across the front. With her free hand, she pushed her hair behind her ear. The other hand held tight to the child.

"What is it, Alvis?" Her voice was soft and tired, lacking the life of his impatience.

"Ma says Grammy's dyin' and we got to go to Kaufman."

"Go to Kaufman?" she echoed. From where she stood, on the slanted porch of a rough board-and-batten shack near Eden in South Central Texas, Kaufman, beyond Dallas, deep in East Texas, might as well be as far as the moon. Then, though, she said softly, "Your grammy's dying?"

He scoffed. "She won't die. That woman's got too much sin stored up in her. She'd go straight to hell, and she's knows it."

"She's not a sinful woman," Sue Ellen said mildly. She looked at him. He was thirty, looked fifty and, she often thought, acted sixty. When she married him, he was twenty-two and stood straight and tall, his eyes sparkling with laughter. But that was before the rain stopped and all of West Texas turned to dust that blew away if you looked at it and the bank took their farm up to Kaufman, where they'd both been raised. Now they sharecropped a tiny, worthless piece of land. Konrad Schwartz, the German farmer who owned the land, provided a tractor, fuel and seed, and they farmed on halves. The parcel of blown-away land was all mesquite stumps and rattlesnakes, and they made a poor crop. She worried about the children, who went too many days without meat and milk, and she worried about Alvis and herself, who were cross, tired and hopeless most of the time.

7

At least, she told herself ten times a day, they lived in a house. Not much of one—a shack some would call it, with slanted floors and cracks so large between the siding boards that she could look out at night from her bed and watch the stars. But there were folks in this region, she knew, who'd lived in half dugouts not more than ten years ago. No, Sue Ellen counted herself lucky to have a house.

"Well," she said, looking at him, "I reckon Grammy Flett can't put it off forever. If it's her time, it's her time." She barely got the words out before a young girl of six banged through the screen door, letting it slam behind her and ignoring the precarious way it bounced on its hinges.

"Don't slam the door," Sue Ellen said automatically, while the girl asked, "Who's got sin in their soul, Papa?"

Sue Ellen gave him a long, hard look and then said to the girl, "No one, Marisue. Your papa didn't mean that."

"My grandmother's dyin'," he told the child, ignoring that he had made his wife unhappy and that the child would instantly know it was his grandmother who had sin in her soul.

"Is she goin' to Hell when she dies, Papa?" Marisue asked.

He opened his mouth, but Sue Ellen spoke too quickly for him. "Of course she's not goin' to Hell, Marisue. How you do talk. You remember Grammy Flett. She always gave you candy, and you used to like to sit on her lap when you was little."

"I disremember," Marisue said.

"Well," Sue Ellen said, turning her back on her husband and leading the children inside, "it's been a long while since you saw her. Grammy Flett's old, near ninety I think."

"Are we going to see her?"

Sue Ellen sighed. "I guess we'll have to." Turning, she asked over her shoulder, "Where's Albert?"

"I left him in town, swamping out Tubbs' store. He'll walk home."

She turned without another word. It was, she knew, a long walk for a child of eight to make alone, but no harm would come to him. And she'd save back a potato for his supper.

That night, to Alvis' back, because now he always turned away from her in bed, she said, "I hope to heaven that rickety truck will make it to Kaufman."

"It'll have to," he muttered.

She wanted to reach out and touch him, rub his back, riffle his hair, but she knew he would flinch and pull away. "Can't feed no more babies," he'd told her the last time she'd tried to touch him in his privates. Instead, she asked,

"Why do you say she's so sinful her soul's goin' to Hell?"

He groaned, a sure sign he didn't want to talk about it. At last, after a long moment, he spoke. "Ma told me. She . . . she was . . . you know . . . one of those women, back when cowboys were the law in West Texas. She . . . ." It was obviously hard for him to bring the words out. "She . . . danced in saloons in Fort Worth, that kind of thing."

"Grammy Flett?" Sue Ellen sat straight up in bed, barely remembering to pull the covers up to hide herself. She thought this was surely the most astounding news she'd ever heard . . . and the very thought of Grammy Flett dancing in a saloon somehow lightened and lifted Sue Ellen's mood. But she could never tell Alvis that.

"Family's been ashamed ever since," he said stiffly. "We don't talk about it."

"Your family's still ashamed about something that happened... what? fifty, sixty years ago?" She could never give voice to the thought that was really on her mind, for it was almost envy . . . envy of Grammy Flett and the good times she must have known.

"Don't do to have bad blood," he said, muffling his voice in the pillow.

"Well, I'll be!" And with that, Sue Ellen lay back down in the bed, pulled the covers to her chin, and lay with wide open eyes half the night.

The truck ground to a stop short of Fort Worth. From Eden, they'd gone north to Ballinger, then angled over to Brownwood, on to Comanche, and finally to Cleburne, all the while bouncing over rutted roads so rough that Sue Ellen ached in every bone in her back and bottom. Dust blew in at them, but Sue Ellen had been covered by dust for so long now she paid it no mind. Her skin had turned a nut-brown color, and fleetingly she sometimes thought of her mother's admonition to always wear a poke bonnet, lest your skin acquire an unbecoming darkness. Hers had, and it was too late to worry about it.

The baby in her arms cried, and in the back, supposedly resting on a pallet, Marisue whined about needin' to use the restroom and wantin' to sleep and when were they gonna' get there. Albert sat stoic, staring over the boards of the pickup bed at the passing dry land.

Sue Ellen looked at her children, their faces wary and unsmiling, their clothes soiled with ground-in grime that would not come out no matter how hard she scrubbed, their feet bare and dirty. She sighed and turned back to stare sightlessly at the road before them.

When the children finally slept, Sue Ellen said, "She wasn't sinful, you know. Grammy Flett's one of the best persons I ever met. I wouldn't have a problem lettin' my soul follow hers."

He gripped the wheel tightly and stared straight ahead at the rutted road. "You can send your soul wherever you want. I know I'm obeying the Good Book."

"It says," she whispered, "love thy brother . . . and that means thy sister . . . and thy grandmother too."

Alvis didn't answer.

They were just beyond Cleburne, some thirty miles from Fort Worth, when they hit a deep rut in the road, bounced badly, and heard a clattering sound. In seconds, the car died.

"What'd you do?" Sue Ellen asked.

"I didn't do nothin'," he said angrily. "The thing just stopped." He got out to study around the car. Finally, at a loss to do anything else, he crawled under it. After what seemed forever to Sue Ellen, Alvis emerged, holding up a squarish metal pan—something, she thought, she might have baked in if she ever could bake again.

"Oil pan," he said. "Guess it got bounced off."

"What's that mean?"

"Means the engine ain't got no oil, and it's froze up. Probably ruined."

"We might just as well walk back to that last town," Sue Ellen said, "get something for the children to eat." Her own stomach gnawed at her, but she would not eat.

"What you gonna buy it with?" he asked. "Your good looks?"

She wanted to tell him there was no call to be mean, but she kept quiet.

10

"No sense goin' backward," he declared. "We'll hitch to Fort Worth."

Leaving the car that much farther behind, she thought.

Hot and dusty, they waited by the side of the road for a ride, the baby crying all the louder when Alvis took him to relieve her and Marisue whining all the more, saying she'd just sit in the shade and wait for them to come back for the car.

"What shade?" Albert asked, scorn in his voice.

Finally a farmer in a Model A stopped for them. Alvis sat in the front, while Sue Ellen and the youngsters crowded into the back. The farmer made laconic conversation about car trouble and having a passel of kids, and it was plain to see he was glad he was not part of this pitiful family. In Fort Worth, he let them out at a garage where he, personally, recommended the honesty of the owner.

"Lost the oil pan?" The man snorted. "Aint' no use to go look at it. Bet you ruined the motor."

Alvis nodded sagely. He thought so too.

Sue Ellen protested. "Can't you at least go see if you can fix it?"

"Lady, you want me to charge you $30 for telling you what I already know? The engine's burnt out, running with no oil, even for a little bit."

Sue Ellen stared off at the concrete around her and clutched Marisue to her.

The mechanic took them to a church with a soup kitchen for the homeless, and they were fed the best hot meal they'd had in months—soup, corn, potatoes and fresh homemade bread—and Sue Ellen tried to ignore Alvis' mutterings, "We ain't like these people. Don't need no charity."

Finally, she poked him hard in the ribs and said, "Without it, we wouldn't be eatin'. I ain't too proud to feed my children on charity if I got to."

When their plight was made known to the pastor of the church, bus tickets to Kaufman shortly appeared.

"Don't know when I can repay you," Alvis muttered.

"No matter," the pastor said. "It is our mission to help those in need. Go with God."

They rode to Kaufman, Sue Ellen holding the baby, Albert staring out the window, and Marisue dozing in her seat.

"You gonna' be nice to Grammy Flett?" Sue Ellen asked him.

"'Course I'll be nice. She's my grandmother, ain't she?"

"You think she's sinful . . . and I, well, I just think it's sinful you feel that way."

"Who's sinful?" Marisue asked shrilly. "Are you talking about Grammy Flett again. What'd she do?"

"Hush and go to sleep," her father told her. "Don't be tellin' everyone on this bus our family business."

There were three other passengers, none of whom appeared to have heard the outburst.

From Kaufman, it was no trick to find a ride to the Flett family farm.

Mama Flett greeted them at the door, hugging the children and telling Alvis, "It's good you got here, son."

"Thought you might need me," he muttered, and that was as close to affection as the two of them came.

But Sue Ellen got a hug and a murmured, "I am glad to see you, child. You're lookin' thin. I got chicken and dumplings on the stove."

Sue Ellen knew that, from the smell that filled the rambly old white clapboard house that had belonged to Alvis' grandparents and had stayed in the family by hook or by crook all these years. Alvis' father was gone now, some five years—just up and left he did one day, Mama Flett had told them. Nobody knew if he'd run off, though that seemed unlikely, or if he'd hurt himself back in the wilds of the piney woods, hunting alone in some place so remote that nobody had yet stumbled on his body. His huntin' dog had come home three days later, but he hadn't been real communicative about what had happened to his master.

Sue Ellen didn't understand—and never would—how Mama and Grammy lived, beyond that truck garden in the back of the house, but they survived nicely, much more nicely than she and Alvis and the children.

While Marisue clamored for dinner and Albert stood staring hungrily at the stove, Mama Flett reached for the baby. "She's in there," she said to Alvis, motioning with her head toward a room off the kitchen that had apparently been turned into a sickroom. "But she's outa' her head, talkin' strange, she is."

With a finger to the lips to caution the children to be quiet, Alvis led his family into the sickroom. Grammy Flett barely made a bump under the thin coverlet spread over her. She lay on her back, eyes wide open and staring at the ceiling, hands folded over her chest as though she were anticipating death and willing to save the undertaker at least the chore of arranging those hands with their paper-thin skin.

"She's singing," Marisue stage-whispered, and Alvis drew back a hand as though to cuff her.

But Marisue was right. A weak, high, reedy sound came from the bed, and looking close, Sue Ellen could see the thin chest rise a little and the pinched mouth moving ever so slightly.

Alvis was clearly disconcerted. "How're you doin', Grammy Flett?" he asked in a voice so loud and hearty that even Albert jumped a little.

Her eyes turned slowly, as though making an effort to focus on this new person. Then, smiling ever so slightly, she said, "I been dancin'. You know, at Uncle Windy's in Fort Worth . . . in the Acre." Her voice was whispery.

"Hush, now," he said too harshly. "We don't want to be hearin' about that."

She paid him no mind and what back to her singing.

Back in the kitchen, Albert carefully asked, "What was she talkin' about? Uncle Windy's and the acre?"

"Nothin' for you to know," his father told him harshly, and Albert subsided, but not before Sue Ellen saw the resentment in his eyes. Had it been up to her, she'd have filled Albert with the little knowledge she had: Grammy Flett had been a dancehall girl in Fort Worth before the turn of the century, when Hell's Half Acre was the flourishing sin district in that town. Oh, Grammy had never been a whore—Alvis had made that point clear and Sue Ellen chose to believe it. But Alvis did not want his son to know even the varnished truth.

They ate mightily of chicken and dumplings, fresh tomatoes off the vine, green beans that had cooked their way to mushiness the whole day, and a blueberry pie. "I'm sorry I ain't got no cream for the pie," Mama Flett apologized.

"Is she all right at night?" Sue Ellen asked as she dried the dishes for her mother-in-law.

Mama sighed. "I been mostly sleeping in that chair in her room. Don't sleep too good, but if I was to come and find her gone some morning, I couldn't live with myself."

"I'll sit with her tonight," the younger woman volunteered.

"Land's sake, you had that hard trip. I'll hear no such thing."

"I want to, I really want to." And Sue Ellen found that she did want to, indeed was almost desperate for time alone with Grammy.

"You sure?"

"I'm sure."

And so, by ten o'clock, they were all packed off to bed, even the baby whom Mama Flett took to sleep with her. Albert, feeling big and manly, took a blanket and went to the loft in the barn, and Marisue curled into a big double bed all by herself. Alvis chose to sleep on the sofa, lest he be needed in the night, so he said, but Sue Ellen knew after that big dinner she wouldn't be able to rouse him if she needed him.

She took a last cup of coffee and went to sit by Grammy's bed in a big old rocker. Setting her coffee down, she reached for one of those thin, frail hands that were all bone and no flesh and held it in her own browned and roughened hand. "Sing to me again, Grammy."

Grammy had been dozing, but she roused now, turning her head ever so slightly toward Sue Ellen and staring at her. Then the thin voice raised in a song Sue Ellen knew was not a hymn. Sue Ellen closed her eyes and let her mind drift, holding that hand and listening to the weird music.

"We danced, you know," Grammy said, suddenly stopping her singing.

The sound of her talking voice startled Sue Ellen awake. "Yes...yes, Grammy, I know you danced. . . . I . . . I think it must have been wonderful."

"Not always," she said, "but sometimes . . . not when you were dancing for pay with men you didn't like. But when we'd dance for ourselves . . . and the music made you feel free and alive . . . and I wasn't beholden to no one then . . . no parents, no husband, no children, just me!" She paused to catch her breath.

"I was young . . . and pretty"—it seemed not to shame her to

14

admit that openly—"and I had lots of young men courtin' me. I've carried those memories all my life."

"Were you . . . Grammy . . . did you do anything sinful?" Sue Ellen bit her lip, knowing she'd overstepped the bounds with the question.

Grammy snorted. "Sinful? Not on your life. I was raised Baptist and dancing was sin enough . . . but no, I was never wicked."

And they both knew what she meant.

"Tell me," Sue Ellen said, "about the music again and how you've heard it all your life."

And so, late into the night, Grammy Flett—spurred by an energy nobody thought she had any longer—talked about life in the city. And sometimes she'd stop talking to sing a while. And then she'd talked again.

Listening, her eyes closed, Grammy's hand still clutched in hers, Sue Ellen ever so briefly felt that she too heard the music and that she was free and young and beautiful and happy. And she knew that Grammy was giving her a dream that she would carry through her life.

In the morning, Mama Flett found Sue Ellen sound asleep in the rocker. Grammy Flett had gone to her reward, her hand still clutched in Sue Ellen's and the corners of her mouth lifted as though she were smiling . . . or singing.

Sue Ellen and Alvis never went back to Eden. Abandoning the car outside Fort Worth and the furniture and clothes in their shack at Eden, they stayed in Kaufman, where Alvis farmed and eventually, when the Depression wore itself out, became a man of some small means, free of debt at least, though he never lost his dour and pessimistic streak . . . and he never liked to talk about Grammy Flett. Sue Ellen fixed chicken and dumplings and blueberry pie for her children and grandchildren and tended the truck garden and kept the house . . . but sometimes, they'd find her staring off out the window, singing a strange song none of them recognized. And when they'd call her back to the present moment, she always had a smile.

Fool Girl

"Josie!" Pa's voice boomed out so loud and sudden that I almost dropped my broom.

"Yes, Pa?" I was in no hurry about sticking my head out the door of our dogtrot cabin. Pa always wanted something—a horse's hoof held while he repaired a shoe, someone to carry the other end of a log, someone to curry his two workhorses. Pa should have had ten sons, but he only had me, a fourteen-year-old daughter. Still, I thought I was about as good at most chores as any boy.

"The workhorses are gone!" he thundered, and it's a wonder every Indian from here to the reservation didn't hear him.

Pa had set our cabin square in the middle of the North Texas prairie when he first came home from the War Between the States. He was determined to farm, but three years running his luck had been bad and there'd been no crops to speak of, nothing but a small garden that was mostly my doing and kept us in table food of a sort. First it was a hard freeze, then the seed was moldy, and then Ma died and he couldn't work for grief. This was the year he was going to have oats and corn, he told me, and this day he had set his mind to plowing.

"The workhorses are gone," he repeated, mad as he could be at everyone—me, the horses, the world in general. "You'll have to go get them."

"Yes, Pa." Pa was in one of his moods, and when he got that way, there wasn't much I could do to change him. Ever since Ma died, he just seemed to get stubborner and stubborner. I wanted to ask why he didn't go after them himself—after all, he couldn't plow until he found them—but experience taught me better than that.

"Don't come home until you've found them," he said.

"What if . . . what if I can't find them?" I blurted that out as a vision rode in my mind of endless days on the prairie looking for two workhorses too dumb to come home.

"You'll find them," he said grimly and stalked away. "Better take the six-shooter." He threw the words over his shoulder.

Figuring I might be gone long enough to get hungry, I gathered up some corndodgers from breakfast in a clean handkerchief, one of Ma's that I treasured. Now it would have grease all over it. And I

16

got the six-shooter off the shelf where Pa kept it. Heaven knows what he thought I'd shoot from horseback with that unwieldy weapon. By the time I got it loaded, any self-respecting Indian would have scalped me and a jackrabbit would be clear to Oklahoma. But Pa had taught me well, and I knew better than to ride with it loaded.

As I got my things together, I thought bitterly that if Ma hadn't died, I wouldn't be goin' out on the prairie. Ma always wanted me to be a lady, and she was the one person Pa never stood up to. When I was younger and he wanted me to ride with him, Ma would say, "Hush, Luther, she's practicing her stitches. A lady must sew neat and fine." I was almost angry at Ma for dying and leaving me.

Outside I whistled for Maisiebelle, the mustang Pa had given me three years before. He'd been disgusted when I named her, said she needed a short name 'cause she was a short horse. Pa never did like her since she tried to bite him 'fore he even got her home to me. But Maisiebelle and I understood and trusted each other. She was about my only friend living way out alone like we did, and I told her all my hopes and dreams, for all the good that it did me.

Pa had waved his arm east, and east was where I headed, pointing Maisiebelle across the vast Texas prairie. We loped along, my eyes scanning the horizon. All I saw was the great empty land covered with rolling prairie grasses and dotted with an occasional clump of mesquite or blackjack oak, treacherous outcroppings of rock, and straggly little creeks, seldom enough for fishing and sometimes, in the hot summer, nothing but baked dry earth.

Expecting the horses to materialize out of the land at any moment, I rode straight on, moving at a fairly good clip. In spite of her name, Maisiebelle was all mustang and could go forever. Not, I thought, like those two heavy-footed animals that Pa linked to the plow. At first, the sun was warm and good, and I forgot all my anger in the freedom of being out on the prairie, smelling all its good smells, and being away from Pa and his mood.

"Maisiebelle," I said, "we ain't always goin' to live like this. Someday, I'm gonna have me a fine house, a big house with two stories and servants to run up and down the stairs, and I'll wear beautiful gowns, and you'll eat sweet clover all day long." The little mustang nickered, and I knew she understood my dream. Content with the perfect day and my perfect dream, I almost forgot how mad

I was at Pa.

But the sun climbed straight overhead, and it turned from warm and good to downright hot. I wiped my sleeve across my face and used the old battered hat I wore to fan myself. Shielding my eyes with my hand, I searched the empty land once again. I could see forever and there were no horses. No men nor houses either. Just emptiness.

What kind of a father, I thought, would send a girl out into such emptiness? He didn't care what happened to me, I told myself. Maybe he hoped I would get lost or Indians would get me—one less thing for him to worry about. But then I straightened—Pa sent me after the horses 'cause he had confidence in me. He just didn't recognize that I was a girl, with a girl's dreams.

When I judged the sun was direct overhead and it must be midday, I nooned, sitting quietly in the shade under Maisiebelle, for there were no trees nearby at that point, not even a scrub oak. It was what cowboys called a dry camp, with no water, and the corndodgers, now hard and cold, stuck in my throat with nothing to wash them down. I threw the last one on the ground, and even Maisiebelle sniffed disdainfully at it and turned away. I wondered if Pa had warmed the dodgers on the stove and had them with cool buttermilk that had been stored in the crock. For a moment, I wished fiercely that I was back in the dogtrot, Pa's temper and all. But I moved on.

Even the poor meal made me sleepy, hot as the sun was, and as Maisiebelle, now moving a little more slowly, headed even farther east, I nodded in the saddle, overcome by weariness. Two or three times, I startled myself awake and looked frantically about the prairie, as though by dozing for seconds I had missed those darn horses. But there was nothing—just me and Maisiebelle and emptiness.

I must have slept soundly however briefly, with the saddle providing a strangely rocking kind of cradle, for this time when I came awake, I did so with great clearness of mind, the fuzzy sleepiness gone. And instantly I knew that I was alone and, though I would not have told Pa, afraid.

Loneliness and fright are like a fog. They settle all around you, resting on your shoulders like an invisible cloak, and matter how you think about it logically, you cannot shake that fog. I lectured myself again and again, and I even shook my shoulders a time or two, as though to chase away that feeling. But I'd find myself checking over my shoulder more and more often as the afternoon wore on.

Ahead of me I could see the Crosstimbers, that irregular, narrow band of trees that stretched up across North Texas to the Red River and into Oklahoma. The Comanches used the timbers as a hiding place I knew, especially in times of the full moon when they seemed more prone to raid. Fear clutched at me as I remembered that it was now a full moon, and just two days ago we'd heard of neighbors who'd lost their horses to Comanches. They were lucky, however, for they kept their scalps.

I looked around almost frantically, determined that I'd find those horses before I reached the timbers. I was convinced that once out in the open, into the woods, I'd not only lose the horses, I'd lose myself and, likely, I thought, also my scalp.

The sun was well on its way down when I rode within a mile of the first trees, my desperation increasing. There seemed no way I could turn and make it home before the middle of the night. I'd lose my way on the prairie a thousand times. And besides, hadn't Pa said not to come home without the horses? Yet to enter the timber went beyond anything I was capable of in my wildest imagination. I wished desperately for Pa, unpredictable as he was.

I'd seen not so much as a pile of dung to indicate that the workhorses had come this way. Perhaps Pa had been wrong, and they'd gone west and I'd been on a fool's errand all day. Half expecting the horses to be plodding along behind, I turned in the saddle, sort of standing in the stirrups as though that would give me a better view. I did not see two heavy workhorses, but I saw a lone rider coming at a good clip.

He was not a Comanche, that much I could tell even from a distance by the way he sat a saddle and the broad hat on his head. I could, of course, have headed quickly into the timbers, for I had plenty of time to beat him and lose myself among the tees. I stopped Maisiebelle and simply sat, waiting for the rider to approach.

Within minutes, I saw that it was Pa. Had he come to harangue me for my failure to find the horses? Would he holler that I was sitting still when I should be pushing on? Common sense told me I should make some last-minute effort to find those horses, dig them out of a hole in the ground if I could, but I sat frozen, waiting for fate to come to me.

Pa reined his horse to a stop in front of me, raising his hand in the traditional sign of friend ship. Then he sat and stared at me, his expression unreadable.

"You've come a good twenty miles," he said. "Why did you come so far?"

Defiantly, I asked, "Why did you tell me not to come home until I found the horses?"

"Fool girl," he muttered, "don't know no better than to ride halfway to hell and gone."

Years later I figured out that was the closest he could come to showing his concern. Then, though, I took it for condemnation and burned under the phrase, "Fool girl."

We rode home together in silence, though Pa did tell me that the workhorses had come home of their own accord, shortly after midday. He never did tell me, though, and it was years before I figured out for myself that two slow workhorses could never have gone as far as my mustang and I had that day.

Josie Parker finished her story and sat silently on a bale of hay, her elbows resting on her knees as she stared at the horizon and a prairie now dotted with fences and buildings. She was a tall, lean woman, hardened by years of hard work. Today was a working day like any other, and she wore a pair of faded jeans, scuffed boots, a kerchief around her neck, and a battered Stetson.

The young man had come from a city newspaper to interview her. His assignment was to find out how she felt about having spent her life—eighty long years—running a ranch with the help of no man, save her father who had died years before and now the few she hired.

"Why. . .?" He stumbled over the question. "Why did you want to be a rancher, Miss Parker? Most women of your generation .married. . .or taught school. . .or. . . ." He was getting himself in trouble and he knew it. "Why did you choose to run your father's ranch?"

She stared at him as though he were a fool. Then she spoke very slowly, "When I was young, I lost two workhorses on the prairie."

Sweet Revenge

The woman in the bed next to me lies curled in a ball all day, moaning for her lost baby. The child, as I understand it, died at birth, and the mother went mad with grief. On the other side of me is a woman who calls out stridently, "Release me this minute! I do not belong here! If my daughter knew how you were treating me . . . ." In truth, it was her daughter, unable to care for her any longer, who put her here, saw to it that she was tied each day in a rocking chair, untied only to take care of personal needs and, sometimes, for a brief walk around.

I've been here six months, and during that long tedious time, I have made it a point to be very quiet, so I am neither tied nor confined. Not that I am free to come and go. No, indeed. I sit here each day, staring out the window at the Texas prairie, plotting my quiet revenge against the husband who put me in the county poor farm, the only place able to care for the "dangerously insane."

That was what the judge said of me at the hearing, "dangerously insane." Howard Smith stood there with all his might and influence—the town's banker who holds the mortgages on every home and business for ten counties—and swore that I'd come after him with a butcher knife when he was sleeping. "Only the grace of God that I'm alive today, your honor," he said humbly. "The woman's dangerous. I tried, Lord knows, I tried to care for her, keep her at home . . ."—here his voice broke a little with emotion—"keep the world from knowing my shame . . . ."

In spite of good old Brother Bacon, the preacher who protested strongly and who is still my champion, the judge ruled that I should be confined in the poor farm where, as he put it, "they have the facilities to care for someone like her."

I did take after him with a butcher knife once, but the story was different than he told it. I never wanted to marry Howard Smith. When I was seventeen, he was a widower of forty, wealthy beyond measure because he was mean as sin to those that owed his bank

21

money. He approached my parents with a marriage proposal which they leapt to accept without consulting me.

My father was a farmer in south Texas and, it pains me to admit, a weak man, bent on doing the Lord's work but never sure which way the Lord wanted him to jump. He was a great deal more sure which way my mother wanted him to jump, for she made it perfectly clear. She also made it perfectly clear that the Lord had not meant her to live the poverty-stricken life of a sod farmer's wife, and she blamed my father for not providing for her in a more fitting manner. That he was a farmer when she married him never seemed to occur to her.

"A perfect marriage," she had crowed, when she told me of Howard's proposal. "You will live a life of comfort, and perhaps your poor dear father and I will not have to scrimp so . . . ."

"Did he offer a marriage settlement?" I asked coldly.

"Oh, now, dear Callie . . . how can you think such . . . " She was off in a flutter of denials, but I had my answer.

I never pleaded nor cried hysterically, neither being my style, but I made it plain that I did not want to go through with this marriage, that I would do almost anything to avoid it. I considered, seriously, running away but reasoned that Mr. Smith, with his wealth and connections, would no doubt find me, even in Dallas. My logical arguments to him had met with bland confidence, "Once we are married, it will all work out."

Work out, my foot! We were married in the church at Brownwood, with Brother Bacon performing the ceremony and me a reluctant bride in white, Howard a beaming groom in his best black suit, though I thought the knees and seat shiny from wear. For me, a kind of hell began with that ceremony. Howard was a randy old man, always pawing at me, sometimes waking me in the middle of the night with his insatiable passion. I learned to lie perfectly still, close my eyes, and take my mind to a faraway place during his rutting. When he rolled over, sated, and began to snore, I rose to clean myself, praying each time that no child had been conceived, for I don't know what I would have done to avoid bringing a child into that household.

Days, I was a servant, though he could well have afforded household help for me. He preferred, he said, to think that his own little wife was taking care of him. So I ran the house, fed him the hearty meals he expected three times a day, made my own clothes and most of his, and worked like a dog from dawn to dark. Howard was as demanding upright as he was in bed, expecting meals on time, whisky when he called for it, my undivided attention when he wanted to recount his latest triumph.

His temper, when aroused, was fearful, and he had his hates and his dislikes. In spite of the fact they had made him wealthy, he hated farmers, swore that they were out to cheat him, that the only honest men he'd ever met were those who refused to toil on the land—just the opposite of what most men believed. And he hated schools, thought young people should be put to work at the age of twelve instead of filling their heads with the foolishness called 'higher education.' When he'd yell and carry on about how the universities were ruining people, I cringed, for I wanted nothing more than to attend the state university in San Angelo and become a teacher. "No school will ever get a penny of my money," he would rage, shaking his mighty fist in the air. He was the epitome of the man who would, as they say, take his fortune with him to the grave if he could.

By the time I'd been married five years, I was twenty-two years old, thin and gaunt, with dark circles under my eyes and, occasionally, a bruise on my cheekbone, a black eye, and, once or twice, cracked ribs. Good Brother Bacon asked often how I was feeling, but I brushed his concern aside. What could he do?

I began to refuse Howard in the night, and then I took to sleeping in a separate bedroom. Twice, he kicked open a locked door to drag me back to his bed, and on those occasions he was rougher than usual. "I'll teach you," he'd mutter between clenched teeth.

The night I took the butcher knife after him, he was drunker than usual and more violent. He'd throttled me until I nearly lost consciousness, and then had forced me to the parlor floor, where he raped me and then fell asleep. I left him on the floor and would have left him all night, but he roused, and I could see from the murderous look in his eye that he was coming for me again. Hoarse and unable to cry out—as though anyone would have helped me—I ran for the kitchen and grabbed the first thing handy, the butcher knife.

He thought I was bluffing, that I was too soft to cut someone, even him, but when he got close enough I sliced at his ribs, opening a long wide cut that bled so hard I was reminded of the proverbial stuck pig, an analogy that fit in more ways than one. Scared, he retreated to his bedroom, and I went to mine, building a barricade of furniture and sleeping with my hand on the knife handle.

Next morning, he was gone. Curious but unconcerned, I set about straightening the house and, unfortunately, had it all tidy and repaired—no sign of a struggle—by the time Howard arrived with the sheriff.

That was how I ended up in the poor farm. Howard said only one thing to me in private and that was "A lot of women would love to have your chances. I'll find one won't come after me with a knife."

My only revenge is that it is against state law to divorce an insane person. Howard is saddled with me, and the next ladies in his life are condemned to illegitimacy. But that's cold comfort as I sit here, rocking away the endless days.

"Brother Bacon!" I fight the impulse to grin, to let my eyes light with happiness—bland is safer in this place—but I am glad beyond belief to see the old man.

"Callie, dear," he says, leaning to touch me on the shoulder, "come with me. You're leaving here."

It is almost too much to believe, too much to bear. "Leaving?" I echo.

"Take me away from here this instant!" the woman next to me demands. "I know you came to get me!"

Brother Bacon ignores her, speaking softly to me. "You're leaving. I've just gotten a court order."

"How . . . ?" I am almost unable to speak, and when I rise my knees threaten to buckle under me.

"Finally had a traveling judge come through," he says, "one that didn't know Howard. I convinced him you weren't dangerous . . . said I'd take responsibility for you myself. Now we must go."

"Howard?"

"He doesn't know."

We go through the formalities, with a disapproving matron frowning all the while she signs the necessary papers, but Brother Bacon is his usual kind and patient self. I stifle the urge to scream at the woman. When we finally are in the buggy and driving away, I demand, "Take me to Howard."

"Now, Callie . . . ."

"I want to see Howard," I say with steel in my voice, though I am not sure what I will say once I am in front of the devil who has engineered my misery.

He protests but finally agrees, and we ride in silence for a long time.

"You can't just go in there," he warns as we approach the house. "It . . . well, it might be dangerous for you."

"It might be dangerous for Howard," I reply, and see in his face the first sign of doubt. Maybe, he is thinking, she did go after him with a butcher knife for no reason, and maybe I've done the wrong thing. By then we are in front of the house, and he has stopped the horse.

"It will be all right," I tell him, heading boldly up the steps of the front stoop.

The door is locked, but I knock loudly, wait a minute, and then knock again. There is no answer, no sound within. After a long wait, I return down the steps, march round the house, and enter through the kitchen door. The kitchen is a mess—dirty dishes, food crumbs, all the signs that no one has been taking care. Howard has been too cheap to hire someone to replace me.

I walk through the dining room, parlor, up the stairs to the bedroom, and there is Howard, dead in his bed, his face beginning to mottle. For a moment, I am furious enough with him to go again for the butcher knife, furious that he has had the final laugh, robbed me of whatever revenge I sought. His empty eyes stare glassily at me, and I turn slowly and with deliberate, measured tread return to Brother Bacon.

"You best come," I say. "He's dead."

"Dead?" He is alarmed. How, he wonders, could I have killed him so soon.

"I didn't do it," I assure him. "I think his own cooking killed him. You should see the kitchen."

When Brother Bacon examines Howard, he suggests it was probably a heart attack. I long instead to see a butcher knife sticking out of his chest, but it's a longing I don't even whisper.

Brother Bacon goes for the sheriff, and I wait. To pass the time, I clean the kitchen, remembering ruefully that cleaning has once before gotten me into trouble. But this is now my house, I reason, and I cannot bear for anyone to see it so ill-kept.

The sheriff is not kind. "I won't offer you sympathy, Mrs. Smith," he says. "I 'spect you're rejoicin'."

"Not quite, sheriff," I say, "I've been robbed."

He is puzzled but won't admit it. "If I could prove you did this . . . ." His threat dangles.

"Sheriff!" Brother Bacon is angry. "Mrs. Smith was at the home and then with me. There is no way she could have any involvement in her husband's death. Ate and drank himself to death, if you ask me."

"I didn't ask," the sheriff says rudely. He used to drink with Howard of a night, and they were friends, which means he has always been my enemy.

I am the nearest relation and so in charge of arrangements. Howard is buried in the town cemetery, with bank employees and a few townspeople in attendance—he was not popular—and Brother Bacon says a few words over the grave. The good man speaks nervously as he commends Howard's soul to God, and I throw a handful of dirt on the coffin and turn away. The sheriff, who has come uninvited, opines that it's a crime not to give a man a proper church burial.

"Not," I say, "a crime for which one can be tried."

Within a week, I have made the house my own, given away every trace of Howard's clothing and personal effects, opened the windows to sunshine and air, beaten the old dust out of the rugs, and put flowers in every room, even the cubicle Howard called his office. His papers have been packed and sent to the lawyer.

Said lawyer comes to call a week later. "Mrs. Smith, you're a wealthy woman," he says and proceeds to outline my wealth.

My instructions are direct: a certain amount to my parents, not generous but enough to insure that I won't have to worry with them daily; another, larger amount to the county poor farm, with the stipulation that it be used for treatment of the "dangerously insane."

"That barely makes a dent," the lawyer says. "Any further plans?"

"Yes. I plan to attend the university in San Angelo and get an education. And I'll build them . . . let's see, a library. Yes, a library. Howard hated books. We'll call it the Howard Smith Memorial Library." I envision Howard, spinning in frustration for all eternity.

The lawyer's face is blank.

After he leaves, I go to the kitchen for the butcher knife. Now it hangs framed, in a place of honor, over my desk in the private library I have built for myself. No one ever asks about the knife, but I find it a great comfort.

That Damn Cowboy

Each day the old man wheeled his chair out to the veranda and sat staring over the distant river and, farther, the purplish, faint mountains. Some days he sat as still as the landscape before him; others, when the wind swept across the plains and struck him forcefully, he would shift restlessly, long bony fingers stroking his white stubble of beard and pulling at his shaggy hair. But always, his eyes, intense and blue, seemed fixed on the river.

He rarely talked, and the family had grown accustomed to his silence. The grandchildren treated him dutifully, their parents a slight bit more tolerantly. Friends and neighbors, visiting the house, nearly ignored him, and everyone generally agreed that his mind was gone. "Addled with age," they called it. Still, he was the first thing newcomers to the small ranching community heard about. After all, he had been an artist—no, not exactly famous, but he had lived next door to Frederic Remington once.

But Rufus Jones wasn't really addled. It was just that in the years of his old age he had found the world less absorbing than his own interior battle. Retreating from everyday concerns, he tried, with a desperation born of old age, to puzzle out some reason for the turn of his life. He had to know why, before death closed the question forever.

Some days when the fire of anger was less strong in him, he would muse on the quirk of fate that led his son, Davey, to settle in Montana, bringing the then-aged Rufus back to the land that had captivated him years ago.

I loved this country from that first trip . . . 1883, no '84, that time I came to follow the cavalry and do some field sketches. Remember thinking it was like the Scottish highlands . . . rolling hills covered with sagebrush and in the distance, those great snow-capped mountains . . . only this was grander, more immense . . . so much space that the very openness could make a man feel caught. And all that light and shade on the whole thing. My first sketches were failures. But they got better, got to the point I was proud of them, thought I had found my place, the subject that was all mine. I was going to be a famous western artist. What happened?

Other days he would think about that damn cowboy, and the flames of bitterness would rise again within him. Too often, he recalled that day when he had first felt the heat of jealousy. It was in New York where he and the great Frederic Remington were neighbors and, in those days, pretty much equals in the artistic world. Both interested in the West, they often sat late at night sharing experiences, swapping Arizona stories for Montana. They tried to joke about their failures and bragged about their successes—like the sale of a painting, the signing of a contract with *Harper's Weekly*. Rufus had never thought of Remington as greater or better than he, at least never until that day. He remembered that afternoon clearly, even now, some forty years later.

Young Davey came running home to tell me that Mr. Remington had a new pony. "And a silver-studded saddle and bridle." I can still see the child's eyes. Overcome with excitement and pure envy. I was working on that portrait of the old man collecting buffalo bones. The surroundings, even the pile of bones, were right but 1 couldn't bring the bone man himself into focus. 1 was frustrated and it wouldn't have done me any good to keep trying, so I told Davey I'd go see the pony.

But as we crossed the lawn, Remington called: " Rufus! Come here! I've done something splendid."

I remember thinking something about egotists, but it didn't really bother me. . . . . I was used to the man, his bluster and roar, it was just part of him. And I went to look—at a mass of clay and a bunch of sculptor's tools, and Remington with that stupid, proud grin n his face. He looked so superior, and all I saw at first was a lump of clay.

"What do you think, Rufus? 1 think this mess is the beginning of something great. In fact, I'm convinced of it. Don't you agree? 1 may give up oils and become a sculptor."

That was when I saw it—that mass of clay was a horse and rider, well done, too. That flash of anger that went through me, it came so suddenly, it surprised, even frightened me. I'd never been jealous before, yet this was almost an instinct . . . 1 remember making the effort, saying all the right things and wanting really to reach out and destroy that lump of clay. But I just stood there and watched, fascinated in spite of myself, as he added a bit of clay here, scooped some away there, and that damn cowboy took shape before my eyes.

Going home I was almost feverish with anger and hate . . . couldn't work at all. That blasted old bone man got worse instead of better, and I even jumped at Davey when he came in for his afternoon visit. Poor kid. He wanted to talk about the new pony, and I flew in a rage, scared him out of the studio.

Wonder if Davey would remember that day now? No, he'd probably dismiss it as old age if I asked him. He doesn't know how I grew to hate Remington—no one knows. I've kept it buried all these years. Everyone assumed all along that Remington and I were the best of friends . . . probably thought it was nice of the great Remington to be so kind to a second-rate artist. Remington sure got so he acted that way, kind of condescending. Or was I touchy?

Sometimes Rufus Jones would relive his own career, the near-success of it, or was it the near-failure? No, success, for he had done some important works, had been known and praised in his day. His mind would begin with that mural in the state capital. . . .

Quite an honor to be asked, and I did them a good job. Was pleased with it. And the one in the Woolworth Building . . . by that time I was known for historical subjects, the history of this great land. Oh, I was riding high.

And then there was that business about cowboys at play . . . I was so proud of that drawing when it came out . . . "Painting the Town Red," four cowboys literally holding a town at bay with their high jinx. Everyone else was so busy painting the cowboy at work, roping cattle, riding herd and all that, but no one paid any attention to the cowboy at play. I was the first—it was my idea!

But barely two years later, Remington did a sketch with the same title. Looked a lot like mine, too. Anyway, the idea was the same. It came out in that book of Roosevelt's about hunting trails or whatever. Why didn't TR ask me to illustrate it anyway? I just had that letter of praise from him saying how much he valued my western work and hoping we could collaborate. Then the next thing TR asked Remington to illustrate the book. I thought that was the final insult—using my sketch and title!

Of course, it wasn't the final insult. The worst came later in

*another of those bronzes Remington did . . . they were all so popular
after that first damn cowboy. This one he called "Coming Through
the Rye," but the figures were almost exactly those of my painting.
And who got all the credit for capturing the cowboy as he really
was—who else?*

Sometimes Davey would come to stand silently beside his father,
staring at the scene that so absorbed the old man each day as though
by looking he, too, could see something. But one late summer day
when the wind off the river promised cold weather soon, Davey
came with something on his mind.

"Dad?" The tall man in jeans and denim jacket bent almost
gently over the older one who sat erect in his chair, fingering the lap
robe that covered him. Davey had to speak twice before Rufus turned
and looked at him, still saying nothing.

"There's someone who wants to come see you tomorrow. She's
an artist, or says she is anyway. The town kind of wonders about
her. But she stopped me on the street today, said she'd heard a lot
about your work and wanted to meet you. I couldn't do anything
else . . . I told her to come on out in the morning.

Rufus turned away as though none of what Davey had said
meant a thing to him. Davey kicked at a cigarette butt with one
scuffed boot, stared at the river for help, and finally went on.

"Sir, did you hear me?"

"Ummmm."

The next that he had to say made Davey uncomfortable, and he
fidgeted a minute before plunging in. "Dad, you will talk to her,
won't you? She says she knows your work, wants to talk to you
about it. Try to be polite, won't you?"

Davey walked away abruptly, only half hearing Rufus' mumbled,
"Can't you tell her I'll be at work on a new painting, can't see
visitors?"

But Rufus had understood that someone had heard of his work,
and he was secretly pleased. Maybe she knew "Painting the Town
Red," or some of the Oklahoma pictures. His mind went back to
reliving his achievements, and slowly he saw himself standing in
the gallery at his 1899 exhibition. Somehow, though, the memories
of Remington's earlier, more successful exhibition in 1893 crept in:

He looked so cocksure, so smug . . . when I congratulated him, he was almost too hearty, telling me that someday I'd have a success like this too. . . . People kept coming up to shake his hand, ooze their flattery all over him, and he ate it up. . . . All I could do was wonder what it would really be like to have that much attention paid to your art, have all those compliments and empty words . . . imagine myself standing there saying, "Thank you, Mrs. Vanderbilt, I'm so glad you like my pictures of the West . . . yes, it's a very exciting land . . . and Mrs. Astor, how nice of you to come . . . You like the sculpture? Well, I'm most humble. . . .

Rufus had thirsted after fame so long, he almost felt himself savoring that of his rival. Bitterly he brought his thoughts back to the present, surprised himself at how far from reality he occasionally drifted these days.

It was midmorning the next day when Rufus, seated in his wheelchair and staring at the river, heard steps approach him from behind. Not Davey, not any of the family. They were womanly, small steps that sounded mincing.

"Mr. Jones, it's so good of you to let me visit. I can't tell you how delighted I am to talk to another artist."

Rufus turned slowly and fixed his stare on her. She wore pink, an outfit so unsuitable it seemed to insult the landscape, and she smiled too much.

"I said, I'm glad to meet you after hearing so much about your work. I've long been an admirer of the great Rufus Jones."

No response for several seconds, then a glance, a barely uttered, "Eh?" and Rufus turned again to the river.

"Mr. Jones, I came to tell you how very much I appreciate your western work—I've seen it in museums, and I just think it's marvellous, so wonderful! Particularly that mounted horse and rider you did in bronze—your first, wasn't it?"

That damn cowboy again! Rufus stared at the river with intensity so great that it even alarmed the lady artist. Finally, long minutes later, he turned to stare at her. Then a wave seemed to sweep over his entire body. The burning look disappeared from his eyes, his face grew calm, and he actually smiled.

"Thank you very much, my dear. I'm glad you like "The Bronco Buster"—that's what he really is. And, yes, he was my first bronze. But I'm afraid you have my name wrong—I'm Frederic Remington."

The Woman Who Loved Too Well: A Romance of Sorts

Here I sit, ninety years old and nary a soul to comfort me. I should have children and grandchildren—even great-grandchildren—around me in my old age. But I've none. I've lived alone in this same house more than sixty long years. Oh, it's not as though I've never loved nor been loved. I loved too well in my lifetime. But there was no choosing between them, and I sent them both away. I'm not sure that memories are enough for a lifetime, but it's too late now to think about that.

Rad Johnson was the handsomest man I'd ever seen, though at seventeen I was a little young for making comparisons. Still, he had black curly hair that tumbled in every direction and fell over his forehead, eyes as black that laughed with joy, and a big wide smile that said the world was his. Mostly I was around people who were worn down and never felt joy—Rad brought a kind of happiness into my life that I'd never known existed.

He rode into Hillsboro one summer night, and nothing was ever the same again. I was helping Agatha Kuchendyll put up supplies in the general store, where I worked so as to bring in a little money. Pa and I lived alone the far edge of town, in a stone house that some sturdy German burgher had built and then left, when he moved on to a bigger and better home. Pa didn't work much these days—old and sick, he said he was, though I said it was the bottle that was making him old and sick. Ma'd been gone ten years or more by then, and I barely remembered her.

"Tobacco, please," the man with the smile said, when Agatha asked if she could help him. Frozen, I sat on the ladder and stared, one hand motionless on the can of peaches I'd been shelving. He saw me, tipped his hat, and went on about his business. Heart pounding, I went back to mine.

"Well," Agatha bristled, soon as he'd left, "that kind never are no good. I hope he doesn't intend to stay in town."

I thought it best not to tell her that I very much hoped he *did* stay. Instead, I simply asked, "Why?"

"Break some young girl's heart, that's what he'll do," she said emphatically, nodding her head so hard that her large bosoms bounced

33

up and down. "Good thing he won't be lookin' at you, Missy."

And why wouldn't he, I wondered. Perhaps Agatha thought I was too young—or too poor—or too ugly. The latter notion pierced, for I was terribly uncertain about my appearance, with no mother to guide me and only Agatha, who meant well but would, I suspected, have clothed every young girl in black from head to foot lest the men notice their sex. "Yes, ma'am," I said.

We shelved the last of the goods, swept up the store, and I went on, even as Agatha prepared to lock up, calling a quick goodnight over my shoulder. Outside the slight breeze was a relief from the heavy quiet hotness of the store, and I spread my arms to feel every bit of moving air as I headed down the road towards home, a bundle for supper tucked under my arm.

"Feels good, doesn't it?" The voice came from behind me, but I had no need to turn and look to see who it was.

"Where might a man find a place to stay in this town?" he asked, lengthening his stride until he was walking along next to me.

"There's the hotel on the main street," I said, eyes down at the ground.

"Look at me. I won't bite." He laughed heartily as he said it, and I raised my face to find myself nearly nose to nose with him as he bent down toward me. Just as quickly, he backed away as if to survey me from a distance. "You're very young," he said, "and—"

"Eighteen next month!" I interrupted.

He laughed again. "Let me finish. . . and very pretty."

I blushed and wondered furiously if it were true or if he were saying pretty things, just as Agatha had warned me men would do.

"May I walk you home?"

"My pa probably wouldn't like it," I said, when in truth I was afraid he would scorn Pa for the drunk he was.

"Aah," he said wisely, "I understand. Until tomorrow then." And he took my hand before I knew it, and was bent over, planting an ever-so-light kiss on it.

I should have pulled my hand back but for the second time within an hour I was frozen, incapable of movement. It must have been just a second, though it seemed a whole lifetime until he released it, laughing wordlessly at me with his eyes, and I turned and ran for home.

Pa asked what I was so het up about, and I told him I thought I'd seen Sam Bass.

Rad Johnson stayed at the hotel three days and then moved into Mrs. Blackingstock's boardinghouse, where he settled down for a long stay. He drank beer with the men and greeted the ladies on the street, attended the Methodist church and did business at the general store. And best of all, he waited for me at the store and walked me home every evening. My self-consciousness fell away, and I soon chatted at him like a magpie, delighted finally to have someone who cared about me, who listened to me, who told me I was pretty.

"They say you don't work," I told him one night. "Agatha says I must stop seeing you."

"Will she fire you if you don't?"

"No," I laughed. "She's just warning me. Says you're a gambler, and that's why you disappear for two or three days every so often."

"Do you think she's right?"

"I don't care!" I said defiantly, and he grinned.

"You look lovely when you're angry," he said. "Just don't ever turn that anger on me."

"I would never," I said.

I remember all the firsts—the first time we took a picnic to the river, the first kiss, the first doubt. The picnic was on the banks of the Brazos River, and by then it was fall. The river was a deep green, sluggish, as though it knew cold weather was coming, and leaves had just begun to drift down from the trees, except for the live oaks. But the sky was very bright, and I laughed and quoted the poem I'd learned in school about October's bright blue weather. I had packed fried chicken and fresh cornbread and pickles from Agatha's barrel by the door—I can taste the brine yet.

"I'm going away tomorrow," Rad said, reaching one hand to brush my hair out of my eyes.

"To gamble?" I teased.

"Yes, to gamble." He said it seriously, though he was grinning, and I could not tell if he was making a joke or not. "When I come back, we'll marry. I'll speak to your father."

My heart fluttered. Marry Rad Johnson? It was too much too hope, like something wonderful had been put in my grasp and then snatched away. "Pa needs me."

"We'll both take care of him," he said, closing his hand down over mine.

The first kiss happened when he came back from wherever he'd been. Listening to Agatha with one ear at the end of the day, I heard hoof beats with the other ear, and my heart jumped. I grabbed my supper bundle, muttered a quick "Good evening," and was out the door with Agatha still in mid-sentence about the new minister's wife and her tasteless chocolate cake.

Standing by his horse he held his arms wide and I flew into them. I kissed Rad Johnson, bold as you please, right there on the street, with Agatha peering out the window. He was even startled for a minute, but then he kissed me back soundly, a fiercely demanding kiss that spoke of a world I knew nothing about.

We were married in the Methodist church on a Sunday in December. I wore my mother's wedding dress, packed away all those years in her trunk, and Pa was sober enough to walk me down the aisle. We spent our wedding night in the house I shared with Pa. He gave us the big double bed that he and my mother had shared, and our lovemaking was fierce and wild, not at all silenced by Ma's ghost or Pa's very real presence in the lean-to which pulled up right next to the bedroom. From the sound of his snoring, Pa had found a bottle after the wedding and wouldn't have heard a gang of thieves if they rode right through the house.

I worried about living with Pa, though Rad told me it would be no problem. But Pa up and died, not three weeks after we were married, and though I grieved for him like a proper daughter, I was secretly glad to have the house alone with Rad.

We were, oh! so happy. I went to work at the store every day and came home every night to find Rad waiting for me, as often as not to whisk me into bed before I could fix him a proper meal.

"Love is food enough for me," he'd say, as he bent to kiss me, those dark eyes laughing at me.

"Rad," I would protest, my proper upbringing getting in the way, "we must eat supper."

"Later, later. . . ."

Inevitably, the next day Agatha would say "You're looking tired this morning, Missy," and I would smile happily at her.

"I have to go away," he said one morning, three months after we married. "I'll be back in a week or so."

"Rad! I'll miss you, and I'll hate being alone. Why do you have to go?"

"To bring you a pretty," he said, bending to kiss me quickly.

Ten long days later he brought me a peau de soie gown of pale green with a gauze bertha—daringly low-cut I thought—and a diamond pendant, which he hung around me neck with a kiss.

"Rad! I have no place to wear such fine clothes," I protested.

"Wear them for me," he said, "because you are beautiful."

I should have felt warmed by love. Instead, I shivered involuntarily, as though someone had walked on my grave.

The green ball gown was the beginning. Rad's trips came more often and lasted longer, though each time he brought me lavish presents—diamond ear drops which I was embarrassed to wear, a beaded evening bag when I longed for a good ticking dress or new crockery for our table, a bottle of French perfume when the roof needed mending. But each time he came home was like a new beginning, and Agatha always asked if I was tired the next morning.

It's hard to say when discontent creeps in or doubts begin, but by the first anniversary of our marriage, I knew I was spending more time alone than with Rad. Finally I gathered my courage.

"Rad, it's no good being married to someone who's gone all the time. I want a husband who's home. Can't you find work in Hillsboro?"

"Would you have me clerk in the store with you? Or perhaps I should muck out the stables?" His voice was steely cold with anger.

"Whatever you like," I said, striving to keep my tone even, "as long as it's honest and it keeps you at home."

"So, now it's honesty you're worrying about, my pretty. A bit late for that, don't you think?" Anger rushed over his self-control, and he actually raised a fist in my direction, though he lowered it quickly when I did not flinch.

After that first fight, Rad stormed out of the house and was gone a week, leaving me to ponder on his question about honesty, a question that only confirmed my worst suspicions. The green gown, the eardrops, beaded bag, and French perfume were all ill-gotten gain. I knew it in my heart.

Fight followed fight, and our reunions lost their joy, became stiff and strained. With the passing of another year, I realized that I valued the time Rad was gone, dreaded his return for the strain and anger it brought. Never really friends, we were no longer lovers, and finally we became enemies.

The last time I saw him, Rad gave me a black eye, just swung his fist in great anger, and then bolted out the door. Stunned, I held my eye and listened to the hoofbeats disappear down the road. I knew without his telling me that he was gone forever, and I felt nothing but relief. I wet a rag and put it over my eye, but Agatha had plenty to talk of the next morning.

After a year, I put up his clothes, packed them in a trunk in the lean-to, put away the spittoon he'd insisted upon, poured out the little left in a bottle of whiskey, and made the house my own. And then I mourned Pa, walked around talking to him, telling him how sorry I was that I'd let Rad push him out of the way. It took me six months to work both Rad and Pa out of my system.

I worked in the store every day, ignoring Agatha's comments, smiling at the customers, stocking the shelves but never counting the money—Agatha trusted no one. Evenings I went home to my empty house and taught myself to enjoy reading. Mostly I went to bed early and wakened with the dawn. In the spring I planted vegetables and tended them. In the fall, I gathered dried grasses and leaves and wove wreaths. And in December Charlie Hall entered my life.

He was the opposite of Rad—big and chunky where Rad had been thin and stylish, blonde to Rad's darkness, shy against Rad's self-confident loving. Charlie came to the Methodist church, and when the minister pressed him—I was shamelessly listening— confessed that he'd taken to farming east of town and hoped to become a part of the community.

"You must come by the general store," I said boldly. "We'll be glad to help you get settled."

"I'll do that," he said, blushing red and touching the brim of his hat.

He was as good as his word, appearing at the store the next day to buy coffee and sugar and three cotton shirts. I folded the shirts carefully and smiled when he thanked me so quietly I could barely hear him.

Charlie Hall never walked me home from the store, never told me I was beautiful, never brought me presents. It was five weeks before we spoke about anything beyond sugar and coffee and cotton shirts. And then he startled me by saying, "I've never met your husband, Mrs. Johnson."

"He's away," I replied vaguely, and then, impulsively, I added, "I think he has been killed and word has not come back to me." It was not a far-fetched idea. Rad had then been gone nearly three years, and given what I suspected was his line of work, a violent end was not improbable.

"I'm sorry," Charlie Hall muttered and hurried away.

Our friendship grew slowly over the next months. "Missy, I. . . I want to fix my place. How do I put up curtains?"

I sewed him curtains—he paid me, of course—and showed him how to put them up.

"Missy, I got me some watermelon, and I've a mind to have some of my mother's pickled watermelon. You know how to do that?"

Yes, I knew how to do that, and I told him. Slowly, I learned to turn the tables. "Charlie, my roof is leakin'. Can you see about it?"

He could and he did, spending half a day up a ladder, nailing down shingles.

"Charlie, my milch cow has the fever. What can you do for her?" And he cut her tail and bored her horns. "Hollow worm and wolf in the tail," he told me. She was better the next day.

Between fixing my roof and seeing to my milch cow, Charlie began to stop of an evening for a cup of tea, and then for supper, and finally for conversation.

"I never felt so at home," he told me one night, "like I belonged someplace."

"I'm glad you feel that way," I told him, pushing the swing so that it moved gently and created a small breeze against the hot of a summer evening.

In July he asked again about my husband, grabbing my hand as he did and then letting it go every bit as quickly, as though he'd touched something red hot.

"I've had word he's dead," I lied, "killed in a saloon fight over a card game." It wasn't a bad lie, for I really believed it was probably true.

"And you? Are you over your grieving?"

Laughter bubbled up unbidden, but the amazed look on Charlie's face turned me serious of a sudden. "You'd have had to know Rad Johnson," I said. Then, "I did my grieving a long time ago, mostly when he was still around. Yes, I'm through with it, and over him."

"Missy, I've never known any woman like you," Charlie said. If it had been daylight, I'm sure I'd have seen a red blush creep up his face and into his hairline. "Would you. . . could you. . . I, ah, well. . . ."

"Yes, Charlie," I interrupted, "I'll marry you. I'd like that."

"Whoopee!" His hat went into the air as he yelled and then Charlie Hall, shy Charlie, pulled me to him and kissed me soundly. It was not the passionate, fiery kiss of Rad but rather a sound, substantial promise of a safe future. I clung to him for a long minute.

We planned to marry in September—less than two months away, but I would have no more December weddings, and I could see no reason for postponement. Charlie was so enamored of my stone house that he asked if we could not marry in front of it, and I agreed—the weather would be warm enough, and my home was always dear to me, in spite of unpleasant memories of Pa and Rad. The minister would pronounce us man and wife, and then Charlie would carry me over the threshold into a new life in an old house.

"Missy, you've added that column of figures twice," Agatha admonished.

I apologized. "Sorry, Agatha, my mind's aflutter."

"Aflutter on weddings, I suppose," she said. Then, reluctantly, "I guess you best abandon those figures and get to thinking about your wedding dress."

It was ecru brilliantine—white not being fitting for a widow—trimmed with satin-bound scallops, the skirt layered over hooped petticoats ordered from Houston. My hair was wound into coronet braids across my head, and I pinched my cheeks for color, though Agatha, her usual disapproval put aside, told me I had no need, for my color was beautiful.

A small crowd gathered, for between Pa and Rad I'd never been close to many in Hillsboro. Still, some that I'd been in school with years before were there, along with church ladies who never missed a wedding, and Agatha, of course—my matron of honor.

A long table held cups ready for the cider punch Agatha had concocted and the stack cake created out of the contributions of several church ladies. Each bought a cake layer, and the several layers were held together with chunky applesauce, made from dried apples, and topped with whipped cream and nuts.

Charlie stood tall and proud in a stiff black nankeen suit, its creased trousers giving it dead away as ready-made and new bought. In nervous hands he held a bouquet of fall wildflowers he'd picked for me, and as I walked toward him I gloried in the thought of long life with him, safe in the protection of his steady ways.

"Ladies and gentlemen. . . ." Mr. McCurdy droned on, but I only half listened because I was staring intently at Charlie who returned my stare with adoration, somewhat marked I must admit by nervousness. Vaguely I heard hoof beats but assumed someone was passing on the road beyond the house. "If anyone have just cause. . . "

"I do!" The frighteningly familiar voice broke into my reverie, and I turned to see Rad Johnson, still mounted on his lathered horse so that he towered over the gathered guests.

I fainted dead away, but Charlie was too flabbergasted to catch me, and I landed hard on the dirt, ruining the beautiful ecru ballantine gown.

Charlie Hall sold his farm and moved on, said he couldn't bear to stay. And Rad, he left after I threatened him with Pa's shotgun, and this time he never came back. Must have been ten years later that I really did get word he was dead, killed in a barroom fight just like I'd told Charlie. But by then Charlie Hall was lone gone and me with no way of finding him.

The Lord moves in mysterious ways, old Mr. McCurdy used to say, and sometimes I've thought the Lord's ways were plain unfair. That ecru gown is in tatters now, but I keep it in the closet to remind me of the two men I've loved.

The Education of Melanie Beaufort

Fort Worth, Texas, early Spring 1857

Melanie Beaufort stood at the window in her sister's small house and pulled back the lace curtain so that she could look out on the dirt street. There was precious little to look at. Two other houses were within sight but neither was as nice as the one Ben Thompson had built for his wife, with its board sidings painted a gleaming white—now dulled with dust, but Melanie would never have mentioned that—and a white picket fence enclosing what might someday, with struggle, be a garden. Knowing her sister Sophie as she did, Melanie could not imagine why she had chosen to marry a man who wanted to be a banker in Texas. Every time Sophie looked at the hot, dusty street with no trees lining it, she must think with longing of Linden, their Georgia home, with its towering pines and magnolias and the green lawns that stretched out beyond forever.

Some six months along in her first pregnancy, Sophie sat in a rocking chair, complacently taking neat, even stitches on a tiny garment. "Anything worth looking at?" she asked idly, her attention riveted on the small garment.

Melanie shrugged. "Two men on horseback. They look . . . well, unkempt, to say the least." She stared at them again. Unkempt they may have been, with long hair spilling out under hats with wide brims and their cotton pants and boots covered with dust, but they were laughing and gesturing as though they were having the time of their lives. Melanie watched them intently and felt a twinge of envy at their freedom. Even here in the wilds of Texas, she was bound by what "a lady" should and should not do.

Sophie rose, a little laboriously, for her new shape was still strange to her, and came to the window. "Farmers," she said. "From the west. Sometimes they come in for . . . well, I guess for some excitement, but they have to come a long way. A hundred miles or more. We don't associate with such people, of course."

Ignoring her sister's last prideful statement, Melanie asked in disbelief, "They ride a hundred miles for excitement?" To herself, she thought she too would ride that far for a little excitement. So far, after three weeks, life with Sophie and Ben had been more than a little dull, and she had promised to stay until the baby was three months old. A long six months stretched before her.

Intent on getting a better look, Melanie pulled the curtain back even further. She was a tall young woman, with reddish-brown hair she parted in the middle and pulled back into a chignon, though tendrils always escaped to frame her face. Her almost severe hairstyle only accented her high cheekbones and large, dark eyes. Her father always said there must have been a Cherokee in the woodpile someplace who had given his dark good looks to Melanie, while Sophie clearly took her rounder, softer blond appearance from their Celtic ancestors.

The riders were by then abreast of the house, still laughing, when suddenly the one nearest the house happened to glance at the window. Seeing Melanie, he tipped his hat in a jaunty gesture and smiled broadly.

The curtain was quickly replaced, but not before his look was burned on Melanie's memory. He was older than she—in his late twenties, she judged, and they had been years of hard living. Even at a distance she could see a certain firm set to his chin, a directness to his gaze that bespoke someone beyond callow youth. She couldn't tell for certain since he was ahorseback, but he looked tall—and there was that thick dark blonde hair that hung to his shoulders. For a reason that Melanie Beaufort would not identify, her heart skipped a beat.

"Melanie, what is it?" Sophie asked.

Red rising in her face, Melanie replied, "Nothing. I just find such men . . . such, well, interesting. You know, they're so free to do what they want to do."

With all her fine Georgia breeding rising to the fore, Sophie said preachily, "They're not the kind of men we will ever know. Even though we are in the wilderness, we must try to live as we did at home. And that includes the people we associate with."

Melanie was tempted to tell her she was tired of the people they always associated with, and since few of them were in Fort Worth, they'd been associating only with themselves, which was getting boring. But she held her tongue, reluctant to upset the mother-to-be.

"Ben says he'll take us to dinner at Hutchins' tonight," Sophie said without looking up. "It's probably the finest dining room in

Fort Worth." Then she giggled, sounding just a bit as she had not too long ago when she'd been but a girl and Melanie had liked her better. "It's the only one decent enough that Ben would take me there."

Fort Worth was then not quite ten years old, a town that began as a military fort for protection of settlements from the Indians. Having never seen any Indian activity, the army soon abandoned the place and left it to civilian squatters. Now, some five years after the army's departure, the city showed signs of growth—a doctor, two lawyers, several saloons, a cotton yard, Steele's Tavern, where ladies could wait in a secluded parlor for the stagecoach which stopped there, the Hutchins' Hotel, hardware and mercantile businesses, and, of course, a new bank. Newcomers these days were not squatters but men like Ben Thompson, men of wealth who came from the South and brought their slaves with them. There was even talk of building a courthouse but so far that had not materialized. But the squatters and the farmers and the drovers—those with not enough money to own slaves and drive fine carriages and build new houses—had not been driven out. They mingled easily with their wealthier neighbors in this frontier city.

They even mingled at Hutchins' Hotel. Ben, Sophie and Melanie had just seated themselves—they chose the table with the cleanest looking cloth on it—when two men dressed in rough clothes entered.

"I tell you, it was Providence," one said to the other. "Meant to be that we came to Fort Worth today."

"If you say so," the second man said, his voice considerably lower. He was dark-headed, not quite as tall as his companion, but stocky and solidly built. He took off his hat and held it nervously in his hands as though uncertain what to do with it. His hair bore the indent where the hat had been sitting all day.

After one quick glance at the men, Melanie quickly turned her full attention to her dining companions who were, unfortunately, totally silent. Then Sophie, too loudly, said the last thing Melanie wanted her to. "Aren't those the two men we saw riding into town today, Mel?"

Before Melanie could shush her, Ben turned his head, then said heartily, "That's Lyle Speaks and Sam November, new clients at the bank." He was instantly out of his chair and across the room.

Ben, Melanie thought somewhat angrily, is a good banker because he flatters his customers. But how, she wondered, had these two men found enough money to deposit in a bank? The next thing she knew, the two men were following Ben back to their table, where the banker made the proper introductions.

The taller, blonde one—the one who had raised his hat to her—was Lyle Speaks. His companion was Sam November. Speaks knew no embarrassment, probably never would in his life. "Ma'am," he said, "I saw you at the window today. You, well, for just a minute there, you reminded me of someone, someone very special."

Was she imagining it or were there tears forming in the eyes of both men?

"I guess, then," she said haltingly, "that it is a good comparison."

"Yes, ma'am, it is, a very good one," Speaks said, his voice cracking. Then, recovering himself, "Well, we won't interrupt your dinner. Just wanted to say hello. Thompson, we'll be in to sign those papers tomorrow."

Melanie felt disappointment—and a thousand questions—as the two men turned away. She kept her attention focused on her dinner the entire evening, never—well, almost never—looking their direction, though the roast beef tasted greasy to her and the potatoes were burnt.

The two men stayed buried in deep conversation, even while they ate. Melanie did sneak enough of a look to see that their table manners were pretty good, somewhat to her surprise. She also noticed that they drank more than a little whiskey with their dinner. When Ben announced it was time to "get poor little Sophie some rest" and they rose to go, a cheery "Good night, folks!" followed them out of the dining room. She knew it came from Lyle Speaks, and on a bold impulse, she turned just enough to send him a smiling thank-you.

"Sam," Speaks said, "I'm gonna' get to know that woman. I may marry her."

November laughed aloud. "Lyle, you get crazier ideas than anybody I ever saw. We come to town to sell our farms, and you decide to get married. You do that and we can't go to bounty hunting for that sheriff, like we discussed today."

"I ain't saying I'm for sure getting married. I'm just saying she

. . . well, she attracts me more than any woman I've ever seen."

"Most of the women you've known have been whores," November said. "This one's a lady, a real southern lady. You wouldn't know how to treat her."

Speaks sobered and his voice softened. "Mama was a lady, and she insisted we learn our manners and learn how to treat women. And Beth, she was fixin' to be a lady." Suddenly his voice got a hard edge to it. "But I don't want to talk about them."

"Man," his friend said, "someday we're gonna' have to talk about them, or they'll haunt us till we die."

"They'll do that anyway." And Speaks left his companion behind.

It had been twelve years since Lyle Speaks found his family massacred. Since then, November, who'd planned to marry his sister Beth, had become his partner and constant companion. They'd farmed, they'd wandered West Texas looking for Comanche to kill in vengeance—and killed a few, they'd even served under General Samuel Curtis Ryan in the Mexican-American War, but none of it had brought them peace. During the day, they laughed and rode and fought and carried on with the best of them, but at night both men were haunted by memories—Pa and Mama and Caleb with their scalps gone and the cabin in flames, and especially Beth, brutally treated before she was murdered on the road. Jeffrey, the youngest, whom Lyle had managed to rescue, had been sent to Tennessee for relatives to raise. It was more than Speaks could do to shoulder the responsibility of a growing brother even while he tried to work his own way out of despair.

"Melanie, where are you going?" Sophie's voice had a whiny tone to it.

"For a walk," Melanie said. "I'm feeling cooped up." She tied her bonnet under her chin and picked up her parasol.

"It's . . . it's not proper for a young woman to walk unescorted," Sophie said.

"Oh, bother, Sophie. We're not in Georgia. We're in Texas, and it's all different here."

"Well," Sophie moaned, "it shouldn't be. You wait, someday it will be just like Georgia."

Melanie resisted an urge to say "Heaven help us!" She also

managed not to slam the door as she left. She was soon aware that Sophie's words were not idle. The rutted dirt street was almost empty but the few people she saw were men. Were there no women in this town? She decided to simply walk the length of the street to the bluff where one could look out over the Texas prairie forever. Then she would turn back, having had her fresh air, dusty as it was. But the going was not easy: she had to pick her way over ruts, dodge wagons careening down the street, even watch out for stray dogs.

When she reached the bluff, she stood for a long time, staring out at the plains, wondering that she found herself in such a strange place. But the view intrigued her, and she felt a longing to ride out on the lonesome land. It was April, and the prairie was covered with wildflowers so that from the distance it looked like a yellow carpet spread over the brown land. She had never seen anything like it.

"Ma'am? Are you all right?"

The voice startled her, and she whirled to find herself staring at Lyle Speaks who stood with his hat in his hand.

"I . . . I'm just admiring the view. Those flowers . . . ."

"You shouldn't be walking alone," he said. "No telling, with all these ruffians in town, what could happen to a fine lady like yourself."

His eyes stared directly into hers, and she felt something deep inside her jump. She didn't know if it was alarm or pleasure or embarrassment, but she sincerely hoped her face had not turned red.

"Thank you, Mr. Speaks. I'm sure I'm fine."

"Well," he said, holding out his arm, "I'm not so sure, and I'm going to escort you wherever you're going."

Slowly, she took his arm. "Home, I guess," she said.

And so, her hand linked in his arm, they paraded the length of what was then Fort Worth. He told her, unbidden, some about himself—though he never told her about the massacre of his family.

"We came to town to sell our farms. Didn't know what we were going to do, but farming wasn't it any more. Just happened the sheriff was looking for bounty hunters. Now that we can do—tracking men down."

"Why would you track men down?" she asked innocently. Bounty hunters were not something she knew in Georgia.

"'Cause they done—uh, have done wrong and need to be apprehended," he said righteously. "And we'll get paid for bringing them in."

The idea appalled her. She turned to stare at him. "You'd turn men in for money."

Something along his jaw line hardened and his eyes turned dark. "Yes, ma'am, if they've killed somebody, I surely would. Wouldn't hesitate an instant."

"Something bad has happened to you, hasn't it?" she asked, having watched his face change.

Without even thinking, he turned toward her, putting his hand over hers that rested lightly on his arm. "Yes, ma'am, it has. But I don't want to talk about it." His eyes were dark and hard.

They walked the rest of the way in silence, his hand all the time covering hers. She made no move to dislodge it.

At Sophie's house, she thanked him for escorting her safely home, and he made a funny little half-bow. Clearly, he wasn't used to such gestures.

She didn't see him again for two weeks. Oh, she saw him, when she looked through the curtain—she was embarrassed now to pull it aside—but she did not see him to talk to. For days, just after the noon meal, he would ride by, and he would always look toward the house. But he never stopped. Then there would be a string of three or four days when he didn't appear. After that, he'd be back again. Once he appeared at the Sunday meeting a visiting preacher held in the tiny schoolhouse, but they had no chance to speak.

Melanie had no way of knowing, of course, that when he didn't appear, he and November were off chasing this desperado or that. Nor did she know that November teased him unmercifully. "'Bout time to go for your ride, isn't it?" he'd say as they rose from the table at whatever saloon they'd chosen for their noon meal. Speaks would just grin and reply, "Guess it is."

What Melanie did know was that Sophie disapproved, loudly, of even a mild interest in "that wild man," as she called him. "I don't know why you keep watching out the window for him," she said, fanning herself. "He's not your type, and he knows it. He best not ever stop at this house."

That was just what he did. Boldly stopped at the house one afternoon when the two ladies sat over a cup of tea.

Sophie answered the door. "My husband is not at home," she

said loftily. "I believe you can still find him at the bank."

Hat in hand, he stood tall, straight, and not the least intimidated by her. "I didn't come to see Mr. Thompson," he said. "I came to speak to Miss Beaufort."

Sophie opened her mouth, but Melanie was too quick for her. "Why, Mr. Speaks, do come in." Her heart fluttered a little but she kept her voice steady. "We were just enjoying tea . . . might I offer you a cup?"

Must be a southern habit, he thought. Aloud he said, "No, ma'am, I never was much for tea. If we could talk for a minute.. . "

"Of course," she said, "Sophie will excuse us."

Sophie made a broad show of picking up her cup and leaving the room, pulling the pocket door almost but not all the way closed behind her. Then she sent Penny, the maidservant, to listen at the door, but as the poor girl reported later to her angry mistress, nothing much was said except that he asked her to ride out on the prairie with him the next day, and Miss Melanie had agreed. Sophie sent Penny for the smelling salts.

"I'm afraid any buggy I could find would be pretty rough," he said apologetically.

"I would much prefer to ride," she said. "Sidesaddle, of course."

He grinned. "I'll see if I can find one of those contraptions. Don't wear your best gown." And he was gone, still grinning.

Next day, he appeared leading a fine chestnut horse with a sidesaddle. Melanie, in a muslin morning dress and matching sunbonnet, met him at the door. "Sophie would greet you," she said with a revealing smile, "but she's resting. She's feeling poorly."

He understood perfectly. At the fence, in a most gentlemanly manner, he placed his hands on her waist and hoisted her into the saddle, backing away as soon as he was sure she as safely situated. She hooked her knee over the horn, draped her skirts appropriately, and nodded at him as if to say, "I'm ready."

"I want you to see those flowers," he said, as he turned his horse westward, away from the settlement.

Soon they were by themselves, the town a speck in the distance. The flowers, she discovered, were not all yellow but all colors— there were deep blues and bright reds, a few delicate pinks, but the biggest and boldest were yellow. "Do they have names?" she asked.

"My mother could have told you," he said with a shrug, "but I can't. Some are Indian names."

At the mention of the word Indian, she looked around in all directions. They were in totally open land, with only here and there a clump of mesquite or black oak, surely not cover in case of an attack. In the distance, she could see a fork of the Trinity River edging toward Fort Worth, but its banks offered no comforting trees. "Is it safe to be out here alone?"

"Indians?" he asked. "There's been no trouble near here since the army came. Indians are to the west." His eyes turned hard, a look she had seen only briefly once before and found frightening both then and now. "Sometimes I wish they'd try," he said. "I . . . well, never mind." He smiled as if to reassure her and then said, "Only thing to worry about here is outlaws, and I can sure to God take care of them. No, you're safe."

She had known all along that she was.

They rode slowly, talking of nothing of consequence and everything of importance. He asked about her home, and she described Georgia and her family—two brothers and a sister, all younger, still at home. She told him she'd come to help Sophie with the baby and then, as though someone else had her tongue, she confessed that she was growing impatient with her sister's complaints and bored with the narrowness of their lives. "Sometimes I just want to ride as far and as fast as I can. Isn't that awful?"

"No," he said, "I've known that feeling a whole lot of late." Then he grinned. "But you can't do it on that saddle."

"Men," she pronounced, "have all the fun just because they can wear pants."

He chuckled. "There's a woman or two 'round here, early settlers they were, that wear pants and ride astride just like a man." He watched for her reaction.

"Why, I'd never!" she gasped. And then, with a slight smile of surprise, "Or maybe I would."

Their rides became a regular thing, two or three times a week, except when he was gone. Then he always sent a message to tell her he was leaving town. When they rode, they laughed and were silly in ways that neither could be in town when others were around. Once he took her to a plum thicket and helped her load her apron with the juicy fruit. Then they laughed because they had no way to carry the plums home.

"You put them on the ground," she said, "until I'm mounted, and then I'll make a bowl of my apron again."

"It would be like riding with a lapful of eggs," he said. "One mis-step, and you be purple from head to toe."

She laughed aloud again at the picture that drew up in her mind.

Lyle never talked to her about where he had come from, and she knew intuitively not to ask. But he talked a lot about his plans for the future. "Rich," he said. "I'm gonna' be rich. Gonna' have a big place somewhere—not in West Texas—and live like a king. Gonna' raise a family just like mine was, a lot of kids, teach 'em all how to work."

"How are you going to get this money?" she asked, eyes alight with merriment. If she had noticed the past tense in reference to his family, she chose to ignore it.

He shrugged. "Haven't figured that out yet. If they ever put a bounty on Comanche scalps, I'll do it that way." There was that hard look again, the one that frightened her. "Meantime, I'll wait and see. Too late to go to California for gold." What he didn't know, of course, was that within another ten years, Texas beeves would turn into their own kind of gold and there he would find his fortune. But neither of them had a crystal ball those days on the prairie.

Sam November would have been amazed by the difference between the laughing, relaxed Lyle Speaks who rode out with Melanie Beaufort and the Lyle Speaks who rode with him after outlaws. Chasing a horse thief or a suspected murderer, Speaks was cold, analytical, all business with never a smile or a joke. When he caught his prey, he tended almost toward cruelty, and November sometimes wondered if Speaks didn't take his deep anger at the Comanche out on outlaws. Once, when a sniveling coward of a stagecoach thief tried to sneak away from their campfire in the night, Speaks shot him once, cleanly, through the head. "Got what he asked for," was all Lyle said.

"You think that southern lady is going to marry a bounty hunter?" November asked him one night.

"Not going to be a bounty hunter all my life," he said. "Neither are you. We . . . we're headed for something, Sam. I just haven't figured it out yet."

Sam November was always ready to let his friend do the "figuring." He just followed along. But always, he wondered where revenge on the Comanche would fit in the scheme of things.

One day as Melanie and Lyle were returning from a ride, they met Ben Thompson, coming home after a day's work at the bank.

"Thompson," Speaks said, raising his hat.

"Mr. Speaks," came the reply. "I've been meaning to talk to you. Melanie, could you leave us for a minute." He made no effort to help her dismount, and Melanie wondered with a hidden giggle if he meant her to leave still ahorseback. That would have scandalized Sophie, if she'd gone off riding alone through town.

Lyle was off his horse in a second, throwing the reins to Thompson, who looked surprised and somewhat indignant at having to hold the other man's horse. But Speaks was already helping Melanie dismount, his hands around her waist, her hands on his shoulders.

Was it Thompson's imagination or did they stay that way just a fraction of a second too long? And did their eyes really meet and lock for just a minute? Before he could be sure, Melanie was thanking "Mr. Speaks" for the ride, and Mr. Speaks was bowing from the waist—a gesture he was getting better at. Then she opened the gate, went up the dirt path and vanished into the house.

"My wife," Thompson began, "is upset."

"I heard she is in the family way," Speaks said.

"No, no, that's not it." He wanted to add that even between men such a subject was not politely brought up, but he refrained. "She is upset at this . . . this relationship between you and her sister."

"I'm finding her company delightful," Speaks said, not at all relieving the other man's anxiety. He considered adding that he intended to marry the girl but thought he'd spare this nervous banker that much.

"It's not proper for her to be riding with you unchaperoned," Thompson said, speaking through his nose as if that gave him authority.

"Well," Speaks said, talking slowly as though to one who might have difficulty understanding, "Mrs. Thompson surely can't ride with us. And I can't see that you'd want to take time from the bank to do it. Now maybe I could ask Sam November . . . ."

"That would hardly solve the problem," Thompson said. "I want you to discontinue the rides and stop calling on my sister-in-law."

Speaks was polite but firm. "I'm afraid I can't do that, banker." With that, he raised his hat again, grabbed the reins of Melanie's horse, mounted his own, and rode off, leaving an indignant banker behind him.

The next time he came for Melanie, she appeared wearing a muslin skirt and white shirtwaist.

"You're a mind-reader," he said as he helped her mount.

"Why?" she asked. "And why do you have a third horse? Is someone else going with us?"

He chuckled. "No, but your brother-in-law thinks that would be a good idea. You'll see what I have in mind."

They rode south this time, where the land dipped into culverts and hidden valleys. At a stream he called Clear Fork of the Trinity, there were trees and shade from the sun, which was almost summer-hot. Carefully, Speaks unrolled a bundle from behind his saddle.

He watched her as he spoke. "If I turn my back and stand on the other side of the horses, will you put these on?" He unfurled a pair of pants, sizes too large for her. Then he handed her a length of rope. "For a belt," he said.

She stared at him in disbelief.

"Well," he said, now uncomfortable, "I thought maybe you could ride astride, and then we could race over the prairie like you been wanting to do. If you don't think it's a good idea . . . ."

Without hesitation she went to him and took his face between her hands. "I think it's a wonderful idea," she said. "And the sweetest thing anyone has done for me in . . . I don't know when."

He was tempted—sorely tempted—to kiss her, what with her face just inches from his, but he didn't want to step beyond the boundaries of propriety. He was saved by her stern command.

"Get behind that horse, and turn your back," she said. "I'll tell you when I'm ready."

"Yes, ma'am!"

In minutes, she called him, and he walked around the horse to look at her. It was all he could do to keep from laughing. The pants could have held two of her, and the rope she had knotted through the loops made them pleat so they were bigger than some of her skirts. The dainty white pleated chemisette she had worn with her skirt looked purely ridiculous on top of the outlandish pants. But, having no mirror in which to see herself, she looked inordinately proud.

He couldn't help it. He laughed, and then he couldn't stop. Then she, looking down at herself, began to laugh. Finally she had to sit down on the ground, panting. "I think next time you should bring me a shirt," she said. "And could you find a smaller pair of pants?"

"Those are mine," he managed through gasps. "It never occurred to me but I guess I could go get some pants made for young boys."

"A capital idea!" She stood up, having finally regained control. "What do we do with my clothes? Just leave them here?"

He nodded. "We'll come back to this spot, and you'll have to change again."

"What if some Indian comes along and decides he wants a muslin skirt and petticoats for his wife?" That idea set her to giggling again.

"You'll have to go home looking like that!" he said, and when he imagined the looks on Ben and Sophie's faces, he too was off on hopeless laughter again.

Finally, they sobered. Lyle tied the sidesaddle horse to a small tree by the creek, draped her clothes carefully over a bush, and held a hand for her to mount. She was awkward at first, riding astride, and had to fight the urge to sling her right leg over to the left side of the saddle. But when he slapped her horse's rump with his hat and they took off across the prairie at a gallop, she shouted with delight. They rode, the world whirling by them in a blur, until Lyle caught the reins of her horse and slowed them both down. "The horses," he said, "they're getting winded."

"Me, too," she panted. "But that was the most wonderful thing I've ever done. You've given me a gift, and I thank you." With a smile, she added, "Besides, the pants are cooler than all those skirts."

He looked at her, uncertain whether to smile or not. Even Lyle Speaks, untutored man of Texas, knew that women didn't ordinarily talk about their skirts with men to whom they were not married. He changed the subject. "We'll walk the horses a bit, and then we can ride back to . . . ah, your clothes."

"And hope they're still there," she said mischievously.

The clothes were there, and so was the tethered horse. After a last hard ride across the prairie, Melanie was as winded as the horses, and when Lyle reached to helped her dismount, she fell into his arms. Without Ben Thompson there to watch, they stood that way for a long minute, and then, forgetting his mother's admonitions about the way you treated proper young ladies, Lyle Speaks bent down and kissed Melanie Beaufort. Her lips were cold and still, having never been asked to respond thus before, but then she answered his kiss tentatively . . . and Lyle suspected she might get a lot better at it with practice.

"You best get those clothes on," he said, pulling away. "I'll step over here and turn my back."

When they rode sedately up to the Thompsons' house, Melanie Beaufort knew that something had happened that would change her life forever. She would never again be the same person who had ridden away from this house only hours ago.

But when Lyle Speaks helped her dismount, he held her properly at a distance. And he said, "I have to go away. I maybe gone three weeks or more. I'll be back as soon as I can."

Impishly, she looked up at him. "Will you bring three horses next time?"

He grinned. "I will." And then he was gone.

Bad things, they say, always happen in threes. Melanie Beaufort came to believe it in early August that year. Lyle Speaks left for three weeks or more, that was the first. Then Sophie's long-overdue baby put in an appearance that involved prolonged labor and much gnashing of teeth and screaming on the part of the new mother. And finally, Melanie received a letter from her own mother.

About Lyle, there was little she could do but worry, and worry she did. He and Sam November were trailing horse thieves to the north, up to what he called "Red River country." She had only the vaguest idea of what that meant, but she was fairly certain it was also Comanche country. The realistic part of her mind knew that what Lyle did was dangerous and that he could just not come back from any of his trips, but that part of her mind also recognized that he was more capable of self-protection than most and that he and

Sam November were an unusual and impressive combination. The imaginative side of her mind constantly saw Lyle staked out on the prairie—hadn't she read somewhere that Indians did that?—or hanging from a tree limb because the horse thieves had lynched the bounty hunters, instead of the other way around. Indeed, if Lyle Speaks could have been privy to her wildest imaginings, he wouldn't have known whether to laugh at their extreme nature or be angry at her apparent lack of confidence in his ability to take care of himself. For Melanie, it would be a long three weeks and she would spend much of it pacing, albeit sometimes with a crying baby in her arms.

The baby was all reality and her presence required no wild imagining, although Melanie suspected that Sophie had suffered through some during the long hours she labored to bring the child into the world. It began late one night, when Sophie complained of indigestion. Melanie wanted to suggest that she had eaten a rather large dinner for one in her delicate condition, but she bit her tongue. Within an hour, indigestion had turned into labor pains.

Melanie had honestly tried to prepare for this moment, for she felt that to be of aid was the whole reason she had suffered through a hellish long trip by steamer and stage from Georgia. She sent Ben for the doctor, hoping he could be found. And she called to Penny.

"Penny, we must get Mrs. Sophie to bed," she said, her voice calm with practicality.

"Lord, Miss Melanie, I don't' know nothin' about birthin' babies. When my maw had her babies, she made us young'uns leave the cabin. Sometimes we was gone two days."

Melanie rolled her eyes heavenward, while Sophie continued to moan. "You don't have to know anything, Penny. Just do what I say. First, put her arm over your shoulders and together we'll get her to the bedroom. Are the linens clean?"

"Yes, ma'am, they are."

Getting Sophie to bed proved more difficult than Melanie had anticipated, for she was limp, dead weight. But at last they had her in the bed, dressed in a flannel gown, even though she had wailed for one of her pretty silk ones.

"I want to look pretty for the baby," she panted between moans.

"Not now, Sophie," Melanie said, realizing she would have to be stern with her sister.

She sent Penny to boil water and bring clean sheets. At home in Georgia when her mother had the younger children, Melanie remembered that a housemaid had tied ropes to the posters at the foot of the bed and given these to her mother to pull on. Improvising, she pulled the draw-cords from the bedroom drapes, allowing them to hang limp over the windows, and tied them to the rail at the foot of Melanie's iron bedstead.

"Here," she said, "pull on these."

"I haven't the energy," Sophie said, her tone indignant.

"Sophie, you'll have to have the energy or you'll never get that baby out. It won't come by itself. You'll have to do the work." Her voice was deliberately harsh.

"Why are you so mean to me?" Sophie wailed.

By the time Ben returned with the doctor, Melanie was tearing sheets into strips to be used for bandaging or whatever. It seemed to her a logical thing to do, but Ben was indignant.

"Those are good linens!" he cried. "What are you doing?"

"I think you have enough bandages," the doctor said mildly. "Might I have a cup of coffee?"

She sent Penny to brew a pot of coffee—"Be sure to put in an eggshell to settle the grounds!"—and sent the doctor into the room with Sophie. Ben hovered at the door of the bedroom until Melanie suggested that he go out on the porch and see if the night air didn't offer the slightest breeze.

"And leave Sophie?" He was aghast.

"You won't be far, and I'll get you if you're needed." Melanie could see that this would be a long night.

The first piercing scream came at one in the morning, startling Melanie from the rocker where she'd been dozing. Her dream had been of Lyle on the prairie with a broken leg, his horse having spooked and thrown him, his companion having ridden on. She could hear Lyle saying, "No, don't worry about me. You go after them." She was almost relieved that it was only Sophie screaming in childbirth.

Things went on that way through the night. The doctor left, saying he'd be back at daybreak, and that there was nothing to do but give her sips of water and lots of encouragement. "Urge her to pull on those ropes. She doesn't seem inclined to help herself."

Melanie spent the night sponging Sophie's forehead and praising her few feeble pulls at the ropes. By daybreak, when the doctor returned, she was more tired than Sophie. The doctor ordered Penny to take her place at the bedside and sent Melanie to sleep, but it was at best a fitful sleep punctuated by Sophie's screams.

By noon, Ben had decided that Sophie was going to die. "It's my fault. I should never have . . . ." He blushed, to think that he was speaking of such intimate matters to an unmarried woman.

Melanie was tempted to put him on the spot by asking, "You should never have what, Ben?" Instead she said, "Nonsense. Most women have this much difficulty with the first baby, and they say afterwards, with a baby in her arms, she'll forget all about the pain."

"Not Sophie," Ben muttered.

By suppertime, even Melanie had begun to worry. Sophie was exhausted and nearly crazy with pain. The doctor had come and gone all day, but when he returned in the evening Melanie asked, "Is there nothing you can do?"

"She's almost there," he said. "She has not . . . ah . . . been the most cooperative patient. And . . . ." He hesitated as though not sure he should finish, but then he plunged boldly on. "Her extra weight does not make this any easier. I can hardly feel the baby."

Sophie, claiming she was eating for two, had put on more pounds than Melanie cared to think about. She had gone from gentle and round to overwhelmingly fat, and Melanie knew their mother would have had a few things to say about that if she'd seen Sophie.

The baby arrived shortly after dark, a squawling, healthy baby girl with a headful of dark hair. Melanie helped to sponge off the baby and get Sophie into a clean gown—silk this time, thank you— and fresh linens, while Penny stood cooing at the tiny handful.

"We done it, missy," she said in a singsong voice. "We done brought you into this world hale and hearty."

Melanie wanted to whirl and say, "What do you mean 'we'?"

With mother and child clean and in fresh clothes, Melanie invited Ben in and shooed the doctor and Penny from the room. Ben stayed no more than five minutes before he came rushing from the room, apparently still uncomfortable about the screams he'd heard. His first, indignant words were directed toward Melanie.

"It looks more like your baby than hers. Where'd she get all that dark hair? Sophie's blonde!"

Melanie gave him a withering look. "But not everyone in our family is," she said. "Your daughter is beautiful, and I hope you told her mother that."

"Yes, yes, of course I did." Nervously, he went out the door to pace the veranda again.

They named the baby Emily, after Mrs. Beaufort back in Georgia. The doctor said Sophie would need to rest a day or two then could be up and about as long as she did no heavy housework. Melanie wanted to assure him there was no danger of that!

But Sophie seemed to require much more rest—days stretched into weeks, and she was too weak to rise from her bed. Ben hovered over her when he was not at the bank, and Penny labored over energy-building meals—fried chicken, mashed potatoes, stew, all the heavy dishes she'd been taught were good for building the blood. Melanie was left with Emily, a responsibility she delighted in.

Sometimes she'd stand on the veranda, the baby in her arms, and look to the west over the prairie, as though she'd see Lyle riding in. She'd imagine him admiring the baby and looking deep into her eyes as if to say he hoped one day they, too, would be the parents of such a beautiful child. But then she'd bring herself up short by remembering that Lyle was probably not the marrying kind and that the differences between them were as great as a canyon which could not be jumped. Sometimes she'd look at the contented sleeping baby in her arms and wonder how those two people had ever produced this beautiful, happy child. "Mean, that's what you are, Melanie Beaufort," she said to herself when those thoughts came unbidden.

The letter from her mother came the day Emily was two weeks old, which happened to be the day that Lyle had been gone three weeks. Melanie knew better than to expect him back punctually on the day he said—his was not work that followed the calendar—but she also knew the longer he was gone, the more she would worry. So she was not in a good frame of mind when she slit open the envelope.

Dear Daughter,
We are anxiously awaiting the news of the arrival of our first grandchild. I know that you will be of great help to your sister, and I am grateful to you for undertaking that long journey to be with

her. Ben will, of course, be of comfort to her, but it is not the same as having a woman from your own family with you at that hour of need. I am only sorry that I could not be with Sophie, as by rights I should have been, if that husband of hers had not seen fit to take her off to the wilds of Texas.

"You should be grateful," Melanie thought, "that you are not here. Sophie would have embarrassed you—or driven you wild."

Then the letter got down to brass tacks.

Sophie has written us about your "preoccupation" with a gentleman from Texas. We are given to understand that you are infatuated with a man who is not your social nor educational equal. While I have always had faith in your good judgment, Melanie, I know that you are sometimes given to impetuosity. I expect you to break off this friendship at once and no longer see this man. I am sure there must be suitable men in that place for you to meet. Surely Ben would not have taken Sophie to a total wilderness.

Your father joins me in sending love and wishes me to tell you that he expects you to behave in a way that will do the family credit. By that I mean, of course, no more unchaperoned rides across the prairie with this rough, uncouth Speaks person.

Your loving Mother, E. Beaufort

Melanie held the letter in shaking hands, uncertain whether to laugh or cry, whether to storm into Sophie's sickroom and accuse her of snitching—and slanting the truth—or ignore it. Knowing that actions taken in haste were often regretted, she slipped the letter into her pocket. But every word was emblazoned on her memory, and she carried those words with her day and night.

Lyle Speaks returned to Fort Worth corraling a herd of fifty horses and packing three dead men on led horses. He and November had caught the horse thieves herding the animals north to sell to the Comanche. Two thieves died on the spot; the third, halfway back to Fort Worth.

"You want to go in another way, so you don't go by her house?" Sam asked at one point.

"Nope. I ain't putting on any pretenses."

So Melanie saw Lyle Speaks return, and all that registered in her mind was there were three dead men draped across the backs of three horses. She fingered her mother's letter in her pocket.

He sent word that night that he would come for her in the evening, being as the days were so hot now. When he arrived, he had only two horses.

Melanie, carefully dressed in a muslin skirt and the plainest shirt she owned, threw propriety to the winds and met him at the gate. "You only have two horses!" she accused.

He laughed aloud. "I'm glad you missed me too!" Then, more seriously, "I decided it was silly to have three horses for two people. I've got a plan."

She believed him, and they were soon cantering out of sight of the village. As they rode, she told him all about Emily's arrival, and she spared nothing about what she saw as Sophie's weakness.

"You won't be like that?" he asked.

"You bet I won't," she said. "Mama always said doctors and midwives are scornful of women who scream."

He chewed on that thought and liked what he heard from her.

When they reached "their spot" on the Trinity, he handed her pants and a loose shirt and walked around the horses.

Once changed, she demanded "Do I have to ride sidesaddle dressed like this?"

"No, I'm gonna' ride bareback, and you can ride my horse."

She smiled at him and, without even thinking about it, she walked into his arms. He kissed her, but gently, and then pushed her away. Lyle Speaks was a man who knew about propriety . . . and understood that things could easily get out of hand right here on the prairie.

They rode fast and hard for only a mile or two, and then she pulled her horse to a stop. "I want to sit," she said.

Obligingly, he helped her dismount, ground-reined the horses, and put the saddle blanket from his horse on the ground. "Don't want to sit on ants," he said.

"I've had a letter from my mother," she told him. "She's as much as ordered me to stop seeing you."

"Does she have some kind of second sight?" he asked. "I mean, all the way from Georgia!"

"Sophie wrote her, the snitch!"

He laughed. "I bet Ben Thompson put her up to it. I'd pull my money out of his bank if there was another bank in town."

"I don't know what to do," she said.

His hand reached to cover hers. "You have two choices. You can stop seeing me, or you can keep on riding the prairies with me."

"It's not that simple," she replied, averting her eyes from his. "I saw you come in yesterday . . . ."

"And you know we killed three men." He said it flatly, without looking at her. "I do my job. I'm paid to bring men in dead or alive. I'd rather bring them in alive, but I'm not going to risk my neck—or November's—to save some outlaw. Men who break the law make a deliberate choice—they know the risks. If I didn't go after them, someone else would. If nobody did, we couldn't live in this land."

"But couldn't you . . . " She almost smiled. "Couldn't you be a banker or something where you didn't have to kill?"

"Nope. It's not in my nature." He wondered if now was the time to tell her about how he'd lost his family, as though that would in some way explain the anger that almost forced him to do what he did. But Lyle wasn't used to confiding, and he particularly didn't want to talk about that day twelve years ago. Instead, he asked curiously, "Do they ever kill men in Georgia?"

"Not the people I know!" she said indignantly.

"I bet you'd be surprised," he said. "What about whipping slaves? Is it worse to kill an outlaw than to whip an innocent slave?"

She grinned at him. "Why do you presume the slave is innocent? They're people. They do bad things."

"What an admission from a southern girl!" he exclaimed. "Slaves are people. Do I take it that you don't approve of slavery?"

"It's not a question of approving or disapproving," she said slowly. "It's the way life is in Georgia . . . and always will be."

"Then you've not been keeping up with the news," he said. "And I suspect you've not read *Uncle Tom's Cabin*."

"That awful book," she exclaimed. "I wasn't allowed to read it. Have you read it?"

"No, but I'll get you a copy. The North is up in arms about this slavery business, and I'm afraid there's more power up north than in the South. I'm no politician, but I think they'll go to war."

"They? Isn't it your country too?"

"Naw." He laughed. "That war won't touch us out here."

"You wouldn't fight?"

"Texas will need take care of its own problems if war comes. Think about Indians, for instance. If the army pulls its soldiers back east to fight, the Comanche will try to take over this country again."

"And you'd fight the Indians but not the Yankees?"

"Reckon so," he said.

It was a loyalty—or lack of loyalty—that she couldn't and wouldn't understand. To her, the South was home and demanded allegiance. Texas was . . . well, frontier, not a country. How could one be loyal to Texas? She stood up abruptly. "Let's ride." It was almost an order.

She set the pace, riding so hard and fast that Lyle Speaks began to wonder about the wisdom of his bareback ride. But he kept up with her, afraid to let her go farther on her own, and at last, as winded as her horse, she pulled to a stop.

"I feel better now," she said triumphantly.

"I'm glad." He would never admit that he felt a lot worse.

They walked their horses back to the spot on the river, talking about nothing serious, avoiding her mother's letter, his killing of the outlaws, even the possibility of war. She told him about the baby and how spoiled Sophie was—"I don't know how she'll manage when I go back."

"Do you want to stay?" he asked.

She shrugged. "I don't know."

Speaks was the first to spot trouble. Melanie's skirt was not hanging on the bush where they'd left it. He looked around to make sure he had the right spot, but it was his business to note signs like bushes and trees, and he had little doubt about which bush was which. Without a word, he pushed his horse into a fast trot. The sidesaddle was gone too!

Melanie approached to find him dismounted and doubled over in laughter. "Whatever is the matter with you?" she asked. Her attention was so riveted on him that she hadn't noticed that her clothes were missing.

When he finally straightened up and calmed himself, he said,

"I'm picturing you riding into town that way."

"This way? Why?" Only then did she look around. "My clothes! They're gone!"

"So's the blasted sidesaddle and I bet the livery will charge me a pretty penny for that," he said.

She slid off the horse, took one look at him, and began to laugh herself. Finally, choking, she sputtered, "Sophie! She'll die of embarrassment."

Lyle Speaks knew at that moment that he loved her. Any other woman would have been furious and would have likely turned that fury on him. Furthermore, most women would have thought of their own embarrassment. She didn't seem to give a fig about what people would think of her.

"We can wait till dark to go in," he suggested.

She began to giggle again. "Then Sophie will think we've been killed by Indians, so she'll have two reasons to be angry—because we made her worry and because I'm a disgrace to the family."

Neither knew how it happened, but the next instant she was in his arms, and he was kissing her gently on the forehead, the tip of her nose, and finally on the mouth. His gentle kiss turned to one of real longing and passion, and she responded much more than she had during their one brief kiss before. Wordlessly they sank to the ground, their mouths locked together.

It was Speaks who stood up. "I don't think we'll wait for dark," he said. Over the years, he and November had visited more than once with the soiled doves in various West Texas towns, but he had never known the desire that raced through him now. It frightened him—for himself and for her.

Equally shaken although less understanding of what had happened, she sat on the ground. "You know those two choices you gave me before?"

He nodded.

"I know which one I want."

He drew in his breath and waited.

"I want to keep riding with you."

Exhaling slowly, he said "I'm glad." And almost added, "And I want to marry you." He didn't know what made him afraid to say the words. It was as though she were a doe that would spook easily.

Instead, he said, "Well, damn, I guess I'll just have to find another sidesaddle."

She rode proudly into town, head high, slid off her horse at the fence, and handed him the reins, letting her hand linger in his just a moment. Then, with a wry smile, she headed for the door, calling over her shoulder, "I'll return the pants tomorrow."

The lace curtain moved back into place.

Sophie waited, hands planted on her hips. In another part of the house, the baby wailed loudly. Before Sophie could attack, Melanie said, "What's the matter with Emily? Why aren't you seeing to her?"

"Don't tell me how to take care of my child, Melanie Beaufort. You're a disgrace to this family."

"I knew you'd say that, and I don't want to hear it," Melanie said crisply. "Nor will I tell you why I happen to be wearing a pair of men's pants." She stormed out of the room, leaving her sister behind babbling to herself. But Melanie thought she heard the words, "Wait till Ben comes home" and resisted the urge to ask, "Why, will he spank me?"

That night, while Lyle Speaks lay on his bunk, hands behind his head, eyes fixed vacantly on the ceiling, Sam November went to Steele's Tavern. When he came in two hours later, smelling of whiskey, he shook Speaks awake.

"Man, you've done it now," he said, his voice full of laughter. "Everyone's talkin' about how you brought that southern girl home wearing pants. Speaks, is there something you aren't telling me?"

Speaks sat up. "They're talking about it? Who?" He reached for his boots.

"No, no," November said, "You'll not go defend her honor against a bunch of drunks. And I'm too drunk to help you."

"She's too good for the likes of them to talk about." Then his face reddened. "Besides, it was all very innocent."

"You need to go to Miss Sadie's?" November asked.

Lyle threw a shoe at him.

The next morning, dressed in his newest breeches and a freshly laundered shirt, his hair clean and plastered to his head, Lyle Speaks rode up to the Thompson residence. For once, he wished he owned a suit like the ones Banker Thompson wore to work every day.

Sophie opened the door when he knocked. "You're not welcome here," she said.

He wondered how two sisters could be so different in looks and temperament. Politely, he said, "I came to see Miss Melanie."

"Miss Melanie is busy tending the baby," Sophie hissed.

Melanie disproved her words by appearing behind her. "Mr. Speaks," she said formally. "May I help you?"

"Yes, ma'am, I came to talk with you if I might . . . in private."

"Mr. Thompson has ordered me not to allow you in this house after you disgraced my sister." Sophie's voice rose in agitation.

He almost bowed. "Then perhaps we can speak on the veranda. Mrs. Thompson, I have come to make amends for embarrassing your sister. It's the last thing in the world I wanted to do." He hated himself for fawning over this bothersome young woman.

"Fiddle, Sophie! If anyone's embarrassed, it's you. It didn't bother me a bit. Now go see to Emily, and I'll speak to Ly. . . Mr. Speaks." She stepped out on the veranda and pulled the door firmly shut behind her. Then, looking at him, she had to cover her mouth to keep from laughing. "Isn't she foolish?" she asked.

To her surprise, he didn't even smile in response. Instead, looking down at the hat he held in his hands—she noticed his still-wet hair— he said, "I came, Melanie, to ask if you would marry me."

Taken completely by surprise, she learned against the veranda railing for support. Finally, weakly, she muttered, "I don't think that's what Mother had in mind in her letter."

"Do you mean that your family would never give permission for you to marry me . . . or for me to court you?"

"I guess that's what I mean." She wanted to throw herself in his arms, tell him she didn't care about her family, beg him to take her away right then. But she stood rooted to the floor.

"And you need their approval, their permission?" He spoke formally.

"I don't know," she said slowly. "May I have time to think about it?"

"Of course." He too felt the strangeness of their situation. He wanted to hold her, laugh with her as he had done on the prairie. Instead, he stood before her, feeling like a wooden doll. A speechless wooden doll.

He inclined his head just a little—the best he could do towards a bow at the moment—and bid her good-day, ramming his hat on his head as he went toward his horse. Although she stared after him, he never looked back.

"Well," Sophie said when Melanie went inside, "I certainly hope you told him you'd never see him again."

"I think," Melanie said, "that I will probably marry him."

"Marry him!" her sister screeched. "You can't!"

"I can." She wanted to add, "He's a lot better than the fool you married," but she kept that thought to herself.

She sent him a message with the simple word "Yes" and her name. He came, dressed in his finest and still wishing for a suit. They sat in the parlor, like strangers.

"I guess I'll have to go to Georgia," he said.

"Why?" She was appalled at the thought. It conjured up visions she'd rather not contemplate. Mostly visions of her mother, who could be as uppity as Sophie.

"To meet your parents, and ask your father's permission."

"Ah, I didn't think we'd do all that. I thought . . . well, maybe I presumed . . . but couldn't we just get married here?"

"I don't think that would be proper," he said. He was remembering his mother and imagining what she would have said to him. The one thing she never would have said was that this girl was too good for him, and that thought never occurred to Lyle Speaks. She was different, he knew that, but they could overcome differences. He didn't know, as she did, that her parents would find him wanting in education, in social graces, and in future prospects.

"Well," she said, rising impatiently, "I'm not to go until October, and it's only August now." Then she exploded. "Lyle Speaks, I don't want to sit in a parlor and speak formally with you! I want to ride and laugh and be like we've always been. Marriage comes up and look what happens!"

He was startled at first, and then he began to laugh. Standing, he grabbed her hands and whirled her around the room. "Will you be ready to ride tomorrow?"

"Will you have a sidesaddle?"

"Yeah," he promised. And wondered why he felt apprehensive.

She wondered why she felt sad.

They rode on the prairie almost every day. Sometimes when they left Sophie stood on the veranda, her arms folded across her chest in a belligerent way, staring stonily at them.

"What's the old saying," Lyle asked, "about if looks could kill?"

"We'd wither like prairie grass in the summer heat," she said.

He laughed. "You're starting to talk like a Texan. That's good."

"It is?" she said, genuinely puzzled. She never intended to talk like most of the Texans she'd met.

Other times they'd arrive home near dusk to find Ben Thompson sitting on the rocker, pushing it back and forth with one foot, his fingers drumming impatiently on the chair arm. Once he saw them, he'd rise and enter the house without ever having spoken a word.

They'd become accustomed to their routine. Lyle brought "her" pants—a smaller, boy's pair—and a cotton shirt for her, and he turned his back in a gentlemanly fashion while she changed, though he had to fight back waves of longing that went over him. They never did find out what happened to the stolen clothes and sidesaddle, but now they were simply more careful about hiding things. They had found a plum thicket that did nicely for that purpose.

By late afternoon, now that it was September, the air had cooled some, and sometimes there was enough of a breeze to ruffle Melanie's hair as she rode. They had survived the beating sun and ferocious heat of the Texas summer, but in spite of the bonnet she had worn faithfully her face had tanned. Lyle thought she glowed with a look of health and happiness, and he told her so, in words that made her blush and look away. She thought he looked handsome as always, but she was embarrassed to tell him . . . or didn't know how.

"Next summer," she said, "I want a hat like yours."

"You'll have it," he promised.

Sometimes they rode without talking, letting the horses amble along companionably; other times, they raced across the prairie, chasing each other and shouting like Indians. Well, at least Melanie thought they sounded like wild Indians. Lyle never would have made that comparison. Other times, they ground reined the horses and sat watching the sky change as the sun went down and light clouds trailed across the sky.

They never talked of serious things like marriage, for they had found the subject turned them both into speechless wooden dolls. Once he felt obliged to tell her about his family. He didn't tell her it was something she had to know if she married him. Instead he just said, in his blunt way, "My family was massacred by Comanches. My mother and father and one brother scalped; my sister . . . well, she was terrorized before she was killed. I saved my littlest brother." She knew what he meant by "terrorized," and she knew that what he had just told her explained the hard look he sometimes got in his eyes, the look that had puzzled her all along. But it left her speechless. "I'm sorry" seemed empty and trite, though she did lay a hand on his arm and say it.

He shrugged. "I've learned to live with it."

She knew he hadn't. She couldn't say "How awful!" nor could she tell him that now she had two visions in her head that would not leave: one of a family she'd never seen, lying scalped in the yard of a house she'd never seen; the other of three dead men across the backs of three horses.

One day as they walked their horses toward home, he said, "In October I'll go east with you. Speak to your father."

"I guess so," she said.

"You don't sound like you put much stock in the idea." He stared straight ahead, as though afraid to look at her. Maybe, if he looked at her eyes, he'd see that she didn't love him.

"I . . . I can't imagine it," she said. "Oh, Lyle, there's so much I can't imagine."

"You don't have to imagine anything," he said. "You just let what's going to happen come."

She shook her head. "I always have it planned out before . . . and I always know if it's going to work or not."

His voice almost broke as he said, "And this isn't going to work?"

"I don't know," she said miserably.

Two days later, she received a letter addressed in her father's bold, scrawling hand.

Dear Daughter,
Your mother is ill. You are needed at home. Please come at once.

Your Father,
William P. Beaufort

When Lyle came for their ride, she tucked the letter in her pocket and went to meet him with her usual smile on her face.

When she had changed in her pants, she came round the horses, grabbed his arm, and reached up to kiss him, a light, teasing kiss.

"What's that for?" he asked, obviously pleased.

"For being you, because I love you," she said. Without waiting for his help, she was ahorseback—a trick she'd learned over the summer. "I'll beat you to that far tree!" and she was off, leaving him to leap into the saddle and gallop after her. She beat him, a triumph that set her to laughing.

"You're sure full of yourself today," he said.

"I have to be . . . or I'll cry." She had put the letter in the pants pocket, and now she fished it out and handed it to him.

He read, then looked at her. "You'll go?

"I have to."

"And it's not a good time for me to go with you."

She shook her head. Then, "I'll come back."

But they both knew at that moment that she would never come back to Texas.

Lyle drove her to the stagecoach. When she walked out of the Thompson house, Sophie followed, wringing her hands. "Poor dear mother, whatever can it be?"

"Serious, if Papa wrote me," Melanie said shortly. "Try to take good care of Emily, Sophie."

"She's my daughter!" was the indignant reply.

To Ben, Melanie said briefly, "Thank you for your hospitality," words so formal that they almost conveyed her distaste. She hugged Sophie quickly and felt a pang over the distance that had come between sisters once close. Then she turned and walked around the wagon, where Lyle waited to help her up. He had already thrown her baggage behind the seat. When they drove away, she never looked back. Melanie Beaufort was wondering if her mother was really sick or if she, herself, had been caught in—or rescued by?—a trap of Sophie's making. She would only know when she got to Tennessee, and she couldn't risk calling Sophie's bluff in case her mother really needed her.

"I'll let you know what's wrong with Mother and when I'm coming back," she said to Lyle, and he replied "I'll be waiting." Then he kissed her lightly on the forehead and handed her into the stagecoach. He drove off in the wagon long before the driver cracked the whip over the horses that pulled the coach.

"Let's go. We're movin' on." Lyle Speaks charged into the room he shared with Sam November.

Caught napping after an afternoon beer or two, November struggled awake. Sitting up and rubbing his eyes groggily, he echoed, "Moving on?"

"That's what I said. I told you we weren't going to be bounty hunters forever."

"What about Melanie?" He asked before he thought, and the minute the words were out he would have done almost anything to take them back.

Speaks' jaw tightened, and his eyes took on that hard look that November knew better even than Melanie did. "Never would work out. We're too different."

"I hope she's not heartbroken," Sam said.

"She's not." Lyle Speaks didn't believe in heartbreak, but this was the second terrible wound to his soul that he would carry the rest of his life.

They rode north at dusk, in spite of Sam's timid suggestion that they wait till morning. Speaks was determined to go then, though he didn't say where.

"Where we goin'?" November asked.

Lyle shrugged, as if to say, "Don't know."

Sam November just sighed and prepared to follow his friend.

Sophie and Ben Thompson were among the many for whom life in Texas was too much. Within a year, they returned to Georgia. With them gone and Lyle Speaks gone north, there was no one in Fort Worth who remembered Melanie Beaufort. But folks talked for a long time, and children heard the story of the wild lady from Georgia who rode astride in men's pants.

The Art of Dipping Candles

My mother doesn't make candles any more. Her candles used to be the smoothest and straightest in North Texas. They burned bright with an even flame and never smoked. Ma ran candles in the late fall, when Pa had killed a steer and she had rendered the tallow. She'd make more candles than we needed for daily use for the whole year, just so we could have them all around the house at Christmas. Sometimes, in the summer if she could find beeswax, she made a second batch, but beeswax was hard to come by.

Ma knew just how much clay from the Red River bottoms to put in the kettle so the candles would have some color, and she knew how long to wait for the dirt to color the tallow and then settle to the bottom so that the candles wouldn't be gritty. In front of our cabin Pa had built a stone pit just sized to hold the kettle above a fire, and Ma spent hours there, dipping a wick over and over again, hanging the finished candles to dry, admiring her handiwork when she was done. Sometimes she poured the hot tallow into a mold and it would set in a hour or two on a cold December day, but there wasn't any art in that, she said. Ma liked to dip her candles by hand.

"Mama, can I dip a candle?"

"No, Elizabeth, you haven't the patience yet to make it smooth and straight. Someday . . . ."

I sat and watched and waited for the day I was grown enough to dip candles. To be able to dip a candle was the mark of a woman to me. It wrapped up in one skill all the things that a woman did, and I dreamt of the day I had a husband and children of my own to care for. When I was grown, I would dip candles.

Ma was dipping candles that December day when Pa had gone for supplies and Jeb came screaming across the prairie.

"Ma! Ma! Indians! Indians!" he shouted, running so hard and desperate that I thought sure his lungs would burst. His eyes seemed near bugged out of their sockets, and his voice, just beginning to deepen, was now higher than mine. Any other time, I might have laughed at him for squeaking. "Mr. Belton says they struck the Simpsons and they're headed this way." He collapsed on the ground, his breath having completely left him.

Jeb was fourteen and used to boast about what he'd do if the Comanche came near our house. Now his boasts had given way to sheer terror, and it was a terror that was catching. As I watched him approach, like watching a dream in slow motion, I felt my stomach lurch. Fear enveloped me—hadn't we dreaded an Indian attack ever since Pa had moved us out to the banks of the Red River in 1866?—and I wanted to run and scream and do whatever I could to shake off that blanket of fear.

If I expected Ma to be as frightened as I was, I was mistaken. Candle in hand, she whirled to look at Jeb. But there was no hesitation, no throwing her hands in the air, no instant of wondering what to do. Ma was in control, as though this moment was something she had been anticipating for a long time.

When she spoke, her voice was calm and controlled. "Get inside, Elizabeth, and take Jessamine with you. Go to the attic. *Quickly!*"

Her voice did what no amount of screaming and running would have done—it quieted my fear, and I did as I was told, grabbing two-year-old Jessamine, who whimpered at my roughness, and pulling her into the darkness of our cabin. It was a good wood cabin—Pa had sent to Fort Worth for the wood, when Ma said she wouldn't spend more than one season in a dugout where bugs and dirt sifted out of the roof into the food.

Behind me I heard Ma say, "Jeb, bring this kettle. Careful, don't spill the hot tallow on yourself."

Jessamine and I peered curiously over the edge of the attic trap door, while Ma closed the outside door to the house and threw the great wooden bar across it, ordering Jeb to climb the attic ladder and take the kettle with him.

"Take this kettle up that ladder?" he asked incredulously, having regained his breath.

There was no arguing with Ma. In that same deadly calm voice, she said, "Take it to the attic. Be careful." Then she pulled the boards tight over each of the windows.

Jeb labored up the ladder, having to use one hand to hold the kettle level while he pulled himself up the ladder with the other. A bit of tallow splashed on his leg, causing him to cry out.

"Hush!" Ma ordered.

He barely made it to the top and set the kettle down, with a sigh of relief, when Ma clambered up the ladder behind him. Once up, she pulled the ladder behind her, while we three watched silently.

"Ma?" I asked. "Will the Indians. . . can. . . will the door hold?"

"Probably not," she said calmly. "Now listen to me. It is very important that you do not move, do not make a sound if the Indians come near this house." She paused and looked long and hard at each of us. "Jeb, you peek out that crack there and keep watch. Elizabeth, you tend to Jessamine. Give her that sugar tit and make sure she doesn't cry. Rock her if you need to."

With those words, Ma set herself down beside the kettle, clutching it with both hands.

I rocked little Jessamine until she slept, while Jeb, less frightened and more filled with the importance of his duty, peered through the crack in the roof boards. Ma sat by the kettle, her face expressionless, her hands still clutching. I wondered if the kettle wasn't hot next to her body.

"Ma . . . ."

She put her finger to her lips and looked sternly at me, so I hushed. Ma wasn't much on discipline—Pa always saw to that, while Ma generally surrounded us with her love. It scared me more, now, to have her so grim and unrelenting, when all I wanted was for her to put her arms around me and tell me it would all be all right. She never did do that, the whole long day.

I wanted to ask Jeb how he knew Indians were coming, and ask Ma if she thought Pa would be home soon, and . . . I just wanted someone, anyone, to talk to me. But we were quiet.

It seemed to me we sat that way forever. My legs began to cramp, and I shifted position ever so slightly, causing Jessamine to wake and cry a little and Ma to give me another stern look. We probably hadn't been there half an hour before Jeb, speaking so low we could barely hear him, whispered, "Here they come. Three of them. On horseback."

Ma nodded and then whispered her first words in a long time: "Our lives depend on how quiet you can be."

I could not see them, but I heard . . . their horses raced up to the house, then the hoof beats stopped suddenly, and there was loud talking which I could not understand. The voices didn't sound angry

. . . more curious than anything, I guess. They stayed outside the cabin so long I was near desperate to ask Jeb what they were doing, but he kept his eyes riveted on the scene he saw through the crack, and Ma sat stone-faced, clutching the kettle.

Then there was a knocking on the door, so loud it startled me and made Jessamine give a whimper. Ma turned the upper half of her body quickly, so that she stared at us, and I clamped a firm hand over Jessamine's mouth while I found the sugar tit and gave it to her again. She sucked happily and quietly.

I looked at Jeb, only to see that he was holding his nose, a desperate look in his eyes. Jeb was about to sneeze! I shook my head at him, as though to say, "You can't!" and he shoulders convulsed but no sound came. Then I had to put my hand over my own mouth to stifle a fear-begotten giggle. Ma looked grim.

The banging on the door kept on, and the next thing I heard was the splintering of wood. Then there was loud, masculine laughter and shouting, still in that tongue that none of us knew. Then came the footsteps . . . not loud, for they didn't wear leather shoes like Pa, but still a tramping sound, accompanied by much talk. They were wandering about our cabin, knocking over the table, throwing crockery on the floor, laughing all the while.

I thought about my doll, the one I kept on my bed, and wished I'd brought her to the attic with me.

I looked at Ma. Her knuckles were white, clutching the kettle tightly, tipping it ever so little towards the trap door opening, though she'd put the board door over it.

Then it came to me—Ma intended to pour that boiling tallow on the Indians if they discovered us. It had been her plan all along, a plan she probably formulated lying sleepless at night, worrying about the times that Pa was gone and she was responsible for her family. Candles were her pride, and candles would save her family.

Ma didn't have to pour the hot tallow on the Indians. Having done all the damage they could and taken all the food they could find—corn dodgers from our breakfast, flour, coffee, salt and sugar—they departed. As I listened to their horses hoof beats fade into the distance, I thought it was a good thing they hadn't come tomorrow, when Pa was just back with enough supplies to help us celebrate Christmas, and I was grateful they hadn't found the steer carcass that Pa had hung in the lean-to.

Jeb watched intently long after the sound of the hoof beats was gone, but at last he said, "They're gone" and then he added matter-of-factly, "We'd best go clean up the mess."

I started to cry, the relief from tension somehow bringing my fear to the surface. I just sat there, clutching Jessamine and letting big tears run down my cheeks, while I sobbed quietly, my shoulders heaving. I knew Ma would come take me in her arms any minute.

Instead, her voice was harsh when she said, "Quiet! They'll be back!"

"Ma!" Jeb complained, "They ain't comin' back. They're gone."

I cried on, and Jessamine began to whimper, and all Ma did was clutch that kettle and command us to be quiet. Short of shoving her out of the way, there was nothing we could do—and we children didn't dare do that. We knew something was wrong, terribly wrong, but she was our mother.

So we sat the whole long day, until dusk began to take away the light filtering through the cracks in the roof. Jessamine was hungry and fretful in spite of my best efforts to quiet her, and she needed to be changed desperately, which made me hate having to hold her. I myself began to need a trip to the bushes so badly that I squirmed from time to time. Jeb drummed his fingers on the board floor and wriggled in impatience, though I thought he too might have longed to run for the bushes. But Ma never moved, never loosened her hold on that kettle.

"Here comes Pa," Jeb said softly.

Within minutes we heard the clop of the mules, the creak of the old wooden wagon, and then Pa's terrified call, "Margaret! Jeb! Where are you?" His heavy boots thundered into the house.

"We're up here, Pa," Jeb said.

Still, Ma did not move. Jeb looked for a long minute, while Pa was downstairs demanding to know what happened and if we were all right. Shrugging hopelessly, Jeb went to the trap door, pulled it up and lowered the ladder.

"You better come get Ma," he said.

Pa had to pry her fingers from the now-cold kettle and carry her bodily downstairs. Jeb followed and then held up his arms to take Jessamine from me.

I had to bolt for that trip to the bushes, and while I squatted there I prayed that when I came back Ma would be her old self again, proudly telling Pa how she'd saved us from Indians.

She never did tell him, and we had to do it for her, Jeb and I both babbling at once, while Ma sat in the rocking chair where Pa had placed her and never said a word, never moved, didn't even seem to recognize us. When at last the story had come tumbling out, Pa looked around at the mess the Indians had made—broken crockery, flour and sugar and salt spilled before they were stolen, blankets ripped off beds—and my doll flung into the fireplace, probably the cruelest blow of all to me—and then he went to kneel by the rocker.

"Margaret, you saved our children. You . . . you are the strongest and most wonderful woman I know."

She smiled just a little and reached a hand out to stroke his beard. I thought that smile meant Ma was back to herself, but I was wrong.

It's been a year now, and she still sits in the rocker. I cook the meals and clean the cabin and care for little Jessamine, but Pa says to give Ma time. "She'll be all right," he tells me. "She's just had a terrible shock."

Pa has butchered a beef, and it's time to make candles. I try, remembering what Ma said about patience, but my candles are lopsided, and they bend in the candlesticks instead of standing straight and tall. I want my Ma to come back and dip candles. It's a fine art, candle-dipping is.

Let's Go to Decatur

At first, Ella Hartsell overlooked the small advertisement in the Chicago newspaper, which arrived in her hometown of Kankakee some three days after publication. Then the word "Bride" caught her attention.

"Bride Wanted," it read. "Texas homesteader, 40, widowed, no ch. Good man." And then there was a post office box in some faraway Texas place called Decatur. She had no idea where that was. Indeed the whole state of Texas sounded like a huge, frightening wilderness to her. Hadn't she read that they still, in 1886, suffered from Indian raids? Then again, perhaps not.

Secretively, she clipped the ad and carried it to her bedroom where, late at night, she wrote a measured response. "I am thirty-three years old and recently widowed"—surely, she thought, there was no need to tell him that Joe had left her and run off with the landlady's twenty-year-old daughter, that she had no idea where her husband was, that, indeed, she was still married as far as she knew. In Texas, that shouldn't matter.

She raised her head from her writing and recalled that night of betrayal. Joe had never made much money, and they had always lived in boardinghouses. Her mother used to cluck about it in private to Ella. "Man can't even put a roof over his wife's head," she'd say, shaking her head in despair. "And you having to work at that millinery shop, and still he can't make ends meet."

"You taught me to sew a fine seam, Mother, and it's fitting that I sew hats for ladies that can afford them. I . . . I enjoy it." Well, maybe that was the smallest of a white lie.

"You should be able to afford hats that others sew!" the older woman fumed.

Ella used to soothe her mother, whispering that Joe was a good man, he'd had a streak of bad luck, but his day would come. Why, didn't he have a new job with the railroad? Took tickets, he did, at the station. A responsible position.

Of course, Ella reminded herself now, it was that responsible position—and the railroad pass that went with it—that gave him the means to run away. She'd come home from the millinery shop one afternoon, a Thursday she remembered, to find a note.

"Ella. I'm not coming back. You go on home to your folks." He signed it Joe, no "Love, Joe," no "I'm sorry," just Joe.

She stayed the night at the boardinghouse, packed her clothes and few belongings, and lay awake staring at the ceiling. She felt as though there'd been a death, as though she'd been widowed. Would she work in the millinery shop and become an old-maid lady who lived with her aging parents?

The next morning as she dressed she heard great commotion below and raised voices, but she could not make out the words. Clearly, though, she could hear Mrs. Clements, the woman who ran the house. Ella descended, prepared to announce her departure, but before she could speak, Mrs. Clements began to scream again. This time Ella understood the words.

"He was your husband," she yelled between sobs, "and you let him take my daughter away."

Ella could feel herself turning pale as she grabbed the back of a chair for support. "Pardon me?" she asked automatically, while her mind tried to register what she'd heard.

"You heard me," the older woman spat. "He's done taken my Loretta with him, the light of my life."

Ella sank into the chair. "I . . . I didn't know,' she said, all the while thinking, *So I've been left for a girl fifteen years younger than I am!* The landlady stared at her but offered no words of comfort, and at last Ella rose slowly. "I'll be moving out this evening. Someone will come for my belongings." She paused then, as the thought of money occurred to her. "I believe my . . . ah . . .. my husband has paid for the entire month."

"Not enough he hasn't," the woman growled. "If I catch him, he'll pay a lot more."

Ella moved home to a never-ending chorus of "I told you so" from her mother and silent displeasure from her father whose only comment, made once, was "I'll kill the sonofabitch if I ever see him again." Her mother worried that she would never find another husband, prayed that the Lord would give her strength to endure her trials, and made Ella miserable each evening by demanding, "Did you meet any one interesting today?"

"There are no men in millinery shops," Ella would mutter.

When she went about town, she was aware that people stared at her. In the millinery shop, she tried to stay in the back and avoid the ladies who came in to try on a hat or buy a bit of lace. But every once in a while, one would catch her, grab her hand, and say, "You poor, poor thing." At church, on Sundays, the minister was always too bright as he asked, "May I do anything for you?" And then he whispered, "If I can help, I am always available." She thought perhaps he leered at her.

And then she saw the ad.

She continued her letter in painstakingly careful penmanship. "I am neither fat nor thin and of average height. My hair is brown, my eyes brown"—was she a farm animal that he would look over carefully before he decided on purchase? In truth, Ella tended toward the plain. She wore her rather dull hair pulled back from her face and rarely allowed herself the luxury of a dusting of cornstarch to soften the shine of her face.

Her eyes were her best feature, a deep brown, and these days big and round and sad. Her mother said men found large eyes attractive, but so far not one man had even spoken to Ella. She knew it was because she was disgraced, and she knew her mother was right—she would never marry again in Kankakee.

The mail-order bride ad might just save her life. She scratched out the description and wrote, "I have no children. I am not unpleasant in appearance, keep myself clean and fashionable, and sew my own wardrobe. I can also make men's clothes. And I am a good cook of wholesome food." She chewed on the end of the quill, then dipped it into ink again and wrote, "I could come with fourteen days notice and train fare."

Next morning, she hid the letter in her reticule and carried it to the post office, where she ignored the questioning looks of Mr. Bradley as she bought the necessary postage. Then she waited.

Two months later, she had still heard nothing. She tried to forget about it, but life in Kankakee did not get any better.

Then one spring day her mother greeted her at the door. "You've a letter," she said, holding out the crumpled envelope. "From Texas." Curiosity raised her voice to a high, whiny complaint.

Much to her mother's disappointment, Ella retired to her bedroom—the room she'd occupied as a child, for heaven's sake!—

to read the letter. His name was Walter Dennison, and he would like her to come to Texas He enclosed a money order for $133 for the train fare, hoped that it was sufficient in amount, and asked that she send a telegram to the Decatur post office letting him know when she would arrive. He wrote nothing more, but perhaps there was nothing more to say. She marveled at his trust in sending the money. Carrying the letter, she went back downstairs to the parlor where her mother sat, pretending to crochet an afghan square. "I'm moving to Texas," she announced.

The protests of her mother and the practical objections of her father were equally tiresome. Her mother cruelly reminded her she'd already made one bad choice in men, and "Now you're about to do it again, only we won't be around to protect you."

Her father growled that any man deserving of a wife wouldn't have to advertise for one. "Like going to a whore," Ella heard him mutter to himself.

As much as she could, she ignored them and made her preparations. After two weeks, she boarded a train, promising to write her parents daily, assuring them she would be perfectly safe. As the train drew away and she saw her mother crying, Ella thought she would probably never see either her mother or father again, and she began to cry softly to herself. Then she stiffened her back and sat up straight. She was about to save her life.

* * * * *

A knot of men stood around a fresh grave in the small cemetery, shuffling their feet, mumbling, uncertain what to say. Three women, parasols held over their heads to ward off the Texas sun, stood off to one side, patiently waiting.

There were not many graves in this cemetery, and even fewer markers. One stone marker commemorated the resting place of the oldest son of the area's biggest ranching family. He'd died of blood poisoning, after accidentally chopping his foot with an axe. But the grave around which they gathered was marked only by a wooden cross and the scratched words, "Walter Denison. Gone to God. May 1884."

"Just stretched out in his bed, he was," one man said. "I shook him, but it was plain he'd be gone a long day. Stiff as a board."

"What'd he die from?" asked someone, and the speaker replied,

81

"Doc don't know. Says could be heart attack, stroke, maybe even something he ate. But it wasn't a gunshot and it wasn't blood poisoning—he didn't have any wounds."

"Maybe he was just tired," one man in overalls suggested. "I could understand that my own self."

"You find any family?" another asked.

Will Campbell, the man who'd found Denison, shook his head. "Nope. Went through every paper I could find. And I don't remember him or Helen—may she rest in peace—ever talking about family. It was like each other was all they had."

A third man joined in with speculation. "What's gonna happen to his place? Who's gonna pay his debts or empty his bank account—did he have one?"

Campbell shook his head again. "Don't know, but I'll tell you what's really strange." The men moved closer to hear. "He was fixin' to get married!"

Cries of "Go on" and "You don't say" greeted this until he held up a hand for silence. "I found a letter from a woman, name of Ella Hartsell, from someplace in Illinois, tellin' him she was on her way."

"Well, you best write real quick and tell her not to come." There was general agreement to that.

"Can't do it. She wrote on April 28, saying she was leaving on the tenth of May. Be in Fort Worth the fourteenth, supposing the train kept on time. She's on her way now. Be here in three days."

There was a flurry of conversation but one man spoke up loudly. "Well, Will Campbell, you always been moaning about being a bachelor, not havin' a wife, and no single women anywhere around Decatur, except schoolgirls too young for you. This here's your chance."

Campbell raised his hand again. "Now hold on here. I'm not marrying a pig in a poke. You know if she answered an ad like this she's mighty plain at best. Besides, I maybe got used to being alone." His tone was defensive.

"Best take those words back, Campbell," said a man named John Stanley. "I never laid eyes on my wife till she got off the train. We corresponded, but that's all. And I like her just fine. Cooks and sews good, willing to work, everything you want in a wife."

"Sorry, John, I didn't mean to tread on your toes. It's just that marriage, it's a serious step, and I ain't gonna rush into it just 'cause Walter Denison had the fool sense to die."

"Well, what are we gonna do with this woman when she gets here?"

"Send Campbell to meet her at the train and tell her what happened," someone suggested.

"I ain't goin' alone."

By the time they finished yelling and shouting among themselves, Will Campbell was going to Fort Worth—alone. His neighbors left him no choice.

* * * * *

When the conductor announced "Fort Worth in one hour," Ella Hartsell felt anxiety rise like a lump in her throat. Walter's money had paid the fare but did not stretch to cover the sleeper, and she had slept, as best she could, slumped on the prickly plush and terribly straight seat that smelled slightly of too many other bodies who'd occupied the same space. Meals at the eating houses adjoining the various depots on the long journey had been, to her mind, questionable and expensive, so she'd eaten little and by now was past hunger and well settled into fatigue. She'd had no chance to wash her face and could only blindly smooth her hair back. The idea of undoing it in public to remake the bun at the back of her neck was not, she thought, to be considered. So she knew that she was rumpled, tired, a bit cross, and not very attractive. And in this fashion, she was to meet the man she would spend the rest of her life with! She considered staying on the train and then dismissed that idea as cowardly. You couldn't be a coward about building a new life!

* * * * *

Will Campbell was dressed to the nines in nankeen trousers, rumpled and baggy as they always were on anyone, a boiled shirt, and a sack jacket. He was painfully aware that his outfit had been fashionable—and new—in St. Louis fifteen years earlier. But he had polished his boots and brushed off his Stetson as best he could.

By the time the train whistle could be heard in the distance, he had been waiting four hours. He'd paced the tracks nearby at least ten times, making a huge circle, stopping periodically to pull an American Horologe watch out of his pocket and study it. Darn train should have been here three hours ago, he thought irritably.

But in four hours Will Campbell was no closer to knowing what he would say than he had been before he got to the depot. "Miz Hartsell, I have some bad news for you." That was hardly the way to greet someone getting off the train. How about a straightforward, "Miz Hartsell, I'm Will Campbell." That wouldn't mean a thing to her.

He watched with a sort of panic as the train slowed down until the passenger car was directly in front of him. The conductor put that big wooden step by the door and began helping passengers off. First came a man Campbell identified as a well-known local gambler; then an elderly woman, bent and using a cane, who took forever to negotiate the three steps.

The third passenger was a woman in her thirties, and Campbell knew instantly that she was Ella Hartsell. Her hair had once been pulled back neatly but now escaping tendrils curled about her face, softening what might have been a stark appearance. The heat of the train had brought a flattering color to her cheeks, and her dark eyes were wide with curiosity—or was it apprehension?

Will Campbell would never be able to explain it to anyone, least of all Ella, in forthcoming years, but he knew right away that he did not want her to get on a train back to Illinois.

* * * * *

Ella thought the old woman would take forever to get off the train, and she chided herself for impatience. She had many more years ahead than that poor women, and besides, she wasn't in a hurry, was she? The longer this moment could be put off, the better.

When at last the way was clear her mind had wandered again, and she was staring into space, trying to imagine what to say to Walter Denison. The conductor had to prompt her with a gentle, "Miss?" She took his hand and descended, her eyes fixed on the steps lest she miss one and enter Texas in a most inglorious manner.

But when she stood on the ground and looked up again, she saw him. He was tall, much taller than Joe. He held his hat in his hands, almost respectfully, and she could see a full head of hair, the brown streaked with bits of grey and gold, probably from working outdoors all the time. His face, though bearded, looked kindly and open, and Ella was suddenly no longer afraid.

She loosened her tight grip on the conductor's hand—she hadn't even realized she had been clutching it—and moved forward, her hand now outstretched. "Walter Denison," she said, and it was not a question.

Will Campbell never knew how this happened either, but he stepped forward, took her hand, and said, "Yes, ma'am. Let's go to Decatur, Ella."

The Fly on the Wall

There I was, pulling myself up into that fool stage to Tombstone one more time, hitching my skirts so I didn't trip and still trying not to show my ankles so I'd get catcalls from the men standing around. When I poked my head into the coach, I looked into the prettiest green eyes I'd ever seen. The only other passenger in the coach was a young lady, and I use both those words deliberately. She wasn't yet eighteen, I didn't think, but she had all the graces of a lady, those graces I knew damn well I didn't have.

Just then my skirt caught on the step of the coach, and I heard a ripping sound. "Damn!" I said loudly, pulling myself the rest of the way into the stage. Then I remembered the young girl and though it was unlike me, I felt just a bit ashamed of my language. I decided to try to start over.

"Mornin'," I said.

"Good morning," she said, with a tentative quality about her voice. Her eyes told me she was both faintly amused and slightly shocked by my unladylike ascent into the carriage.

She wore a very proper brown traveling dress trimmed with silk ribbon, long-sleeved, tight at the waist and uncomfortable looking as hell. Her shoes were high-top affairs of fine leather, white on top and black for the main part of the shoe, with slightly elevated heels—I swore she couldn't walk ten feet in them, especially not on the dirt streets of Tombstone.

Her hair was pulled back and covered with a straw hat that had a brown woven affair hanging down behind it into which she'd tucked the most incredible red hair I'd ever seen. It was curly too, for stray bits escaped around her face in corkscrews.

I was conscious—maybe even self-conscious—of the difference in our appearances. I wore a white shirtwaist—now some wrinkled and with a spot of coffee spilled on it that I'd tried and failed to get out over my breakfast—and a black broadcloth skirt, with sturdy black shoes, the only kind a sensible woman would wear in this godforsaken part of the country. My hair had been neatly piled on my head in the morning with a roll, secured by countless hairpins, framing my face. But I knew by now, in the heat of a July mid-day, limp strands hung about my face and down the back of my neck. They didn't curl into charming corkscrews like hers did. My face was sweaty, and I had to mop it with my tired handkerchief.

I was almost struck dumb by the expression in her eyes— innocence, maybe a little fear. She was too young and too sweet— did I really use that word?—to be on a stage to Tombstone by herself.

I tried again to start a conversation. "Name's Kate, Kate Elder. They . . . they call me Big Nose Kate." There, I'd said it. The reason for the nickname was obvious, and I usually figured I might as well get the name out in the open. It sort of kept people from staring at the prominence of that one feature. Having a big nose didn't make me ugly, and I knew that. In his rare sober moments, Doc Holliday called me a "fine figure of a woman." It didn't seem to bother him that as a good-sized woman I towered over his skinny frame.

Doc Holliday, of course, was the reason I was back on the stage one more time. Although he was only twenty-eight, I thought of Doc as an old man—that's 'cause he was dying of consumption. He was a dentist, but he didn't care much about practicing his trade—once told Allie Earp he couldn't be bothered pulling her "baby teeth" when she had a toothache. Knowin' he was dyin', Doc was one of the best shootists of the West—that was because he didn't fear dying. He was difficult, moody, unpredictable, and violent—and he was the only man I'd ever really loved in a lifetime of—well, okay, I was a few years older than him—of making my living on the frontier in ways that ladies didn't talk about. Doc and I really got together in Colorado where he'd killed a man over a poker game—actually, he'd cut the guts out of the man, and I hated to think about it to this day. But I could tell they were fixin' to lynch him, and I got him out of that jail. No, I'm not telling how I did it. But we'd been together— off and on—ever since.

When he followed the Earp brothers to Tombstone, I followed Doc—though his companions were none too pleased about it. Doc sort of set up practice as a dentist, and I . . . well, I did what I knew best how to do. I opened a "palace of pleasure"—some palace, in a canvas tent, with just swags of canvas hung down to create "private" rooms. Miners didn't care, and the five girls I hired were busy all the time. Me? I ran the business, but I spent my nights with Doc.

But about two weeks before that stagecoach ride, he and me

had one of our classic rows. Doc was usually too drunk to fight by talking, but he wasn't above punching me when he got mad. And I'd just told him I wouldn't take it any more, I was getting on the stage and going to Tucson. He'd said, "Good. Get on that damn stage and get outta' my sight."

I went, but it wasn't easy. I had a business in Tombstone— matter of fact, I had a thriving business. Folks around Tombstone called it "Kate's Sporting House," even though it was only in a tent. But I even left that behind. I was that mad at Doc.

But once I was in Tucson, I began to miss that coughing, tubercular, mean son-of-a-bitch. And when he wrote one of his flowery letters saying he missed me, I took the next stage back.

My traveling companion studied me and at length said uncomfortably, "You're . . . well, it isn't that big. I . . . I didn't even notice it."

"No need to fool an old bag like me," I said. "It's a big nose. I'm used to it." I settled myself in the seat. "Ain't you a mite young to be travelin' off to a place like Tombstone by yourself?"

"No." She didn't look like she believed it herself.

"Well," I said sort of preachily, wanting to impress her with my worldly knowledge, "it's a rough place, Tombstone is. Aren't many ladies there, if you know what I mean."

If she knew, she ignored the comment. "I have business in Tombstone," she said, smoothing back one loose curl with her left hand. A diamond sparkled on her ring finger.

"You looking for a lost lover? Or, sometimes I've heard ladies say they're looking for their brother, when they really mean a lover."

She shook her head. "Neither."

I didn't believe her. The ring was a giveaway. "I'd hide that ring, if I were you," I advised.

She looked at it and shrugged. "I shouldn't mind losing it."

Wyatt Earp used to tell Doc I was a slow thinker, but I wasn't all that slow. She wouldn't mind losing the ring, because she'd lost the one who gave it to her. . .and I bet she'd lost him to Tombstone and the many pleasures and free money that flowed there. I was beginning to know a little more about this young lady—and the more I knew, the more I worried about her. She'd never survive in Tombstone.

"Might not like the way you lose it," I said. Just then there was the driver's loud yell, and the coach took off with a jerk, throwing me sideways against the panel. My feet went up in the air, my head banged against the side of the coach, and I had to brace myself to keep from sliding off the seat.

My companion must have been coiled for the moment. She sat still, with perfect balance, unmoved by the wild motion of our vehicle. "Do you mean robbers?" she asked, but there was little interest in her tone.

"You're damn . . . ah, darned right I mean robbers. They rob this stage more often than not."

"I am prepared for trouble," she said. From a hidden pocket in her dress she pulled a Colt derringer, the small kind of .41 caliber pistol. This one had a pearl handle, like the ones women dealing faro sometimes carried.

I couldn't help it. I laughed aloud. "Honey," I said, "that pea-shooter won't stop any self-respectin' robber. He'll have it off you before you can blink. You best just keep it hidden." I was so curious about this child that I could burst, but I was also beginning to like her. There was a bravado about that small gun that someone like me couldn't help but admire.

She put the gun back in her pocket and turned her eyes out the window, clearly through talking to me. But there couldn't have been much for her to see—desert floor, cactus, dry gulches and, in the distance, some purple mountains that gave the false hope that you might be headed toward a better land. Alkali dust flew up around the wheels of the stage and seeped in through gaping holes in the frame of the vehicle and around the doors and windows. Overhead the sun beat down, and inside the carriage was hot—really hot.

"Usually rob the stage at Contention," I said conversationally, "dry wash just this side of the tiny town. It'll take us better'n two hours to get there."

"Is it always robbed?" she asked, and I thought I caught a tremor in her voice. She began to twist the ring on her finger.

"Not always," I said reassuringly. "Only once about every five or six trips. And it was robbed trip before last. I think we're okay." There was another long silence.

"What you gonna do once you get to Tombstone?" I asked. "I

mean, you wealthy? If you got enough money to support yourself, someone'll steal it from you. And if you don't . . . well, there ain't but one kind of work for a pretty girl like you. And somehow I don't think you're that kind."

"I . . . I don't know what you mean," she said, and I didn't know whether to believe her or not. "I can find work in a restaurant or something," she said, but I could tell she only half believed it herself. She looked so vulnerable that she made me remember myself all those years ago when I was young and innocent.

"I been on the line," I said boldly, "and I've run a house. And I can tell you I'd hire you in a flash, but I wouldn't be doin' you a favor. You'd be old in five years, dead in ten."

It must have dawned on her what I meant, for her eyes grew wide. "I won't do either thing," she said slowly. "I have business in Tombstone . . . and I can provide for myself."

"Honey, I sure hope you're right, but somehow I have the feeling you need help."

Her chin went up in the air, though it was trembling slightly, and her eyes went out the window. Conversation was cut off. I tried to sleep and couldn't because I kept glancing at her. She stared out that isinglass window at the great nothingness around us. We made it to Contention without incident, though I confess I was a little disappointed. I'd wanted to be able to say, "I told you so," and to— well, you know, "save" her by bullying the robbers. It was something I knew I was full capable of. After all, I only had to mention Doc Holliday's name and most folks in the territory would pale and go the other way.

It was a seventeen-hour trip, and I never could sleep on that blasted stage as it bounced and rocked over an excuse for a wagon road. We stopped at two roadside stations beyond Contention, and at each I clambered out to stretch my legs and exchange pleasantries with the driver and station man.

"You goin' back to that son-of-a-bitch, Kate?" they'd ask, and when I'd nod, they'd say something like, "We'll get you a nice coffin, one day."

"Comes to that," I replied, "you best be measuring him, not me. Doc don't scare me."

Even while I bantered with the stagecoach men, relieved myself behind a scrubby bush, and welcomed the chance to be out of that airless stagecoach, my traveling companion sat motionless inside through each stop. Even though she neither slept nor fidgeted, I figured she must have wanted to relieve herself and was afraid to venture out of the coach.

After the last stop, I did my usual ungraceful climb into the coach and ignored the catcall behind me. Heaving myself onto the seat, I said, "You got a name?"

She smiled. "As a matter of fact, it's Kate. Kate Farrell." There was that flicker of amusement in her eyes. "I thought it was strange we both had the same first name."

"Yeah, but you don't have the nickname . . . or the nose to go with it," I said. "Listen, Kate Farrell, you need anything in Tombstone, you tell somebody to find you Big Nose Kate. I got friends there—important friends." Well, Wyatt and Virgil were important—I just didn't have to add that I couldn't stand them and they hated me. Doc was the bond that held us all together.

"Thank you," she said simply. Then she asked a question. "Do you know Morris Tedley? I believe he's a banker."

I nearly hooted. Morris Tedley dealt faro at the Eagle Brewery.

"A banker?" I asked incredulously.

"Yes," she said solemnly. "I believe with the Tombstone American Bank."

"There ain't no such bank in Tombstone," I said bluntly.

Her eyes widened again, this time in unwelcome surprise. "You must be mistaken. We've had correspondence on that letterhead."

"Tedley must have a friend with a printing press," I said, "and there's only one in Tombstone. John Clum publishes the *Tombstone Daily Epitaph*. He could do up some fake letterhead."

She appeared to ponder this, though not without some unhappiness. Decisively, she said, "I'm quite sure he's a banker."

"You can be 'quite sure' if you want," I thought, "but he ain't no banker in the sense you mean." Now I decided right then and there I was going to have to take this chicken under my wing if she was to survive. I didn't know what that low-life Morris Tedley meant to her, but I had my suspicions, and they had to do with that diamond on her finger. If he done her wrong, he deserved his comeuppance, and I was going to see that he got it. Kate Farrell was far too young and innocent be in Tombstone by herself, let alone figure out how to snare someone like Tedley.

"Now, Miss Kate Farrell," I said as the driver sawed on the reins to bring the horses to a screeching halt in front of the Dexter Livery and Feed Stable, "you go get yourself a room at the Cosmopolitan—it's the best place in town. You can eat there without goin' out on the streets, and you'll be safe. I'll come after you in the morning, and we'll find this Tedley fellow." Asleep in his bed after a long night gambling, I thought. Might not be a bad time to confront him. But first I got to find out what he did. I decided I'd deal with that in the morning.

"I appreciate your help," she said. "I . . . I was a little uncertain about what to do when I get here. The Cosmopolitan?"

"Right down Allen Street here, next block as a matter of fact. I'll get someone to carry your bag down there."

Feeling like a foolish old mother hen, I watched as the driver hauled her bag off the top of the stagecoach. I hailed someone to help her with it and threatened to tell Doc if he did anything but take it straight to the hotel. I gave him a silver piece and then trailed them to the Cosmopolitan. Kate Farrell went in that door without turning around, like she never knew I was behind her. But she knew. I found Doc at the Occidental Saloon, two doors down from the Cosmopolitan. It was the place Wyatt partly owned and where he and Doc and Morgan and Virgil spent all their time. Morgan was the one I addressed.

"Morgan Earp, I got a job for you," I said.

"Already got one, Kate. 'Case you forgot, I'm the city marshal." He'd never liked me any better than I liked him.

"It's that Morris Tedley," I said. "You got to do somethin' about him."

"Morris Tedley?" Wyatt hooted. "He's a fly on the wall, couldn't cause any trouble if he tried."

"Well, he's tried, and he's done it. I don't exactly know what, but—"

Doc looked to be a little less drunk than usual, but the thing about him was you could never tell by watching him where he was on a scale of drunkenness. Now, he stared at me and drawled, "Hello, Kate. Nice to see you back in Tombstone." He was perched on a stool and looked perilously close to falling off it even though his skinny legs were twisted about the rungs. He gave me a lopsided grin, and I was glad to see the old fool.

"Doc," I said, going over to him and almost whispering, "I'm glad to see you too. I really am."

He squeezed my hand, which was a real show of affection for him. Morgan and Wyatt looked disgusted.

"Kate," Doc said slowly, "why the hell are you so upset about Morris the fly?"

So I let loose about Kate Farrell and how she was looking for Morris Tedley and how she wouldn't tell me what it was about and no young woman should be alone in Tombstone and they had to do something, 'specially Morgan since he was the law.

"Sounds like a personal problem to me," he said. "I got rustlers to worry about, not broken hearts."

"Doc, you gonna' listen to this?" Wyatt asked impatiently. "I'm goin' across the street to the Eagle and see what's goin' on."

"And warn that snake Tedley," I snarled.

Wyatt just grinned, but Doc took my hand. "Let's go home, Kate. I been missin' you, and you don't need to bother your head about some girl that's foolish enough to come this far chasin' a scoundrel. She'll get discouraged and go back where she came from soon."

Back where she came from! It hit me I didn't know where she'd come from. I tried to remember if her speech gave away a place of upbringing, but she hadn't talked much, and I couldn't place it.

Late in the night, when Doc lay snoring so loud I thought he'd choke and die that way, I lay awake, tossing, turning, wondering about Kate Farrell and her story. She had become my responsibility, no matter how much Morgan and Wyatt and Doc laughed and tried to discourage me.

Next morning I was up early, before Doc even stirred. I dressed silently, pulling a clean but wrinkled shirtwaist out of my carpetbag and putting on the same black broadcloth skirt. This morning, I did take some time with my "toilette," being much more careful than usual to secure the pins that held my hair in place and dabbing some cornstarch on my nose so that it didn't shine. I pinched my cheeks for color, and then gave that up and dabbed on a bit of the rouge I kept hidden from Doc.

Dressed the best I knew how, I went down Fifth Street to Allen and turned right to the Cosmopolitan Hotel. I told myself I was goin' for breakfast. While I was waiting for my flapjacks and sausage to appear, I went to the clerk at the desk. "Is Miss Farrell in?"

He bent his balding head over the register and used his finger to follow name by name down the list, an irritatingly slow process. I stood there fuming, sure that my flapjacks were growing cold and hard. At length, the silly man raised his head, looked me directly in the eye, and said, "There ain't no Miss Farrell here."

"Impossible!" I stormed. "I followed her here to this hotel last night."

"You followed her?"

He seemed genuinely interested by this, and I considered bashing him across the face. Reason somehow prevailed. "Yes. I . . . I was concerned about her and watched to be sure she made it safely to this place of retreat. Young girl, red-hair, too innocent to be in a place like this." I looked around as though in disgust.

"This is the best hotel in Tombstone," he said indignantly. "But nobody named Farrell checked in last night."

"Did any woman alone come into this hotel last night?" I demanded, putting my face across his counter until that nose that made me famous was right up close to his own nose, which wasn't so small either.

He backed away a little and then began again his finger-following of names down the register. "Miss Waggoner!" he said triumphantly. "Miss Dorothy Waggoner. She came in on the stage last night."

Now, I thought, we're getting somewhere. "What room is she in?"

"Oh, I can't tell you that." He rolled his eyes heavenward and raised his hands, as though imploring the Lord to help him.

The Lord had better help him, I thought, before I'm through with him. "Either you tell me, or Marshal Earp will be down here to find out if you been double-lettin' rooms," I said.

It was, of course, the Earp name that threw terror in his heart. "Room 136. Third door on the right, top of the stairs."

Without even thanking him, I headed up the stairs. At 136 I knocked with loud determination, bound to find out why this slip of a girl had lied to me about her name.

There was no response. I knocked again, louder, and then shouted, "This is Kate Elder. You open this door and tell me why the hell you lied to me."

Still no response, until a drummer down the hall opened his doors and came to stand belligerently in the hall. He obviously had had a hard night, for his eyes were bleary, his hair stood on end, and he was totally unaware that he was confronting me in his longjohns.

"She left early this morning," he said. "Quit the damn racket."

Back downstairs I berated the clerk. "Why didn't you tell me she left early this morning?"

He shrugged. "I didn't see her leave. Haven't seen her since she checked in. Maybe she don't want to talk to you."

I turned away in disgust and went to eat my breakfast. The flapjacks were stiff and cold by now, but I ate them anyway.

Not much surprised Big Nose Kate Elder—she'd been around long enough to see it all—but she would have been astounded if she'd seen Kate Farrell—for that was her real name—leave her room at 5:30 in the morning—long before Big Nose Kate was awake, let alone thinking about the helpless girl she'd decided to take on as a cause.

Kate Farrell had darkened her red hair with boot black and tucked it under a beret. She wore baggy work pants held up by a rope belt and a denim shirt that was too big for her and slightly frayed at the seams. Her worn boots were not cowboy boots like most men in the Arizona Territory wore but the square-toed boots of the East. Her face bore blackened smudges, as though she had not washed for a day or more. Instead of going down the main stairs and past the desk, she ever so gently eased open the back door, clambered gracefully down the back stairs, and landed in a gentle jump in the alley behind the hotel. Then, with a quick look over her shoulder, she headed determinedly around the hotel to Allen Street and back to the livery, a woman—or young boy?—with a definite destination.

That destination was Dexter's Livery and Feed Stable. Body loose, walk confident, she strolled in to find the owner barely awake, rubbing his eyes and contemplating the day.

"You use someone to muck out the stables and harness horses?" she asked, pitching her voice so low that had Big Nose Kate heard her she would have denied it was the same voice.

Sam Dexter looked startled. "Why you lookin' for a job so early in the morning?"

"I figure that's when people need help. You don't get goin' in the morning, you don't get goin' at all." The young person stood with arms akimbo, almost challenging the owner to hire him.

"What's your name?" he asked. "Where you from?"

"Name's Tom O'Toole. Where I'm from doesn't matter. I'm sixteen years old, and my folks are long ago and far away. I got to take care of myself." Well, it was only part a lie, Kate reasoned. She did have to take care of herself. And what better place to find out what was goin' on in town than a livery stable?

"You been around horses a lot?"

"All my life," came the reply.

Sam Dexter considered. "Let me see your hands," he demanded. A pair of thin white hands were held out, but Dexter could see where calluses had been, the kind that came from holding reins. Big Nose Kate had never thought to look at the hands of her traveling companion. If she had, she'd have been even more puzzled.

"Been a while?" Dexter asked.

"Yes, sir," O'Toole replied. "I been on the road, catching rides where I can, walking when I can't. I . . . I want to stay one place for a while. And in town they tell me . . . well, they tell me you got a good reputation for taking care of horses. I like that." This last bit of flattery was delivered with disarming innocence.

Dexter nonetheless puffed with pride. "That I do, lad, and I'll not tolerate anything less than the best care of the horses entrusted to me."

"Yes, sir," came the reply.

"Pay's ten dollars a month and found."

"Don't need no found. I . . . I hooked up with somebody, and I got a place to stay. But I'll work whatever hours you want, however long."

Dexter considered for a long time, staring at this young boy, wondering if he was strong enough, had the endurance to muck out all the stalls, exercise the horses that didn't get ridden, keep the tack polished and shiny. "Okay, we'll give it a week," he said. "You can start now."

So Tom O'Toole spent the day hard at work. In each stall, he stopped to stroke the horse's nose, talk to it gently, even affectionately. When he exercised the horses, he showed no fear even of the rank ones, and he rode with a confidence that Dexter had seen on few young men. He watched, seated at his desk, feet propped on the desk, hat pulled over his eyes. But not much missed his gaze. He was satisfied he'd found himself a sure-enough gold mine of an employee.

When someone came for their horse, Dexter hollered out, "O'Toole bring that bay from stall seven . . . " or whatever, and Tom O'Toole saddled and bridled the horse and led it forward. There was only one untoward incident in the day.

"O'Toole? Bring Tedley's horse from stall ten," Dexter called out. He was too far away to see the shaken look on his new employee's face, but soon the young boy came leading a skittish black thoroughbred that pranced and offered twice to rear up on its hind legs.

Morris Tedly watched in disgust. He was a medium-sized man, slender to the point of being dapper, with carefully pomaded hair, neatly creased nankeen trousers which, to anybody in Tombstone, identified him as a dandy. And he had an air of taking himself too importantly. "You there, boy! Can't you control that horse."

The "boy" said nothing but, talking gently, tried to calm the horse, leading it slowly toward the front of the stable. Just in front of Tedley, the horse reared, lashing out with its front hooves. Tedly ducked and ran for cover, while Tom O'Toole hung onto the reins and finally calmed the animal.

When Tedley approached, he had his arm raised to cuff the errant stable boy.

Sam Dexter grabbed the upraised arm. "Now, I wouldn't be doin' that, Tedley. This boy done a fine job of calming that horse. Maybe you best see about training him yourself . . . or find another livery."

"There's not another livery in Tombstone," Tedley protested, his tone verging on a whine.

Dexter just nodded and walked away. Tedley threw a dirty look at the stable boy and roughly pulled his horse into the street, where he mounted with the awkwardness that showed his unfamiliarity with horses and then slammed roweled spurs into the animal's side, making it take off in a great leap that nearly unseated the rider.

Watching, Tom O'Toole fervently wished that the horse had really bucked and thrown Tedley. The incident gave him an idea.

"What kind of a man is he?" he asked Dexter.

Dexter shrugged. "Mean as sin, but there's no stuffin' to him. Poke him or threaten him, and he'll fall apart pretty fast."

Pondering this, Tom O'Toole went back to work.

At seven, Dexter said, "You best go on now, Tom. Been a long day. Don't want to wear you out the first day."

"Yes, sir. Horses are all settled for the night. You sure there's nothing else?"

"I'm sure. Be here at seven in the morning—five-thirty's a mite early for me."

Kate Farrell walked slowy back to the Cosmopolitan Hotel. She was tired, though she'd never have admitted to anyone else that it had been a long day. And her hands were raw with blisters—it had been too long since she'd held the reins of reluctant horses. And she'd never worked this hard from dawn to dusk.

At the Cosmopolitan, she once again entered by the back stairs. In the communal bath on the second floor of the hotel, she cleaned herself of the day's dirt but left the boot black in her hair. Back in her room, she turned herself into a woman again, albeit a dark-headed one. She dressed carefully in a fresh broadcloth dress and again tucked her hair into a net—she didn't want that nosy clerk to notice the change from red to black. Then she sat at the tiny desk to write a note. Folding it into an envelope, she sealed it carefully and scrawled a name across the front. It was eight-thirty when she stopped in front of the clerk at the desk.

"Miss Waggoner?" the clerk said eagerly. "Did you have a good day. I mean, in your room all day. . . ."

"I had a fine day, thank you," she answered serenely. And then, "Would you see that this is delivered by hand?" she asked, folding a dollar bill under the envelope so that he could see it.

"Yes, ma'am, Miss Waggoner" he said perfunctorily. And then he looked at the name. "You want to send something to Big Nose

Kate Elder? Doc Holliday's woman?"

Dorothy Waggoner smiled blandly at him. "Yes, I do."

"She . . . she was here looking for you early this morning. I 'spect it was just too early for you to answer the knock."

"I imagine so," she said. Her manner was ladylike, almost slightly timid, and you'd never have known how she spent the day.

"Big Nose Kate Elder," he said, wrinkling his own nose a bit with distaste. "It don't seem like you'd have anything to do with the likes of her."

"Is that so?" Miss Waggoner said blandly and sailed into the dining room.

Had the clerk been able to read the note he held burning in his hand, he would have known it said simply, "Can you come to my room at the Cosmopolitan Hotel, room 136, tomorrow night at eight? With appreciation, Kate Farrell."

Dorothy Waggoner ordered pheasant for dinner. She found it well prepared and of good flavor. Shortly after finishing her meal, she retired to her room. Seven o'clock, she knew, would come early.

* * * * *

I about leaped out of my shoes when some no-good yahoo handed me that message.

"Clerk at the Cosmopolitan paid me to deliver this," he said and disappeared as quick as the words were out of his mouth.

We were at the Occidental, and Doc was drunker than a skunk—belligerent drunk. "What the hell's that?" he demanded. "You gettin' mail by special delivery?

"None of your business," I replied, turning my back on him to open the envelope.

Wyatt and Morgan stared at me, their expressions half amusement and half distaste. I swear if I'd had a gun I might've shot them both right then, thinking I was a no-good whore like they did.

My back turned to all of them, I smoothed out the note and read it. To me, it was a real puzzle. There was no Kate Farrell registered at the Cosmopolitan, and yet here I was invited—practically commanded—to appear there to see her the next night. Of course, there was no way in hell that I wasn't goin' to be there.

The next day, when I was filled with anticipation anyway, was a day that Doc chose to turn ugly. "No good whore," he yelled at me. "Just waitin' around for me to hit it big in the mines."

Since he never worked the mines, I thought this was kind of funny, and I made the mistake of laughing.

He hit me broadside across the face with the flat of his hand, and I spun backwards into the door frame. Within ten minutes, I could feel my eye begin to swell up. Doc, meantime, collapsed on the bed and began to snore.

Wonderful, I thought, I'll go see Kate Farrell with a black eye.

When I got ready to leave that night, Doc was still angry. As I started out the door, one skinny but strong arm blocked the doorway, and I was forced to stop. "It's that woman after Morris Tedley, isn't it? I'm tellin' you, Kate, you stay out of that. Whatever business she has with Tedley, she can handle herself. I don't want to have to be beggin' Morgan to look out for you."

"I can look out for myself," I said angrily.

I appeared at Kate Farrell's room right on the dot of eight— breezing by that dumb desk clerk without so much as a "How d'ye do?"

She answered my knock immediately and the door opened to admit me to a room tinier than I thought it would be. Kate Farrell wore a calico wrapper and looked like somebody's kid sister. She didn't look like someone mixed up in two identities and heaven knows what else-except that gorgeous red hair was now sort of a dingy black and looked like it needed washing.

Before I could blurt out my questions, she said with a small gasp of sympathy, "Kate! What happened to your eye?"

"Walked into a door," I said. "Just wasn't watching." What I wasn't watching close enough was Doc's hand coming toward me. She shook her head, and I knew she wouldn't have understood about Doc punching on me. In the world she came from, men didn't hit women.

"How come you registered as Dorothy Waggoner?" I asked bluntly, ready for the truth to be out. "And why is your hair black?"

She laughed lightly, "I don't want Morris Tedley to recognize me," she said. "I was sure you guessed that."

"He did you wrong, didn't he?"

She considered for a long minute. "Do you promise not to tell anyone?"

"Cross my heart," I said and made the appropriate gesture. I was about to jump out of my skin with curiosity. I lived in a world where men did women wrong, but not the kind of wrong she was talking about.

"He . . . he took money from . . . ." Her eyes watered up, and she could hardly get the words out. She paused a minute, seemed to get control of herself, and said, "He took money from my father to go into business in Tombstone. We were to be married once he'd made a success of himself."

That no-good scoundrel, I thought. Hangin's too good for him. "Where's your father? And why'd he trust that low-life?"

"Father's in Ohio—that's where I was raised, and where Morris grew up. We've known each other all our lives. He was always churchgoing, respectable . . . I just can't believe he's not a banker here, like he told Father. I had to come see for myself . . . and maybe try to get the money back."

"Your father let you come this far alone?" I asked suspiciously.

"He thinks I'm visiting an aunt in Kansas. By the time he finds out I'm not, I hope I'll be back home."

"So what's your plan?" I asked, my mind whirling with ways this poor thing might get her money back from Tedley. "You'll get it back," I said confidently. "He's nothing more than a fly on the wall."

"Fly on the wall?" she echoed.

"Yeah, that's what the Earps call him. They say he ain't got no stuffin', ain't no more of a threat than a fly on the wall."

"The Earps?" she asked.

"Earps are three brothers recently come to Tombstone. Morgan's the marshal, and Wyatt owns a gambling house, and Virgil . . . well, he's just here. They spend a lot of time with . . . my friend, Doc Holliday."

She wasn't interested in any of them at the moment. "I don't know what to do, but I'll have to get that money back for Father. It was all he had in the world, and he's . . . well, he's getting on in years." She dabbed at her eyes.

"Well," I said, "you could always try to beat him at faro."

"Faro?" she asked, clearly puzzled.

"Card game. With a board. Banker—that's Tedley—draws two

cards at a time, and players put bets on the board against what the banker draws."

"I . . . I don't think I could learn to beat him at that. I suppose by now—" she let out a small sob—"he's learned to be very good at that."

"Only medium," I said, "from what I heard. But I doubt you could count on beating him. Might cost you more than you make. You got to watch to make sure the dealer's honest about where he takes the cards from . . . and I doubt that's the case with Tedley, that fly on the wall." I proceeded to tell her everything I'd learned from Doc about faro, and she took it all in wide-eyed.

"I can't risk money like that," she said, shaking her head. "I'll have to figure some other way to get Father's money back from Morris. . . . The marshal you mentioned. Would he help?"

I shook my head. "The Earps don't get involved with what they call 'domestic matters.' They're too busy gettin' rustlers and the like, building themselves a big reputation." My bitterness showed in my voice.

Kate Farrell was clearly disturbed. She put one hand up to brush her hair away from her face, and that's when I saw it. She had blisters on her hands, raw, weeping blisters that must have hurt like hell.

"What've you done to your hands?" I demanded.

She looked at them ruefully. "A little honest work, that's all. They'll toughen. I've . . . I've had blisters like this before."

"Only thing I know that would cause blisters like that is a pair of reins," I said, waiting for her to tell me something that would answer some of my questions.

She smiled. "You're too smart for me, Kate Elder. You promise not to tell?"

I nodded. "I already made that promise once," I reminded her, "and Big Nose Kate keeps her word."

"I'm sure," she said hastily, not wanting to offend me. "I got a job at the stables, disguised as a boy named Tom O'Toole. I . . . well, I've always known horses, been around them. Father trained horses. It was his business until. . . ." Her voice choked, and then she recovered. "Until his health failed." She looked down at her hands. "Working at the livery seemed better than being a . . . what do you call them? . . . a biscuit-shooter?"

Now how she knew that word for a waitress I never would figure out. I was dumbfounded by this girl.

It was near ten o'clock when I left the Cosmopolitan, past the hour when a respectable woman should be on the street alone, but that never bothered me. I went two doors down to the Occidental in search of Doc—and secretly hoping Morgan would be around.

They were all there, even Virgil this time. All three Earp brothers greeted me with nods and expressions that were almost sneers, but I was used to it and paid them no mind. Doc said, "Lo, here cometh the lovely Kate."

"Stop that foolishness," I said, batting his hand away from my waist. "Order me a whiskey."

"Say 'please,'" Morgan said, and I gave him what I thought was a withering look. I'd heard a lot about withering looks and never known what they were.

"Is there a new stable boy down to the livery?" I asked as casually as I could.

"Now, Kate, why would that matter to you?" Doc asked, frowning at me.

"Just heard a rumor. Always feel bad when a young boy hits town—they're running toward what they think is glamour, and it's more often disaster."

"Didn't know you were so soft-hearted," Morgan said. "Yeah, there's a new lad down there. Nice kid, name of Tom O'Toole. Works hard, knows horses and can take care of them."

And she's ruinin' her hands, I thought.

The next night, long about eight o'clock, I said to Doc, "I believe I'll go on to the Eagle."

"Goin' to play faro?" he asked suspiciously.

"I might," I said, "I just might. You gonna' give me any money?"

He snorted in disgust and forked over $25.

"I won't get rich on this," I said, "but I'll try."

It was just as I thought: Kate Farrell, disguised as this Waggoner woman with dark hair, was at the Crystal Palace. This time she'd added a pair of wire-rim spectacles to her disguise, and the dress she wore was pale blue with a bit of lace at the neck. It made her look—well, virginal—but of course she was! Now a new woman, unknown in Tombstone and unescorted, usually drew a lot of attention at a place like the Eagle, but Kate looked so young and innocent that nobody paid her any mind after looking once at her in surprise, as though wondering what a girl like that was doing there. She drifted from blackjack table to roulette to faro, apparently fascinated by each game. But at the faro table where Morris Tedley was dealing, she lingered, slightly back of the players.

Tedley looked up. "Want to play, ma'am?" His voice was oozing with charm and he had that seductive look that dealers use to lure people into their games. He sure didn't recognize her, though I was holdin' my breath.

She shook her head to indicate no, and then seemed to change her mind. "I . . . I've never played," she said in a sweet young voice. "Will you tell me what to do?"

Tedley knew opportunity when he saw it. "I certainly will, young lady," he said. "Just sit right down there. Now you place your bet on this board, and when I take two cards from the bank here. . . ."

Kate appeared to be listening to him as intently as she had listened to me the night before. Something told me Morris Tedley's run of good luck might have just run out.

I dodged behind people and pillars and kept Kate from seeing me. I didn't figure it would help our relationship for me to be caught spying on her, but that was what I was doing. And I watched in amazement as she cleaned Tedley out.

Each time she'd win, she'd say, "Ooh, is that money mine?" like a little kid who'd just been given a piece of candy.

"Yes it is," Tedley said smoothly, raking it toward her.

Now I knew he was playing that old game of letting the beginner win until he was hooked—only this time it was a she—and then taking him for all he was worth. I was in a terrible quandary—interfering with gambling was strictly against the code of behavior in Tombstone, but how could I watch this poor girl lose whatever she had?

I eased up behind her and put my hand on her shoulder.

She turned, looked up at me, and her face lighted. "Why, Kate, you're my guardian angel. I'll win if you stay by me."

Tedley looked at me with clear disgust. "You don't be coaching her now, Big Nose Kate?"

"Me?" I asked innocently.

I tried to slip her Doc's $25, but she pushed it away.

There came a point when it was suddenly clear that Tedley had lost control. The pigeon he thought he was working was winning. I watched the sweat gather on his forehead, watched carefully as he shuffled the cards—and had to remind him sharply once, "From the top, Tedley, not the bottom." He threw me a dirty look.

An hour later, Kate Farrell was ooohing and aaahing over the $500 she'd won. "I can't imagine all that's mine," she said. "I best be going now."

Tedley was desperate. "It's . . . it's usually not done to leave with that much of the house money," he said.

He must have been thinking, *What the hell! She's young and green, and I can bluff her.*

Kate gave him her sweetest smile. "Well, I'll come back another night, and I'm sure you'll take it all back from me."

"That a promise?" he demanded.

"Surely," she replied. Then, "Kate, will you walk back to the hotel with me?"

"You bet I will," I said roughly, throwing Tedley one of my withering looks. "You need protection." Once we were in the street, I demanded, "How did you do that? You never played before!"

"Why, Kate, I just listened to everything you told me, and it certainly worked. I'd . . . I'd like to give you some of this money."

"No," I said roughly, "I don't need it. Is that . . . does that satisfy Tedley's debt to your father?"

She laughed merrily. "Oh, my, no. Not anywhere close. But it's a start. I'll put it in the safe at the hotel."

"Ought to put it in the safe at Morgan Earp's office," I told her.

"The hotel will be fine," she said serenely. "And thank you for walking back here with me." She said good night and disappeared through the doors.

I stood outside, dumbfounded. Somehow there was something about this story I wasn't getting.

I didn't see Kate Farrell for several days, not until I began to hear about what she done.

At first I was too busy with troubles of my own to worry about that sweet little girl. Things were heating up between the so-called rustlers—the McLaury brothers, and Johnny Behan, and Ike Clanton—and the Earps, and Doc was right in the middle of it. Some said he knew about this murder and that, and it was said that Ike Clanton was gunning for Doc.

Now, having a man gunning for him never made Doc nervous. As I said, and I may repeat myself, Doc wasn't afraid of dying since that what he was doin' anyway. And a bullet would be a lot faster and neater than coughin' himself to death. But havin' a man call him a liar made Doc frantic . . . and he took his frantic out on me. I had another black eye, and I told him I was tired of bein' his punching bag.

There's folks to this day will tell you Doc and I split because I got . . . what's the word? abusive? yeah, that's it. But that ain't the truth. Doc got abusive, real bad so.

Anyway, in the midst of this, we're in the Occidental one night, and Wyatt says to me, "Your friend Tedley's having a run of bad luck. I heard he lost a bundle the other night."

"Yeah," I muttered, "I heard too." I wasn't about to tell him I'd been there and what I saw.

"Now his horse pitched him ten miles out in the desert. Broke his leg, and he lay there half a day 'fore anyone found him. Sorry fool is lucky he didn't die."

His horse pitched him? The horse he stabled at the livery? Something else was strange here. My mind spun with possibilities, none of them good.

"He dealin' with a broken leg?" I asked.

Wyatt aimed for the spittoon. "Naw, the doc's got him laid up in traction. Can't deal for two months or something. He'll lose a lot of money." He chuckled, to show that Tedley's loss of money meant nothin' to him.

I took myself down to the Dexter's livery that very day and told Sam Dexter I wanted to see his new stable hand. "O'Toole," I said, triumphantly pulling the name from my memory. "That's it. The O'Toole boy."

"Now, Kate, what business you got with him?" he asked.

"Don't you be bothering me, Sam Dexter. Just call that boy."

He hollered to the back of the stable, and pretty soon a young boy in baggy clothes and a beret kind of hat came runnin' up between the stalls.

"Lady"—did I hear Dexter hesitate over that word?—"wants to talk to you," he said, jerking his head in my direction.

"You be sure I do," I said, approaching the "stable boy" with menace.

"Yes, ma'am?" he said, all innocence. "What can I do for you?"

I didn't even recognize her voice. This was a soft voice, but that of a young boy not a girl, and there was a difference to the words— I couldn't put my finger on it, but I figured Kate Farrell was as good an actress as she was a gambler.

I looked at Sam Dexter, with his ears all perked. "Not here," I said. "Come out on the street."

Allen Street was crowded with people coming and going, talking, shouting, all involved in their own business. Nobody paid us any mind, except to shove by us. I pulled "Tom" east toward Chinatown, where nobody would for sure bother us.

"You do somethin' to spook Tedley's horse?" I asked bluntly.

He looked directly at me. "No, ma'am, Miss Kate. I . . . I never would do that. I heard what happened, and I'm just surprised it didn't happen sooner." Wide, innocent eyes looked directly at me. "That horse was too much for him to begin with."

"You didn't put a burr under the saddle so that it would be all right at first and then finally work its way into that horse's hide?" I knew the tricks, you see.

He gave me an amazed look. "A burr? Why would I do such a thing? 'Course I'm sorry Mr. Tedley's hurt. But Kate Farrell, she wouldn't be sorry at all." And with that, he said, "I have to get back to work, now. Nice to see you, Miss Elder." And he was gone.

I didn't even tell Doc about the encounter.

I forgot about Morris Tedley and even Kate Farrell a few days later when Doc got mean drunk and told me to pack my bags and get out. "Go live in that tent whorehouse of yours," he said. "It's where you belong."

My Irish—well, all right, it was Hungarian—was up, and I warned him. "You throw me out, you old fool, I'll tell Sheriff Behan you were one of the four that held up that stage outside Contention two weeks ago."

He yawned. "Go ahead and tell 'em," he said. "Nobody'll believe a drunk like you."

"Drunk?" I exploded. "Who's the drunk? You'll see, Doc, I'll get you in trouble."

Well, I did just that. Swore out a affidavit that Doc had been in on that robbery. Probably that was the dumbest thing I've ever done in a long career of dumb. Next thing you knew there was a warrant out for Doc's arrest. That made me sober up—well, I mean, sober up in my thinking. I never was drunk! Trouble was, Morgan and Wyatt were pushing me to leave town.

"If I leave town," I said, assuming my most haughty voice, "I can't tell them I was wrong about Doc being involved."

Morgan's voice was tight. "You'll tell them that and then you'll leave town."

"I'll tell them that," I said, "then I'll decide what I want to do."

"You leave town," he said in a straight tone, "or your tent whorehouse is likely to burn just like Morris Tedley's tent."

I was astounded. "Morris Tedley's tent burned?"

"Yeah, the one he lived in. Yesterday afternoon. He's lyin' there with a broken leg, and the thing catches fire. No one knows how. Only reason he didn't go up in flames with it was that stable boy you was asking about, he walks by and pulls Tedley out of the flames. Close call." Earp shook his head, though there wasn't much sympathy on his face.

Kate Farrell had set fire to Morris Tedley's tent! I wondered if she'd stolen his money first, and I made myself a promise to go to the Cosmopolitan that night.

"Where's Tedley now?" I asked.

"Got him a room at the Cosmopolitan. He screamed he couldn't afford it, but wasn't much else to do." He shrugged.

"I'll sign your new affidavit," I said. "I got other business to see to." Both of them at the Cosmopolitan, I thought. Morgan didn't even know what trouble could happen. But I was beginning to suspect.

"You're gettin' on the afternoon stage," Morgan said with real menace in his voice. "I don't care about that 'other' business." He grabbed my arm. "I'm goin' with you to Doc's while you pack, and then I'm escorting you to the stage."

"You can't run me outta town!" I yelled indignantly, jerking my arm to pull it loose. Morgan held firm, and next thing I knew I was being marched down Allen Street at a good clip—away from the livery and the Cosmopolitan both.

With Morgan standing over me, I threw some clothes in a carpetbag. Took everything I had at Doc's. "What about the stuff I got at my place? And who's gonna run my place?"

"I'll find someone to buy you out, and I'll send your stuff to Tucson. You ain't comin' back to Tombstone, Kate."

"Don't you go bettin' too soon," I said under my breath. The real reason I was lettin' Morgan do all this—even though I was fightin' and complainin'—was that I was ready to get away from Doc, and I knew right then he would take Morgan's side against me. In a week, he'd be begging me to come back to Tombstone.

But what would happen to Kate Farrell/Dorothy Waggoner/Tom O'Toole in a week? Better yet, what would happen to Morris Tedley?

Morgan literally shoved me into the stage, even before I could hoist my skirts out of way. I was about to turn and give him a good slap when I saw the other passenger in the coach.

Kate Farrell herself! Red hair and proper brown traveling outfit. She smiled complacently at me.

"You!" I said. "Did you finish your . . . uh . . . business with Morris Tedley."

She smiled, and there was no pretense of innocence about her any more. "Yes, I did, thank you. Quite satisfactorily."

I paid no mind as Morgan slammed the door shut—almost on my foot—and the stage lurched forward. "Who are you?" I asked. She shrugged. "It's only fair you know. I am Kate Farrell, and I am from Ohio . . . but by way of some other places. Morris Tedley and I, we were partners . . . we ran games in St. Louis, Kansas City, finally Tucson. But he double-crossed me." Her eyes turned steely when she said that, and I wondered how stupid I could have been ever to think of her as innocent. Clearly she was more sophisticated than I would ever be . . . and more clever.

"I had to reclaim the money he stole from me," she said. "And

I decided to make his life difficult while I did it. He won't try anything like that on me again."

Little did I know how seriously she meant that!

We rode in silence. There wasn't nothin' I could say to her. I sure as hell wasn't one to pass judgment on one of my fellow sisters. After all, hadn't I just gotten revenge on Doc in a pretty unfair way, accusing him of robbing a stage? And yet . . . there was something so calculating, so cold about the Kate Farrell who now sat opposite me.

I recalled that when we rode out, I was the big mouth, telling her all about how it was in the Wild West. Now I was quiet, silenced by her cleverness and her . . . what was the word I wanted? Something to do with the devil.

Once again, she never set foot out of the stage, never had to relieve herself or eat the greasy food at the stops, never slept. I did all of those things . . . otherwise seventeen hours on a stage would have driven me crazy. Or, as Doc would have said, crazier than I already was.

As we pulled into Tucson, I managed to stammer, "Well, I wish you luck, Miss Kate Farrell. Doesn't seem to me though you need my good wishes. You make your own luck."

She took my hand and looked me straight in the face—only this time, those eyes weren't so innocent. "I'm sorry I tricked you. You were a good friend, and I took advantage. I don't usually do that to friends."

I had just one question for her. "How old are you?"

"Twenty-eight," she said without flickering an eye.

"You fooled me," I said as I jumped down from the stage. The driver threw down my carpetbag and I headed off to find lodgings, without ever looking back to see where Kate Farrell went or if she went alone.

Just as I'd said, Doc wrote within a week, begging me to come back, saying the business about the affidavit was all cleared up, and no one suspected him any more of anything except bein' a drunken fool—some admission from him!

I took the stage back one more time—not knowing it would be my last trip to Tombstone. No one met me, and I hefted my bag to

Doc's by myself. He was really glad to see me, the old coot! It sort of pleased me.

But then he said, "Let's go to the Occidental and celebrate your homecoming."

"Morgan'll just tell me I have to leave town," I said. "Let's just stay here."

"I don't have a bottle. We're going to the Occidental." That was how quick his mood could turn.

So we went to the Occidental, and there was Morgan and Wyatt and Virgil.

"Hey, Kate," Morgan said, "that girl on the stage with you. Who was she?"

"Name's Kate Farrell," I said and wondered if I should go into all her aliases.

"You know," Morgan said slowly, "I done some investigatin'. But you already knew she was that new stable boy, and she was that dark-haired young woman at the Cosmopolitan."

I didn't say anything.

Morgan went on. "In one disguise or another, she seemed connected to everything bad that happened to Morris Tedley. And the day he dies, she leaves town."

"Tedley's dead?" I said.

"Yeah. I'm calling it suicide. Couldn't take losin' his money, breakin' his leg, and all that. Man reaches the breaking point pretty quick out here. Shot himself."

"What caliber gun?" I asked

"Why? It was a .41," he said.

I was tempted to tell him, "That wasn't no suicide." But I kept my peace. Sisters under the skin had to stick together. And I knew without asking, that Morris Tedley had died penniless.

The Damnyankee

A wet norther blew through four days before Christmas of 1908. Standing by the window I watched the wind pile snowdrifts around the fence posts and the road disappear into a field of white. Seven miles down that road was the Sweetwater railroad station where, in two days, Edward Patrick Smith would arrive to visit for the holidays.

"Lookin' won't make the snow change," Papa grumbled from behind the back issue of *Livestock Journal* in which he had buried himself. "Snow either'll stop or it won't."

"Either way," I said firmly, "we'll be going to the train station."

"Not goin' to risk my horses—and my own life—for some damnyankee," he muttered.

Edward Patrick Smith—Ned—was a New York lawyer I'd met when I'd visited the East with my Aunt Edna. "The girl needs an eastern shopping trip," she'd insisted, "and since she's no mother to take her, I'm going to see to it." And off we'd gone. Ned had been having tea at the Waldorf Astoria Hotel at the same time we were, and a look had turned into a conversation and then a shared dinner. For three wonderful days, Ned showed me "his" city and since then— a long five months—we'd been corresponding. Now, my "damnyankee," as Papa called him, was coming to Texas for the holidays.

By December 23rd, the weather was warm again, and a bright winter sun had turned the road from ice to mud.

"Horses'll bog down," Papa said.

"No," I said firmly, "they won't." I was tying the last of the red and green ribbons to the mantel, which I'd decorated with prickly pear and dried grasses. We had no Christmas tree, and I'd rejected the idea of a tumbleweed tree, settling for ribbons around almost everything I could think of, from lamps to furniture and even the picture of Mama that sat on the sideboard. Remembering New York with its glittering lights and imagining what it must look like at Christmas, I desperately wanted our house to look festive.

"I'll send Jake." He turned his back on me, busying himself with something on his desk.

"No, Papa, you and I are going to meet Ned."

112

"Ned," he muttered. "What kind of a name is that for a grown man?"

The train was over three hours late. Papa spent the time in the general store, swapping stories with several other ranchers and telling them, no doubt, about the "damnyankee" who was arriving on the train. I sat in the train station and reread Dickens' *Christmas Carol.* I thought Tiny Tim's cheer might banish my fears about how my father would greet Ned.

Papa greeted him properly, of course, and shook his hand—he knew his manners—but he did it quickly, and his "Howdy" was almost mumbled into his beard. Then he grabbed one of Ned's satchels and said, "Sallie, get that other satchel." He clomped off, his boots smacking the mud, his Stetson set firmly on his head.

Ned, dressed in a dark wool greatcoat, shoes polished so high the lamps reflected in them, stood open-mouthed. He had no way of knowing that I'd been Sallie all my life on the ranch and Sarah only when I was masquerading as something I wasn't. Nor could he know that my father had been barking similar orders at me for years: "Sallie, get that saddle!" or "Sallie, fork some of that hay over here."

"I'll take the satchel, Sarah," Ned said firmly, picking it up with one hand and offering me the other arm, which I took reluctantly, knowing the gesture would bring a withering glance from Papa. It did.

"Had some bad weather, eh?" Ned asked as the wagon slipped and slid through the mud, only Papa's firm hand on the reins keeping us from going off the narrow road.

"Yep," Papa said and slapped the reins at the horses again.

"Sarah's told me a lot about your ranch," Ned said, trying again.

"That so? Didn't tell you her name's Sallie though."

Ned shrugged and gave me a wry grin. I tightened my hold on his arm and kicked Papa hard with my boot heel. He didn't even say "Ouch!" We rode in silence for over an hour until our house rose out of the horizon before us.

Trying to look with Ned's eyes, I saw a square stone house, a chimney jutting up through the roof on one side, a roofed verandah wrapping around three sides. The house stood alone on a slight rise of ground, surrounded by nothing more than bare ground and the barbed wire fence which marked the near pasture. It looked . . . barren. Glancing at Ned, I saw his eyes sweeping the landscape.

"So much space," he whispered. "Is . . . is it all part of your ranch, sir?"

"Most of it," Papa answered, pulling the team to a stop. I knew he was biting his tongue to keep from telling the young whippersnapper that you never ask a man how many acres or head of cattle he owns. It's like asking how much money he has in the bank.

Inside, I showed Ned the guest room, with its ruffled yellow curtains and flowered bedspread. Clearly, a lady's room. "I hope you'll be comfortable."

"I'm sure I will." He opened a satchel and began to shake the wrinkles out of shirts and pants.

"I'll help." Why, I thought, are we so formal, so distant? Is this the man who made me laugh until I cried, bought me flowers from a street vendor and once called me on the telephone to sing "Ah, sweet mystery of love"? It was Papa, I thought. Papa has scared us both.

Papa harrumphed, and we joined him in the parlor, where he was pouring three cups of black coffee so strong it tasted like it'd been made over a cousie's fire. Ned sipped his gingerly and let it cool.

"Where's the Christmas tree?" he asked, looking around at all my ribbons, which now seemed to droop foolishly.

"No tree," Papa said. "No trees around to cut."

Ned got a wistful look in his eyes. "My family will be gathering around a six-foot tree tomorrow night," he said.

Anger at Papa welled up in me. Here was a man who had come clear 'cross the country to see me, left his family at the holidays, and Papa couldn't even make him welcome! It didn't cross my mind that I knew nothing of Ned's family, not even where he'd grown up.

"Christmas Day," I said bravely, "we'll gather a group here to shoot off firecrackers."

"Firecrackers?" He was obviously amazed. "It's not Independence Day!"

"We always shoot them at Christmas," I said defensively.

Papa went to bed early that night, having grumbled his way through the roast chicken I'd fixed. Ned and I sat in the parlor, on facing chairs, and found that the magic of our Waldorf Astoria meeting did not repeat itself in a Texas ranch house. He told me what he'd done since summer, even though I already knew every detail from his letters, and I told him what I'd done—or rather, being stuck on the ranch, what I hadn't done—but he already knew that.

Gradually though, our talk went back to my New York visit, and we fell into conversations that begin with "Remember?" Remember when we skipped along Fifth Avenue? Remember eating oysters at that tiny tavern? Remember walking in Central Park? I remembered all right . . . and knew that it was both Papa and Texas that made things different. Papa was cross—Aunt Edna had been cheerful and invisible—and Texas was plain—there was no Fifth Avenue, no Central Park, no romantic small tavern in the basement of a brownstone.

Next morning, Papa announced that he was taking the team to the far pasture to check the cattle there. "See if they survived the norther," he said.

"I'd like to go with you," Ned said.

"I . . . I can be ready in ten minutes," I said, looking at the wrapper I wore and figuring I could change that quickly into boots and a split skirt.

"No," Ned said gently but firmly, "you stay here and give me a chance to visit with your father."

Papa looked grim, but all he said was, "Better change pants."

"I didn't bring workpants," Ned said. "These will be fine."

I spent the morning listening for the wagon to lumber back up to the house. Part of me was convinced that Papa would do something to test Ned—ask him to help hold a reluctant steer or tell him to drive the wagon team, which he couldn't possibly know how to do.

It was near mid-day when I heard not a lumbering wagon but one being driven at full speed, the horses' hooves pounding the ground, the wagon creaking ominously. Before I could reach the door, I heard Ned shouting, "Sarah! Sarah!"

Whatever test Papa had put him to, Ned had obviously passed— he was in one piece and able to shout. As I threw open the door, he was yelling, "Your father's been hurt. Broken leg, I think. I need boards to splint it."

"Boards?" I was absolutely stupid in my confusion.

"Bed slats," he said impatiently, "and a sheet I can tear into strips." He rushed past me to the guest room, where he proceeded to remove the slats from the bed and would have pulled off the sheets had I not shouted, "Wait! I have some old ones!" I got the old sheets and my coat and met him at the wagon.

"It's too cold for an injured man to lie long on the ground," he said as he slapped the reins and put the horses once again into a run.

"What happened to Papa?" I asked, shouting over the wind that whipped my hair into my face.

"Tried to talk to a bull that wasn't conversational," Ned shouted back. "Tripped over a root trying to get away. I had to drive the team between him and that bull."

"Showing off," I muttered, "that's what he was doing. Showing off for the damnyankee."

"What'd you say?" Ned asked loudly.

"Thanks," I said, "Thanks for saving his life."

By evening, Papa was sitting up in his bed. The doctor had come from town, pronounced it a simple break, and praised Ned's splint. "You'll be off that leg six weeks," he told Papa.

"Won't be off it six days," Papa said. "Got too much to do around this place." Then he looked at Ned. "How'd you drive the team?"

That wry look again. "I grew up on a farm. I wasn't born a New York lawyer."

"Did a damn good job today, son, that's what you did." It cost Papa to say that, and he couldn't look Ned in the eye as he did.

Ned blushed and said a low "Thanks."

"I'm glad," I said late that night as we sat by the fire, "that you and Papa became friends...even if it was in such alarming circumstances."

"We were always friends, Sarah," he said. "I understood him perfectly . . . and I fancy he understood who I was and where I come from, except maybe the part about the farm." He paused and stared at me. "The one I wasn't sure about was you."

"Me?" My voice squeaked.

116

"You. You're different out here."

"Oh, well, I ride horses, and work with the cowboys, and they all call me Sallie . . . ."

"That's not what I meant. You . . . you're self-conscious and reserved—and stiff. From the minute I got here, you . . . I don't know how to explain it."

"I do," I mumbled, looking away from him. "I was so worried about Papa making you welcome, that I forgot to make you welcome myself."

Just as he leaned toward me—he was going to kiss me, I know he was!—Papa called out: "Sallie? Sallie!"

"Yes, Papa?"

"I want some syllabub!"

"Syllabub? At this hour?"

"It's Christmas morning, isn't it?" he demanded, yelling from his bedroom.

Ned went to the door of his room. "My family always drinks syllabub," he said. "I'd be pleased to make it."

I got a pitcher of rich cream from the shed where it kept warm enough not to freeze and cool enough not to sour, and then I brought Papa's sherry, some sugar, and a little grated nutmeg. Ned mixed them with the air of a scientist bent on a great experiment, saving aside some of the cream to whip until it was frothy enough to top each of three glasses. He placed the glasses on a silver tray, draped a white towel over his arm like a waiter, and paraded into Papa's bedroom.

And so, the three of us sat, early on Christmas morning, sipping our syllabub, saying rarely a word until Papa said, "Not bad for a damnyankee."

"I was born in South Carolina," Ned said.

Papa shooed us out, said he was tired, and as Ned and I parted in the hall, he leaned down to kiss me. Not a peck this one, but a kiss as light and gentle as though a butterfly had landed on my lips.

"Merry Christmas," he said.

"Merry Christmas," I answered. "I'm glad you came to Texas."

"So am I," he said, "and so is your father."

Pegeen's Revenge

I wasn't in the saloon the night Louann got shot. If I had been, I'm sure it wouldn't have happened—or at least, that's what I tell myself. But she had this thing about making me go to bed, so I was upstairs in my room, pretending to be asleep. It was a hot night in August, and I couldn't have slept even if I was tired. The big old hand-me-down man's shirt she'd found for me was so hot it felt like being wrapped in a wool blanket. So I did what I did a lot of nights—I listened to the singing and shouting from the saloon. Usually it was good natured, but not that night. Somehow as I lay there I sensed a menacing tone in the buzz from downstairs, like low, angry voices.

My name's Pegeen—oh, its Mary Margaret, but everyone called me Pegeen back then. I was twelve years old in 1877 when all this happened. Three years before my mama went to sleep and didn't wake up. I heard someone say the word "laudanum," and Louann told me she left a note saying I belonged to her now. I missed my mama a lot, but by then I was fiercely attached to Louann. We lived upstairs from Miss Ellie's saloon in Fort Worth, Texas. And no, don't be thinkin' that. Louann wasn't no lady of the night, though Lord knows I know about that. My mama had fallen that low, and that's why she took her life. But Louann, she sang and sometimes she danced on the top of the big grand piano Miss Ellie had bought. But mostly she went around the room, hugging the cowboys, inviting them to have another drink, watching them play cards, and making each one of them think he was the best-looking, most important fellow she'd ever seen.

And some lowlife shot her over a card game!

I heard the shot—it was a loud, muffled sort of a bang, not the clean crack of a rifle shot—and when I threw open the door to the balcony, I saw the smoke, thick and dirty, rising over the poker table. Everyone was yelling and screaming, and I screamed, "Louann!" as I lunged down the stairs. I heard someone else yell, "Get Doc McGarrity," and yet another voice cry out, "Find Marshal Courtright."

Strong arms grabbed me and held me. "She's been hit, Pegeen. You can't help her."

"She's not dead!" I screamed.

"No, at least not yet." The voice belonged to Eddie, one of the bartenders. "They've sent for Doc McGarrity. You need to stay out of the way."

I squirmed and wriggled, but he held tight. I was convinced that Louann would be all right if I could just get to her, hold her hand, tell her how much I needed her. Of course, I was wrong. That wouldn't have done a thing to help her.

The knot of people around her parted to make way for Doc McGarrity. He bent over, listened with his stethoscope, seemed to study Louann from several directions. Then he spoke to the men around him. Someone ran up the stairs and returned with a blanket from which they made a makeshift sling, and four of them carried her upstairs.

"Louann!" I wailed again, but I guess even then I knew that she couldn't hear me.

I was still sitting on the stairs, arms propped on my knees and head buried in my arms, when Randy Spurlock came down the stairs. Without a word, he sat down next to me.

"Who shot her?" I asked, raising a tear-stained face.

"Gambler. Fella I'd never seen before. Looked like he came off a riverboat on the Mississippi—you know, creased trousers and a black vest with a big gold watch chain. A real dandy." Randy's voice was bitter. He was sort of Louann's special friend, though I guess both of them would've denied it if you asked them. But I thought Randy was just about the best-looking man I'd ever seen— tall, strong, curly headed with eyes that usually laughed though now they were so sad it hurt me to look at him. Still, he was everything a twelve-year-old girl dreams about.

"Why'd he shoot her?"

"She was . . ." Randy's voice almost broke. "She was tryin' to help me. I was losing bad . . . and you know, Pegeen, I don't lose at poker. She saw the reason. He was dealin' out of his shirtsleeve. When she called him on it, he pulled this little tiny gun . . . ."

"If it was a little tiny gun, then it didn't hurt her too bad, right?" I was figuring all this out in my mind.

He laid a hand over mine. "Wrong, Pegeen. It was a derringer—

little but deadly at close range. Big bullet—about this big—" He held up the stubby end of his little finger. "Big and slow, so it hits hard." He was quiet for a minute. "Hit her in the upper arm, aimed for the heart and missed. If it had been her heart . . . ." He shuddered.

"Shoulder!" I scoffed. "She'll be all right then. It'll just have to heal."

This time he put a comforting arm around me. "Probably shattered the bone so's Doc can't fix it right. If she lives, she'll never have use of that shoulder again. She won't be dancin' on the piano anymore like she used to."

"What do you mean 'if she lives'?" I asked indignantly. "Louann's gonna' live."

"Sure she is, honey, sure she is."

We sat there in silence, each of us avoiding looking at the other. I studied the saloon, which had been turned into a shambles. Chairs and tables were overturned, and cards and beer bottles were scattered everywhere. I looked toward where Louann had fallen and saw blood on the floor. Not a lot, but it was still blood. I couldn't bear that so I looked the other way.

Suddenly I grabbed Randy's arm. "Look, what's that there on the floor."

Almost relieved to have an excuse to move, he got up, walked to the far side of the overturned table, and bent down. Then came a low whistle. "It's the gun," he said, coming back to where I sat. "He must have dropped it just before he got away in all the confusion."

I reached for it.

"Un-huh. There's still a bullet in the second chamber." He broke it open and dumped the cartridge into his hand. Before handing me the gun, he looked through both barrels, just to be sure. Then he clicked the gun together and gave it to me.

The derringer was ugly. Stubby and short, like a fat man. I'd seen fancy pistols lots in the saloon. Sometimes men would come in to play and lay their pistols on the table as a show of good faith. I'd seen 'em with gold scrolls and filigrees on them and sometimes brass plates with the maker's name. This one was black steel, with a rubber grip where you put your hand. And it was so small.

"This little thing?" I asked.

"That little thing is a Remington .41 rimfire double derringer, if you want to get technical. And it's deadly. I can still see the flash when he fired it. Like a burst of flame."

I put my hands over my ears.

A plan began to take shape in my mind. "Randy, how do you fire this thing?" I was pulling the trigger but nothing happened.

"Pegeen, you don't need to be knowin' how to fire a derringer."

"Ah, come on, show me."

Reluctantly, he took the gun back. "You got to cock the hammer"—he showed me—"and then pull the triggcr."

I tried, but the hammer was too stiff for me, and the gun, small as it was, was awkwardly heavy in my hand. "I could never shoot this."

"Good," he said, reaching for it.

I jumped up and moved away, stuffing the gun into my overall's pocket. "I'm gonna give it to Louann. I think she ought to have it."

"Pegeen. . . ." His tone was threatening as he moved toward me. "A girl your age has no business with a gun."

I climbed up a couple of stairs. "You've got the bullets," I pointed out. "I'm just gonna save it until I can give it to her."

I spent the next three days sitting outside Louann's bedroom door. Nobody would let me in to see her. "You'll upset her," they said.

"Leave her be," the doc said. "She's having a hard time."

Once as I dozed on the floor, I heard the doc talking to Miss Ellie. "Infection's set in, just like I feared. Those damn derringer bullets are greasy on the outside, and they pick up lint and stuff and carry it right into the wound. Sometimes it's a blessing if they bleed, carry that stuff out. But Louann, she didn't bleed enough. The wound's puffy and red and hot. I dug out the bullet and drained as much pus off as I could, but we'll just have to wait for the crisis.'

"What crisis?" I wanted to scream.

Fortunately Miss Ellie asked, "Crisis? What do you mean?"

I peeked one eye open, hoping they'd still think I was asleep if they even saw me, and saw Doc shrug his shoulders.

"We'll see if the bullet's gonna beat the body or the body's gonna beat the bullet."

"That damn lowlife!" Miss Ellie said vehemently and turned and went downstairs. Doc followed her. They'd forgotten about me, and if I'd kept good track, no one was with Louann right now. I reached into my pocket and held the derringer until it felt warm in my hand. Somehow that reassured me. Then ever so carefully I eased open the door to her room and slid in, gentling the door closed behind me.

Louann lay on her back, so motionless that I thought they were all wrong, and she'd died after all. I crept to the bedside and put out my hand. With one finger, I stroked her cheek lightly. She wasn't dead—her cheek was burning hot with fever.

"Louann," I whispered, "there's a crisis coming. You got to fight."

All I got in response was a moan, low and miserable. She moved just slightly. Her left shoulder was all tied up with bandages, I guess to keep her from moving it. Once while I watched she grabbed at the bandages with her good right hand, and I had to take the hand and pull it back down. Had I remember to wash my own hands, I wondered? I hoped so. Louann was always after me about bathing more often and being more ladylike, and it wouldn't do to carry even more germs to her.

"Louann, I got something for you to fight the crisis with. It's the lowlife's gun, the one that shot you."

She moaned, and I thought her eyes flickered a little. I tiptoed around to the other side of the bed, so's I could put the derringer into her right hand. "There now, you feel that. It'll make you well, 'cause you and me, we got to go for revenge. We got to find that no-good son-of-a-bitch that shot you." Louann would've washed my mouth with soap if she heard me say that! I squeezed her good hand added, "And he shouldn't have tried to cheat Randy."

I thought she tried to say "Pegeen," and I quickly whispered, "I'm here, Louann. I'm gonna wait for the crisis with you. We're gonna fight it."

Of course, I slept right through the crisis and never did know it. When I woke up, curled in a ball on the far side of her bed, I heard Doc and Miss Ellie talking. I wanted to stretch my cramped muscles so bad I near cried out, but I sure didn't want them to know I was there.

"Crisis passed," Doc said, relief spilling over in his voice. "She's gonna' make it. I don't know how she got the stamina or the will or what, but she's gonna make it."

Well, I knew. It was because I'd given her the gun and talked to her about revenge. Louann was going to get well so we could shoot that scoundrel with his own gun. Now I maybe was only twelve, but I knew that it wasn't something we could do tomorrow or the next day. Louann had a long time of recovering ahead of her, and it was up to me to keep her spirits up by talking about revenge. I could hold out to her a mental picture of shooting that Mississippi gambler in the shoulder, just like he shot her. I guess I was so bent on encouraging Louann that I never thought about the reality of shooting someone. At least not for a while, I didn't.

It was two more days before Miss Ellie "officially" let me in to visit Louann. By then, she was propped up a little in the bed, and Miss Ellie was feeding her broth. I just thanked her for letting me come in and didn't tell her I'd spent the last three nights sleeping by Louann's bed.

"I can feed her," I offered.

Miss Ellie sniffed. "You'll need to go take a bath, get clean clothes, and wash your hair before I let you any closer to her."

Now I would have been downright offended by that, except I knew that was exactly what Louann would have said. In fact, I think I saw Louann look sideways at me as she opened her mouth to receive broth. But if she could talk, she didn't let me know it.

"Yes, ma'am," I said obediently and left the room. It wasn't no time at all until I was back, freshly scrubbed—well, maybe I'd cheated a little but I really had tried to scrub every inch of my body. And I'd washed my hair—it was still wet. And the most serious sign of my good intentions was that I'd put on that blasted dress that Louann bought me last year. It was too small now, tight across the shoulders, and so short around my ankles that if it was pants folks would have thought I was expecting heavy rain and high water. I may have been uncomfortable, but Miss Ellie thought I was now acceptable.

"You sit here by her, Pegeen," she commanded, "but don't you go to wearin' her out by talkin'."

"Yes, ma'am."

The minute she was gone, I asked, "You got that derringer

Louann?"

She was too tired and hurt too much to laugh, but something told me she would have if she'd had the energy. She moved the covers back with her right hand, and there lay the gun. "Hard to hide when they change the bedclothes," she managed to say.

Well, of course I hadn't thought of that. I just knew it was important that she keep that gun by her . . . I don't guess I knew the words symbol or incentive, but they were what I meant.

"Can you hide it in the folds of your robe?"

She nodded and took the spoonful of broth that I offered her.

"You know," I said conversationally, "I . . . well, I figure when you're well, we can take a wagon and go looking for this guy. I mean I'm sure he didn't stay in Fort Worth after shooting you. They'd have lynched him."

She nodded as though in agreement.

"But we can't let him get away, so you got to hurry about this mending business."

"Tired," she said, "So tired."

"Well that's partly the pain medicine Doc is giving you, I suppose. You just sleep and gather your strength. But you be thinkin' about how we're gonna find that guy. And every time you touch that gun, it'll remind you of what we have to do."

She nodded, but she was asleep almost before I could take away the soup and tray.

Randy came into the saloon that night. Just as he was about to sit at the poker table, he saw me, sitting in my usual place on the stairs. Eddie had fixed me lemonade and put it in a beer bottle he had rinsed very carefully—he did that for me sometimes, and it was our little joke. I loved to watch men come in and see this young girl in coveralls drinkin' a beer. They gaped and stared and never knew how funny they looked, even when I laughed at them.

"Pegeen, you better not be drinkin' beer!" He knew I wasn't.

"Who's gonna' stop me?" I answered like a smart aleck.

"Me! I'll tell Louann on you."

"You seen her yet?"

He shook his head and slumped down beside me. "Miss Ellie won't let me. Acts like I'm gonna attack her or something. I . . . I just want to see how she's doin' and tell her I hope she gets better soon. I'm real glad she's gonna' be okay."

"Doc says her left arm will never be much good, but I figure she can still shoot with her right hand."

"Shoot?" he exploded. "Who's she gonna' shoot."

"Oh, I mean shoot pool and do stuff like that. You know." I thought I recovered very quickly, but Randy was looking at me real skeptical.

"You ain't thinkin' of shooting anyone, are you, Pegeen?" His voice was stern. Then he suddenly remembered. "What'd you do with that derringer?"

"Gave it to Louann like I told you I would. I just thought she should have it. And, no I'm not gonna shoot anybody and neither is she." I tried to treat it lightly. "Well, if that sidewinder that shot Louann came in here, I'd sure shoot him."

"Well, that ain't gonna happen. I guarantee he's in Fort Griffin or Abilene by now. . . or someplace on down the road from there."

"You aren't goin' after him?" I asked, intending to suggest that it would be manly of Randy to seek revenge for Louann.

He shook his head. "Nope. And Louann wouldn't want me to. If she'd died, I'd have probably helped the law find the guy. But now she's gonna be okay . . . shoot, I don't even know his name."

"You know what he looks like." I was nothing if not persistent.

"Yeah, so does she." He sat for a minute. Then he said, "I got to go play some cards. You see if you can sneak me in there sometime, Pegeen. You do that?"

"Sure, Randy, I'll do that."

By the end of the second week, Louann was sitting on the edge of the bed and talking to me almost like her old self.

"Tell me about that guy that shot you," I said. I was sprawled in the one chair in her room, wearing my coveralls again. After that one time, Miss Ellie had quit worrying about getting me into a dress.

"He was mean looking," she said. "Had the coldest eyes I ever saw. I don't think it bothered him one bit to shoot me. Only thing that would bother him is being hanged."

"Or shot," I offered.

She grinned. "Or shot." She reached into the bedclothes and

pulled out the derringer. With her right hand, she rubbed it as though for good luck. "I don't know I've got the strength to shoot this, Pegeen. These little guns have a kick to them. That's why you have to be right on top of what you're trying to shoot—you can't aim with any kind of accuracy."

I watched her as she raised the gun. Trouble was she couldn't use her left hand to cock it, and it was near impossible to cock and hold in the same hand. "You keep working at it," I said.

Randy got in to see Louann about that time, and try as I might to sneak in behind him, I couldn't. "Pegeen," he said in his sternest voice, "you stay outside. I want some private time with Louann." He looked at me. "And don't you be peeking through the keyhole or listenin', either one."

I stomped off in a pout.

He must have been in there an hour. I know because I sat at the end of the hall and watched the door. When he came out, his face was red and he was rubbin' his chin, like he was confused about something. He brushed right on by me without saying anything.

When I went into her room, Louann was lying there staring at the ceiling. I thought her face looked kinda' red too. "How's Randy?" I asked.

"What?" She was startled by my voice, and it was like I was calling her back from some far place. "He's fine," she said with a shrug. "You know that. You've seen him a lot more than I have lately."

The first day Louann came downstairs in the afternoon, the few men in the saloon stood and cheered. She came slowly, dressed in a cotton wrapper, and clinging to me with her right hand. Helping her was kind of awkward, because you didn't want to touch her left side at all, where her shoulder was bound into a sling. So I just let her hold on to me and hoped that she was steady on her feet.

She was almost winded when she sat down at one of the tables.

"Hey, Louann! Whisky?" Eddie called from behind the bar.

She gave him a wan smile. "Lemonade, Eddie. And not in a beer bottle."

Everyone was awkward around her, not knowing what to say

beyond, "Gee, you're looking good," and "I'm glad you're okay," and stuff like that. I wanted to shout at them that she wasn't suddenly deaf and dumb. She was still Louann who wanted to know what was going on in Fort Worth and who was winning at the poker table. She began to call them by name, ask about this one's wife or that one's child, and pretty soon they loosened up.

Randy came in just by accident, and he was delighted to see her sitting there. He plopped himself down in the chair next to hers and said, "I knew there was a reason I wanted a beer in the middle of the day, just didn't know what it was."

"And what was it?" she asked with a smile.

"So I could see you sitting up and acting like a person instead of an invalid," he said with a grin, and Louann raised her good arm as though she'd swat him.

I wished Randy hadn't come in, and I know that's selfish. But I kind of wanted to be her guardian all by myself. Now she turned her attention to him, and when she announced, after an hour, that she was "wiped out," it was Randy who helped her back upstairs. I sat and nursed my lemonade and my pout.

Louann came downstairs every day after that, each time staying a little longer, and pretty soon she was taking her meals with the rest of us at the table where Miss Ellie had Idabelle serve us. I sometimes had to help Louann cut her meat because she couldn't use both hands, but other than that she was pretty good one-handed.

One day when I walked her back upstairs and followed her into her room, she sat on the edge of the bed and stared at me.

"What's wrong?" I finally asked. "My overalls dirty again? Idabelle just washed them."

"They're too small, legs are too short. And your hair needs cutting. I haven't been doin' much about taking care of you."

"I can take care of myself," I mumbled, and I wanted to add that I could take care of her too.

"Soon as I get my strength back, young lady, you're gonna start your studies again." Louann, who had more education than you'd expect from a dance-hall girl, had been supervising my reading and arithmetic. I liked the reading all right but not the arithmetic, and missing lessons was about the only good thing I could see about her being laid up.

But the next thing she said really threw me. "Tomorrow I want to go for a walk."

By now it was late September, and that awful Texas heat had pretty much gone, especially in the early mornings. "You want me to go with you?" I asked hopefully.

She smiled at me. "Well, Pegeen, I don't think I'm quite ready to go alone yet."

That first day we only went a little ways—not even a city block—before she was ready to turn around and go back. "I bet you don't know how hard it is to walk with one hand," she said with a wry smile.

"Why? You don't walk with your hands."

"Nope. But two free arms give you balance. I feel like I'm gonna topple over toward my left, and I can't stop myself. You try holding your arm tight against your shoulder and see."

I tried it but I didn't get the effect she was talking about. We did get some funny looks from people on the street.

When she was back in her room, Louann said with great determination, "I'm going to rest now, but this afternoon I want you to come to my room. There's something I need your help with."

I wasn't exactly looking forward to that, 'cause I knew what she wanted—not my help with anything. She wanted to "help" me with schoolwork. I was so sure of it that I went and dug out the books we'd been using before Louann had declared a summer holiday last July. As I sat there and tried to read *McGuffey's*, I got to thinking about Louann's recovery. She hadn't mentioned the gun or revenge lately, and yet she seemed to be getting a lot better faster and faster. So maybe we didn't need my revenge plan anymore. Maybe she was going to get well just to be well and not to find the man who shot her. A corner of my mind felt a little relieved. I'd enjoy the adventure of setting off to find the man, but I had some qualms about shooting him. And I thought she did too.

Boy oh boy, was I wrong! When I went into her room in the late afternoon, she was sitting up in the chair, fingering the derringer. "I can't do it!" she said in frustration. "I can't cock it. It's too stiff for one hand."

I took it, but I remembered I couldn't cock it when Randy gave it to me. I tried again, nothing. I held the gun with my left hand and tried to pull the hammer back with my right. Still couldn't get it. Finally I braced the gun against my leg and used both hands.

"Try not to shoot yourself in the leg," Louann said. "Even I know that's not how you're supposed to do it."

"It worked," I said, handing her the gun carefully with the muzzle pointed away from both of us. "Can you pull the trigger?" I asked. Randy would probably have shot both of us if he'd been there, because we didn't check the barrels. But I was sure it was unloaded—and it was.

She held the gun away from her, pointed at the wall, and pulled the trigger. "Easy," she said. "But I won't be able to tell that lowlife to stand still while I get Pegeen to cock my gun."

"Maybe you could carry it cocked once you find him and know where he is."

She laughed aloud so hard that I began to laugh too. "What's the matter with that?" I asked, when I could talk again.

"It shows that neither of us knows a thing about guns," she said. "Nobody, but nobody, goes around carrying a cocked pistol."

"Well, this is an unusual case," I said lamely.

"It surely is," she said. Then, "Where are the cartridges?"

"Randy took them."

"Can't ask Randy," she said, "but I know how to get some."

I never did ask where or anything, but one day she showed me two cartridges and explained carefully that she kept them separate from the derringer. But I knew this: Louann hadn't given up the idea of revenge, and since it was my idea, I was honor-bound to help her with it.

As fall moved into October, Louann was pretty much on her feet. Her shoulder was no longer bandaged so tight. Now she could get a dress on both arms, if the sleeves were loose, and then she put a loose sling to hold her wrist and keep pressure off the wounded shoulder. She couldn't use it, of course, but she didn't look as much like an invalid. And could she walk! I was tired sometimes when we came back.

One day as we walked through the Acre, dodging garbage in the streets and turning away the children who offered to shine our shoes or sell us the apples they'd stolen off a vegetable cart uptown, Louann suddenly said, "I won't be able to drive a wagon, you know."

"I can drive a wagon," I said.

She turned to look at me. "Have you ever?"

"No, but how hard can it be? You pull on both reins to stop the horse, the left one to make it turn left, and the right one to make it turn right."

"Well, that's the basic idea," she said. And without another word, she led me to Mr. Standifer's stable, where she brushed away his congratulations on her improved health and said, "I'll need a horse and wagon two days from now, in the evening. I'm liable to need it for some time, maybe even a month."

"Now, Miss Louann, you can't drive a horse with that arm."

"I'll have someone who can," she said crisply. "Meantime, Pegeen here will lead the horse back to the saloon."

Mr. Standifer and I were both astounded, but for different reasons. He looked skeptically at me, but Louann headed him off with "She's very familiar with horses."

Now that was a slight exaggeration! But what got me was that suddenly not only were we really going to hunt for the gambler, we were going in two days! That made everything much more real. My stomach had just dropped to my feet.

On the way back to the saloon, Louann laid out her plan. We would take two days to put together the things we need to travel. We'd travel light, putting things in her carpetbag. She would secret some biscuits and cheese from Idabelle. Then I'd lead the horse and buggy back to the saloon, where she'd come down the back stairs and meet me.

"Where we going?" I asked.

"Didn't you once say Randy thought the man was probably at Fort Griffin? That's where the hide hunters bring their goods for sale and gamblers wait to get whatever money they get from the sale. We'll start there. Believe me, I can describe him thoroughly."

Well, for two days I lived on pins and needles, jumping every time someone called my name, sure that our plan had been discovered, convinced that Miss Ellie would ask why I all of the sudden wanted all my clothes clean. I was so wound up that I couldn't sleep at night and lay tossing and turning. I wanted this waiting to be over, the way you want the wait to be over before something bad happens—you just want to go on and get it over with.

That night she chose was a Thursday night, which Louann figured would be kind of quiet both in town and in the saloon. It was darker than pitch. Clouds covered the moon, and the air had a winter nip to it. I shivered as I edged along the street, keeping close to buildings so no one would see me. Louann had sent me off with a joyful, "We're going, Pegeen, we're really going. You hurry!" I wanted nothing more than to crawl into my bed and pull the covers over my head.

I sidled into the stable and edged toward the corner where Mr. Standifer had his desk. Actually he had it in an empty stall, so it was sort of hidden when you came in. "Mr. Standifer?" I called.

"Right here," he said. "Come on over here."

I did . . . and there sat Randy! To this day I don't know how he got there, but I guess Mr. Standifer must have told him about Louann renting the horse and buggy. She was going to be furious when she found out, and I didn't want to be in Randy Spurlock's shoes for anything!

"Uh . . . hi," I said.

"Well, Pegeen, what a surprise." He stared at me, his mouth split in a wide grin. "What you doin' here at this time of night?" Ostentatiously he pulled a big watch out of his pocket and stared at it. "Nearly ten o'clock. I'd a thought Louann would have sent you off to bed by now."

"I came . . . to get something for her."

"Yeah," he said dryly. "A horse and buggy. But, Pegeen, my love, I don't think you can handle that. The horse, maybe yes, but not pulling an empty buggy. You just go on and hop in, and I'll drive the horse."

I heard the clip-clop of a horse's hooves and knew that the stable boy was bringing up the horse and buggy. Looking desperately at Randy, I said, "I'll be all right. I don't want to trouble you."

He stood up. "No trouble at all, Pegeen, none at all. You just go on . . . well, here, let me help you."

And the next thing I knew I was sitting in that buggy, Randy was beside me, and we were parading down Rusk Street. Without asking he turned the horse behind the saloon. He waited until Louann stepped out of the shadows, and then he tied the reins and jumped down. "Hey, Louann, I thought you girls might need some help. It's a far piece to Griffin."

She stared at him without speaking for so long that Randy almost lost his joking good-natured attitude. Finally she said, "Randy Spurlock, I may never speak to you again."

"Yeah," he said, "you will." Without another word, he lifted her by the waist and set her on the seat beside me. Then he heaved the carpetbag into the back of the buggy, walked around, and climbed in. He tapped the reins gently on the horse's back, and we were headed toward the street.

Three made a crowd on the seat of that tiny buggy. Louann and I were tense and silent, but Randy whistled like he hadn't a care in the world. Only thing is, he didn't head west out of town. He headed uptown. Next thing I knew he stopped in front of the marshal's office.

I almost blurted out, "We ain't gonna shoot anybody!" I figured we were gonna be arrested in advance, guilty for having planned a crime even if we didn't get to carry it out.

"Randy . . . ." Louann began, but he cut her off.

"Something you need to see in here," he said. "Then I swear I'll take you to Fort Griffin if you still want."

Silently she let him lift her out of the wagon. I scrambled out on my own and followed them inside. Marshal "Longhair Jim" Courtright sat at his desk, his feet propped up on the top, his hat pulled low over his eyes. I thought he was probably asleep and wondered that this was the man that was supposed to clean crime out of the Acre and Fort Worth.

Randy merely said, "Marshal," and headed right past him to the jail cells, pulling Louann by her good hand so fast that I thought she'd trip. The marshal never even looked up, which I thought was odd. In one of the cells a man in rumpled clothes sat on the bunk. His hair was messed, and his eyes were bleary. I had no idea who he was or why we were there, but Louann did.

She screamed, long and loud, and then she buried her face on Randy's shoulder and began to sob.

He put an arm around her and asked, "You got that derringer,

Louann?"

She nodded.

"Well, get it out. Here's your chance." When she didn't respond, he reached for her reticule and drew out the derringer, holding it carefully so as not to point it at anyone. In an elaborate gesture, he broke it apart and checked the barrels. "Two cartridges. Good girl. Here."

He handed her the gun, and she took it woodenly.

"She can't cock it," I said.

"Oh," Randy said cheerfully, "'course she can't. I'll do it." And he did.

The man in the jail cell was getting alarmed. "Marshal! Marshal! You got to help me. This man, he's telling that woman to shoot me."

There was no response from Longhair Jim.

"Now Louann, you get as close as you can, you know, like he was when he shot you."

Then, and only then, did I know for sure who that man was and why we were there.

Louann's hand shook but she raised the gun and pointed it at the man. He began to blabber and beg, even fell down on his knees, crying about how she couldn't shoot a man in cold blood. Louann just stood there, pointing that gun at him. I held my breath and my stomach hurt something fierce. I really thought I was about to see a man die, and I didn't want Louann to pull the trigger. But I couldn't speak. Randy seemed unconcerned.

After what seemed hours but probably wasn't even a minute, Louann lowered the gun and said, "I can't do it."

"I know you can't, honey," Randy said, carefully taking the gun from her. He closed the hammer, broke the gun apart, removed the cartridges, and put everything in his pocket. Only then did he wrap his arms around her, careful always of her shoulder. "Not that he don't deserve it, that lowlife, but I knew you couldn't. Look at him snivel like the coward he is."

Louann turned toward me. "Pegeen?"

I looked at the ground. "I only wanted you to have some reason to get well, Louann. I didn't really want you to kill anybody."

With her good arm, she hugged me fiercely. "But you'd have gone with me all the way to Fort Griffin."

I nodded.

"Now," Randy said, "aren't you glad I saved you the trouble? He never was as far as Griffin, but he killed a man in Weatherford. You don't have to shoot him, Louann. I reckon he'll hang sooner rather than later."

We left, and the sounds of the gambler's sobbing followed us out the door of the office. Marshal Courtright didn't look up when we left either.

An Old Woman's Lament about War

War is unforgiving, they tell you. Old women who had lived through the first big war shook their heads and told me it'd take my boys and I could only pray to God they'd come back. But war took my daughter too, and that's a bitter pill to swallow, even now all these years later.

Oh, it took one of my boys—Charles never did come home, lost somewheres in France they said when they gave me the gold star to hang in my window. I got the star even now, put away with his report cards from grammar school and his high school diploma that never did him any good. Seemed a mite silly to keep that star in the window all these years, and so I took it down one day. Guess it was Willard who told me to take it down.

War didn't take Willard, exactly, but it sent him back to me changed some—not the limp which testifies to a German hand grenade but the look in his eyes. Maybe only a mother can tell, but I see a thin layer of fear way back there in the depths, a fear that he hides well but that never goes away.

But Sharon—Sharyn, she calls herself now—that was the loss that tore at my soul. What's that old verse? "A son is a son/Until he takes a wife/But a daughter is a daughter/All of her life." Whoever said that hadn't met Sharon. . .or maybe they hadn't ever lived on a ranch with the men gone.

The crying woke me, great gulping sobs coming from Sharon's bedroom. I pulled on my old chenille robe and poked my feet out on the cold, bare wood floor, trying to find my slippers by feel without turning on the light. The wind blew through our frame house with nary a thing to stop it on a cold winter night, and I'd banked the fire to save a few pennies. No sense heating a house full of people under bedclothes, Lewis always said.

That great loud crying made me frantic, and I hurried down the drafty hall without finding my slippers, my feet as cold as my heart.

She lay on her bed, still dressed from the day before, her head buried in a pillow and blonde hair fanned out around, one clenched fist pounding the bed in rage so strong I was surprised not to hear the pounding. Stretched full length, she clearly was no child but a woman, and tall at that.

"Sharon? Stop that. Cryin' never solved nothing." I remember wishing I'd been the kind to go put an arm around her and rock her like I did when she was a little baby—and like I'd do now if I had her before me—but that wasn't my way. "What ails you, child?"

"It's not fair," she screamed, gulping for air as though her sobs were about to suffocate her. "It's not fair."

"What's not?" I asked as gentle as I knew how, reaching a tentative hand to brush the wet hair back from her forehead.

"War!"

I shook my head. "No, it isn't. It isn't fair both our boys had to go and leave us here alone to wait and wonder."

"And Robert," she said intensely.

Robert was her boyfriend—fiancé she went so far as to call him, now that he was clear off in Europe somewheres. "You afraid Robert won't come back?" I pulled the blanket out from underneath her and tried to cover her—a motherly gesture—but she flung it off.

"Yes." Rage had turned to a whimper now. "I'm afraid we won't get married and. . .and I'll live all my life on this place." Jumping from the bed, she began to pace, long legs taking long steps so that she came full circle in that tiny bedroom with every four steps.

Didn't sound too bad to me. I'd lived all my life on two ranches—down the road some twenty miles where my momma and daddy raised me and then this thousand acres near Quanah where Lewis brought me when we married, back near thirty years ago. Lewis had been gone six years—heart attack they said—and I still loved the land, wondered sometimes if I didn't love it more than I'd loved him.

"No sense worrying about that today," I said practically. "Get out of your clothes and get some sleep. I'll do the morning chores."

I half-ran back to my bedroom, trying to convince my feet they'd soon be warm again.

Charles went to war in February of '42, right after Pearl Harbor, and Willard the next fall, both of them as soon as they turned eighteen, and Sharon and I'd been doing the chores morning and night ever since. Only hired man I could get was old Jake—the army didn't want him 'cause he was fifty-eight, near blind in one eye, and sick half the time—arthritis, he told me, or was it rheumatism?

"I'd go serve my country, iffen they'd let me," he'd cackle proudly, sitting at my kitchen table of a cold morning and wrapping his hands around a cup of steaming coffee. "Don't take but one eye to shoot a rifle nohow." But the army didn't see it his way, and he was reduced to taking care of two fool women, too many head of cattle, six horses, and a ranch bigger than it should be.

The next morning when Sharon came downstairs she seemed better, though she looked like you do after crying too much. Her face was puffy, and her eyes seemed big and dark. She ate some toast with wild plum jelly from last year's crop and gathered her schoolbooks without talking, managing a slight "bye" over her shoulder when she heard the school bus honk. That was the winter of '44, her last year in high school. War had done her a dirty trick for sure, turning her senior year into an endurance lesson rather letting her enjoy the final moments before she took on responsibilities like any other adult.

"How was school, honey?" I asked that night as I dished up the same stew we'd been eating for almost a week—it just doesn't pay to cook for two women, as I kept on finding out the hard way. Sometimes I sent the extra home with Jake, but even he had got tired of that stew.

"Fine," she said, toying with a chunk of potato. "Billie Sue's gettin' married." Her blue eyes had a wistful look in them, and she kind of stared off in space, that potato chunk speared on her fork.

"Married?" I asked, pouring myself a cup of strong, black coffee. "And who would marry that silly girl?"

"Alvin Thompson. He's gonna' sign up with the army, and he

told her he wanted to marry her first."

"Probably leave her with a child to care for and him too far away to help," I scoffed, without turning from the sink where I'd started to run the dishwater.

"Oh, Mama!" Wailing at me over her shoulder, Sharon ran up the stairs to her room.

Standing downstairs, I heard her slam her bedroom door. With a sigh, I put on my coat and shoved my feet into my old worn boots, wishing for once that Lewis—or Charles or Willard or someone—was there to tell me how to raise that girl. In the barn, I talked to the horses as I put out oats, and when I milked, I told Edna Louise—the milk cow Charles had raised from a calf—all about how worried I was. She studied me with those big eyes so intent that I truly thought for a minute she'd comfort me if only she could talk. But when I went back into the house, I never did tell Sharon how worried I was. Just called "'Night!" through the closed door and went on to bed. Seemed to me six-thirty came earlier these mornings.

Life went on that spring. I milked and fed in the mornings, took the truck into the pasture to toss hay for the cattle until the prairie grasses came up to feed them, cleaned and cooked and went on the way I always had, Lewis or no Lewis. Wednesdays I went into town to the church to roll bandages—"for the war effort," they told us. Said if we rolled lots of bandages, it would shorten the war and save a life. I never could figure how a bandage could shorten a war, but some nights I drove that old Ford home down that rutted dirt lane with my hands purely aching from folding and pressing and worrying if my bandage was as good as Mrs. Fowler's. She was the preacher's wife and a dedicated bandage-roller.

Jake mended fence, fixed the leak in the roof that came with the spring rains, and talked about the war while he drank my coffee. "Bet them boys are givin' those Germans hell," he'd say, and I'd agree, "Bet they are," even while my heart stopped cold to think of my sons in a war. They should have been home in their beds, safe, taking care of me and Sharon. . .and there they were, off fighting an enemy that didn't seem real to me yet.

"I don't ever intend to do this again," Sharon said one evening after we'd ridden the length of the ranch, checking fence and cattle, and had to get off our horses a time or two to look at a broken fencepost or a cow with screwworms that Jake would have to doctor—I drew the line at some things. Slapping dirt off her pants and kicking her shoes against the step to dislodge the mud, Sharon declared that what we'd done was men's work and she didn't intend to work like a man the rest of her life.

"Where's Robert gonna' take you to live?" I asked, knowing the answer.

"He's gonna' ranch . . . already owns two hundred acres," she said reluctantly.

"You're gonna' work like a man again and again," I told her with no sympathy and watched as she sashayed away, her behind twitching in anger.

Sharon went to school everyday, and like as not she fed in the evenings for me. Sundays she was good as gold about going to church with me. Maybe it was 'cause Robert's parents were usually there, and they always shared the news of him. I was a mite envious, for I had no one 'cept Sharon to tell about Charles and Willard. But then, they neither one did write much.

"Sharon, how pretty you're looking!" The minister's wife came up to us after church one Sunday.

"Thank you, Mrs. Fowler." She was all smiles and polite, using those manners I'd drilled into all three of them as youngsters.

"About to graduate from high school, aren't you? And what will you do then?" The flowers on Mrs. Fowler's hat bounced up and down as she talked, but her smile never faltered.

"I. . .don't rightly know," Sharon said. "I guess I'll help Mama." Desperation crept into her voice, but maybe I was the only one who could hear it.

"We all have to do our part for the war effort, don't we?" Mrs. Fowler said brightly, and I saw her again, folding bandages so fast that she always did more than any of the other ladies. Smug about it, she was. "Staying home to help your mama, what with those boys off fighting for our freedom, is the best thing you can do, Sharon. I'm real proud of you."

"Thank you," Sharon managed softly, just before she turned away and strode to the Ford faster than I ever could have thought of walking. When I finally caught up with her, she drove home without saying a word.

Sharon graduated in May. She should have had Lewis and Charles and Willard there to smile at her and be proud, but all she had was me. I did my best, telling her how proud I was—Willard never had finished high school—and how proud her daddy would have been. After the graduation and after she'd hugged and kissed all her girlfriends, I took her to the cafe and we each had a chicken-fried steak in celebration.

"How's Robert?" I asked, not really because I was so interested but just because I wanted to make conversation.

"He's fine," she said. "Says we wouldn't believe the atrocities he's seen."

"Atrocities?"

"Yeah. Man being cruel to other men. Says war is hell."

Somehow that didn't sound new to me. "Bet he misses you," I said heartily.

"Yeah, he says he does. But who knows when he can come home." She focused her attention on her fried peach pie.

I couldn't have said it for the world, but I knew even then that Robert wasn't coming back.

"I've been thinking of goin' to Fort Worth," she said. "To get a job in that defense plant."

Long as I live, I'll never be able to tell how those words cut into me. I wanted to stand up, right there in the cafe, and scream, "You can't go! You've got to stay home with me! Didn't you hear Mrs. Fowler tell you that staying home on the farm was the best contribution you can make to the war effort?" Instead, I said, quiet as I could, "What about Robert?"

She grinned, that soft girl kind of grin that says plain as day she knows a secret. "That's why I'm not going."

I wondered if Lewis had ever made me grin that way. If he did, I sure couldn't remember it any more. I gave up trying to remember and said a silent prayer that it would be a long time before Sharon found out that Robert wasn't coming home.

Sharon started to work three days a week at the post office in Quanah—started sorting the mail at six in the morning, she did, and came home by noon, more tired than I was after doing ranch work. But she was good about helping me—said she'd even bake pies, but I told her we didn't have anyone to eat pies anymore, and that made me sad. Pretty soon with her helping out so much and Jake's arthritis doing a little better I had enough time to spend two days a week rolling bandages. I hated that, but I kept telling myself that my rolling bandages was keeping my boys safe. After word came about Charles, I never did roll another bandage—but that gets ahead of my story.

Robert wrote to Sharon regular as clockwork, so every Monday night she had a letter to read at the supper table, and like as not she read parts of it to me. And then there came the night she half-screamed, half-cried when she opened the letter.

"He's been wounded! He's hurt! He's in a hospital in England." A look of amazement was on her face. I guess every one of us who sent someone off to war thought they'd be immune to bullets and never did believe they could be hurt.

"Long as he's well enough to write, that's a good sign," I said heartily.

"Un—huh," she muttered, silently devouring every word of the letter.

I turned back to the lard I was making into butter—mixing in those little packets of color that were supposed to fool you into thinking it was real butter. I'd gotten so I mostly ate my toast dry, but I felt like I ought to keep butter—or what passed for it—for cooking and for Jake to put on his toast of a morning.

"He says the nurses are wonderful," she said, "and he expects to be home soon. Oh, Mama, isn't it wonderful he got wounded? Now he can't get killed!"

I wanted to agree with her strange logic, but my heart was crying out, "Don't you know he isn't coming back to you?"

Sharon lost weight during the fall, growing thin and looking pale, and I worried some about her, but I didn't rightly know what to do. I guessed it was the waiting that was getting to her, but those letters from Robert came regular every week. I was grateful she didn't have to worry about a telegram from Uncle Sam. 'Course that was before I knew that was how they notified you—just a cold telegram, saying "Lost in Action." The telegram about Charles didn't come until long after Sharon was gone. When it came, I had nobody but Jake to console me, and all he said was, "Well, at least you got Willard," and I couldn't cry out to him that Charles was my first-born and that I'd never get over the loss of him. To myself, I thought *I should have Sharon.*

"Got your letter from Robert, I see," I said one Monday in December. Christmas was almost on us, and she was staying later at the post office these days. I guess she carried that letter home unopened so she could read it in private and quiet.

"Yeah," she said, slitting the envelope with her fingernail. "Maybe he's coming home soon. He oughta' be better by now."

"Sure should," I agreed without paying much attention. I envied Sharon in a way—she had her whole life before her, and she believed Robert was coming back, even if I knew it wasn't true. There was a sense of optimism about her, when I couldn't see much hopeful for myself. Just working this ranch, with Sharon and Jake to help me, until I was too old to sit a horse.

"Goddamn son of a bitch!"

I'd never allowed any of my children to swear in my presence, and Sharon's outburst came at me like a cannon blast. "Sharon Elizabeth Grimes," I said, turning toward her to lay down the law, even grown like she was. But she was already gone.

That bedroom door upstairs slammed again, and I was left not knowing. Robert's letter still lay on the kitchen table, though she' crumpled it some in anger. I hesitated a moment—no longer than that—and then, one ear cocked up the stairs to hear if she came back down, I smoothed out the wrinkles so I could see what he said.

Dear Sharon,

It pains me to write this, but I must tell you that I have met someone who is more important to me than life. You won't believe this, but her name is Sharon—maybe that was why I was attracted to her. Anyway, she is an Irish nurse here at the hospital in England, and we were married three days ago.

I want you to know, Sharon, that you are a wonderful person and that I will always love you. But I could not deny my heart. I hope you will find someone with whom you can be as happy as I am with Sharon.

Sincerely, Robert

Sincerely, I thought, what kind of a way is that to sign a "dear john" letter?

From upstairs there was a continuous banging and slamming, and I wished I could figure out what Sharon was doing. I sat at that kitchen table, worrying a cup of coffee in my hands but not drinking it, until nearly nine o'clock at night. Then, the banging proceeded down the stairs toward me, and Sharon stood in the kitchen, a suitcase beside her. She wore her best grey wool skirt and a clean white blouse, with the gold jewelry that I'd given her for graduation. She looked a lady, I thought, but I could do no more than stare at her.

"I'm going to Fort Worth," she said. "Robert ain't coming back, and I'm not spending my life here with you."

"Isn't," I corrected automatically, and then looked blankly at her. Maybe then was when I should have wrapped my arms around her and told her it would be all right, but I didn't know how to do that. "You can't go," I said. "I need you here." At least that part of it was the truth.

"I can't stay here, Mama," she said. "Robert will bring his Irish wife back here, and I'll be the girl he forgot, and everyone will feel sorry for me, and I'll live the rest of my life on this ranch. I won't do it. I've got to find me a life of my own."

"Can you wait until morning?" I don't know if I thought she'd change her mind by morning, but it seemed like the thing to say.

"There's a bus at ten," she said, "and I'm gonna' be on it."

I can't tell you the things that went through my mind. I should have been worried about my nineteen-year-old daughter going off alone on a bus in the middle of the night—why, who know what could have happened to her? Robbery, rape, murder—none of those things went through my mind. All I knew was that I didn't want her to go and leave me alone on that ranch—and I had no words to say that to her.

"Will you drive me to town?" she asked, fierce determination written on that face.

"Sure," I said, and so that's what I did. I drove her to town, and I sat in the Ford across the street from the bus station and watched her board the ten o'clock bus to Fort Worth.

"Write to me," was all I said to her, and she answered, "You know I will" and gave me a quick kiss on the cheek. And that was it—she was gone out of my life.

Oh, she comes to visit now, bringing that rich husband with her, but they don't stay long. Says Quanah's too small for them. And I've been to Fort Worth a time or two—they live in an area called Rivercrest, by a big country club, in a house that would have bought four ranches the size of ours. Her daddy would have been uncomfortable in it, and truth to tell, I never do settle down any of the times I go to visit.

Robert came to see me, once he came home from the war. Sharon was right—he brought that Irish bride with him. Named Sharon, just like he said. All blonde and rosy-cheeked and much more plump than my Sharon, and I wondered what he saw in her. Except I watched them, and she looked at him like she absolutely adored him. I know I never did that for Lewis, and I doubt my Sharon would have done it for Robert. But still, I blamed him because she was gone.

Willard's a comfort to me. Never did marry, that shy boy of

mine, and now he lives in the old frame house with me and listens to the wind whistle through the cracks of a winter night. Jake's passed on—I always thought he died just to prove to me that he really was sick—and Willard and I do the work. All these years, and I'm still working like a man.

But Sharon isn't—she's sitting like a lady in a big house. The war did me a bad turn, taking my daughter from me, but it gave Sharon a new life where she didn't have to work like a man.

Prisoners

By the time the Italian prisoners of war came to Umbarger to decorate the church, VE day was past and Freddy had been gone nearly three years. Later, it struck me as strange that we watched for Freddy to come home from war and instead, a large group of Italians came, not to Umbarger but to the POW camp at Hereford. Italians! In the midst of a German community! It was, some of the old men said, an outrage.

I'd seen Freddy march off to war, proud as the brass buttons on his uniform. I remember standing there in a cold rain in Hereford and watching that straggly band of men trying to march like soldiers. If we had to rely on the likes of them to defeat Hitler's troops, we were in real trouble, I thought. Besides, how could they fight the Germans when every last one of them was German himself? Umbarger was a German community in the Texas Panhandle, as out of place as a bunch of Martians would have been in Fort Worth. When I was in high school in Hereford, we always laughed and poked fun at the German kids from Umbarger. Called them krauts, we did. And then I went and married one—but that's another story.

When the new and undisciplined soldiers broke ranks, Freddy came over to where I stood with his parents, holding Elsa in my arms. His blond hair was cut so short he almost looked bald, and when he held the baby up against him, the contrast of her darkness against his pale coloring made me smile in spite of myself. Her name may have been German, but Elsa favored me in looks.

"I'll miss you," he said, almost formally, leaning to give me a distant kiss.

"Ah, Freddy," Papa Peterman said, as though his son had been talking to him, "we'll miss you too." It was the most emotional Papa would ever get.

Why, I wanted to ask, do you let them call you Freddy when you are twenty-six years old and ought to be called Fred like a grown man? How could I say that to a man who shortened my given name of Isabel to Bell and called me his "Tinkerbell"? Now his whole family—in fact, the whole town—called me Bell, and I wanted to scream each time I heard it.

"I'll miss you too," I said, looking down at my foot, my shoe making designs in the dry dirt. I didn't know if I meant it or not.

The train pulled out, soldiers leaning out of every window, waving madly, shouting to families left behind. I spotted Freddy and waved Elsa's arm mechanically in the air so that she could tell her daddy goodbye.

"We'll go home now," Papa said, and we turned and drove the thirty miles back to Umbarger in the Peterman family car, a '39 Ford—steady, dependable and dull. I slunk down in the back seat and sang a song from my childhood softly to Elsa . . . "From this valley they say you are leaving, We will miss your bright eyes and sweet smile, For they say you are taking the sunshine, That brightened our lives a while." She was entranced, and I didn't mind that Mama Peterman scowled at me over the back of her seat.

War, they say, is sheer hell on those who fight. For me, it was a hell of a different kind. Boredom was my problem. Elsa and I kept house in the small cottage that Papa had provided behind the Peterman farmhouse, but how long does it take to clean three rooms? And how much cooking can you do for one three-year-old and one woman so discontent that she was never hungry? Besides, we ate most of our meals with Freddy's parents—I picked at sausages and kraut, veal cutlets and pork roasts, applesauce and boiled potatoes, longing always for the food of my childhood—steaks and great pots of beans simmered with salt pork, cornbread and cold buttermilk.

"You are not hungry, Bell?" Mama Peterman would ask, and I'd shovel in another mouthful of kraut. Elsa, the little traitor, ate as if there were no tomorrow and grew fat and happy under the care of her devoted grandparents, which seemed to somehow cancel out the ambivalence of her mother. Oh, don't get me wrong—I loved that child with a fierceness that defied description. But the whole rest of my life was wrong.

Three days a week I joined the other ladies of the parish at St. Mary's Church in rolling and sewing bandages for the war effort. Catholicism was maybe the only thing that Freddy and I had in common, besides a quick animal passion one night after a college dance and the daughter that resulted from it. I felt guilty about that moment, for it went against the teachings I'd been raised with, but I would never regret it—Elsa was too wonderful.

Joining the church ladies in their do-good service was a natural way to pay my dues to the church and I did it willingly, though I doubted that an entire army could go through all the bandages we made. The women gossiped about people in the community—who was expecting, who would marry who, what soldier had written home from where, what teenager had gotten into perilous trouble with liquor. I generally sat working my hands and letting my brain wander, while my tongue remained quiet. I had nothing to say, for I knew none of the people they talked about . . . and cared less.

"You surely are a silent one," Mrs. Marks said one day.

Before I could answer, Mama Peterman said complacently, "Yes, she is, isn't she?" and went right on rolling bandages.

Some days my mind took me away to be Rosie the Riveter, or at least a Texas version. One girl from Umbarger—Janelle Smith, who had anglicized her family name of Schmidt—had gone off to work in the Convair plant in Fort Worth where they made bomber planes. I envied her mightily and dreamed of following in her footsteps. But then, Elsa, playing quietly at my feet would look up at me with a huge smile, and I would remember that I was a prisoner. I would reach down and hug her, and then I'd pinch myself to think how lucky I was that this child of light had come into my life.

Freddy's letters came dutifully, though the names of places were cut out so that I had no idea where he was. Probably I wouldn't have had much idea even if they'd left the names in, but I knew that he was cold and wet a lot of the time, only rarely in the path of bullets—for which we were all thankful—and that he was anxious to be home. He ended each letter with kisses for Elsa.

Once I went home to my family's hard-scrabble farm for Christmas, taking Elsa with me. Freddy never liked to go there—both the poverty and the exuberance of my family made him uncomfortable. Now, in this my second visit in four years away, they made me uncomfortable. Even before Freddy, three years at the university in Canyon had changed my perspective on my family. Six of my brothers and sisters still lived at home in the five-room house which Papa worked hard to maintain on a tiny and unprofitable dryland farm. They were noisy, careless, and utterly happy, without regard for privacy or personal property—my sister used my toothpaste—and within three days I was ready to return to the dullness of Umbarger. It was strange to me to think that my family lived only twenty-three miles from Umbarger. They might as well have been a thousand miles way, for all we had in common or for all we saw each other. I knew why I'd married Freddy.

Don't get me wrong. I loved Freddy Peterman better than a German hausfrau would have loved him. I gave him more love than he'd expected in his life or his bedroom, and he gave me security like I'd never known. We each got what we'd lacked in our family homes, and it worked well—except for that gnawing discontent in me. Still, we had Elsa to bind us together, and I was fierce in my determination to give her the best childhood I knew how, a childhood free of uncertainty, poverty, noise, confusion—all those things I'd grown up with. Freddy, on the other hand, was determined in his own blind way to give her all the things he'd grown up with—security, stability, regularity, and, though he didn't recognize it, dullness. So at least we agreed on Elsa's future. She, sunny and charming, seemed blissfully unaware of our dull plans for her.

We were rolling bandages on a fine October Thursday when Father Krueger announced that seven Italian POW's would begin work the next Monday. "They will decorate the sanctuary," he said.

"Why?" Mama Peterman asked, her tone harsh and suspicious. "Why should we have foreigners in our church?" It never apparently occurred to her that she was a foreigner.

"For food," the priest answered simply, ignoring the criticism in her voice. "We will feed them a midday meal . . . a large midday meal. And I will need volunteers."

We didn't know it then, but the prisoners came because of "La Fame"—the famine—at the prison camp. These were the unrepentant followers of Mussolini, those who refused to recant their Fascist beliefs, and one way they were punished—or coerced—was with shortened rations. Ah, America, land of the free! So they volunteered to paint murals in our plain church not for the greater glory of God but for their stomachs. I thought it a wise bargain on their part. Of course, like Mama and Papa Peterman, I had no idea what Fascism was or why it was different—worse or better?—from Nazism. I just knew that it was unAmerican and we should be angry at its soldiers.

"Bell and I will help," Mama Peterman said, as though she were determined to be at the head of the line.

I shrugged. It mattered little to me if I cooked for farm hands or Italian POWs. There is only so much one can do with sausage and potatoes.

"You'll feed wops?" Papa Peterman shouted incredulously when Mama told him the story. "When our boy is fighting to make this country free, you'll feed his enemies?"

Maybe, I thought, he knows more about Fascism than I thought.

"Papa," she said serenely, "they will paint holy pictures in the church. It is for God."

Papa went shuffling off, grumbling about God's mistakes being compounded by the folly of women.

"Mama? Can I see the holy pictures?" Elsa tugged at my skirt.

"Of course," I said, "but it will be a while before they are painted."

Four days later, I presented myself in the common room of the church, prepared to do my duty for a gift to God. . .and to feed the hungry Italians. I expected sullen dark men who ate ravenously but were otherwise resentful, maybe even hostile. They were, after all, our enemies. Instead, I found men with almost unbearably thin bodies but exuberantly high spirits. Laughing and joking, they called to each other in Italian from one table to the next.

"Hey, Paulo, bambino!" one shouted, and then let loose with a long string of cheerful but unintelligible syllables.

Paulo raised his eyes to answer but looked first, almost by accident, at me, and our eyes locked. He was as dark as me—as I thought Italians should be—and his hair was so curly as to be unruly. But it was the smile that leapt to his face when he looked at me that caused my heart to stop cold. Freddy had never looked at me with such. . .such frank longing in his eyes. And surely I had given Freddy more encouragement.

Flustered, I turned away, hearing too loudly their laughing cries of "Paulo!" and their shouted words that I could not translate but feared I understood. I spent the rest of the morning in the kitchen, serving plates and washing dishes and, when necessary, sending sixteen-year-old Elise Brachman to our guests.

150

Coffeepot in hand, she stopped by Paulo and inquired politely, "More coffee, bambino?"

The men exploded in laughter, and she ran, red-faced and embarrassed, into the kitchen. "They called him that!" she exclaimed. "Isn't that his name?"

"It's an affectionate nickname," I told her. "It means 'baby'."

Elise never again volunteered to feed the prisoners.

He was waiting outside the church the next time I came to serve. He leaned against the building, wearing paint-splattered clothes, and never took his eyes off me as I approached. "I wondered when you would come again," he said boldly, his gaze locked on my face. His English surprised me. If I'd thought about it, I would have expected halting English liberally sprinkled with Italian.

"You had no need," I murmured, wanting badly to look away and yet drawn to those intense black eyes.

"I had a strong need," he said. "I think you are beautiful."

"My mother-in-law will see me," I said, hating myself for sounding so subservient.

"Your husband? He fights the war?" This almost seemed to amuse him.

"Yes," I said. "Well, no, not now that it's ended."

He laughed aloud, long and uninhibited. "It's wonderful," he finally said. "He is over there fighting to make you safe, and I am here enjoying your company."

"He will be home soon," I said almost defensively, one nervous hand smoothing at the back of my cotton dress. The day was warm, and I was beginning to feel heat creep into my face.

"Will you be glad?" he asked with directness.

"Of course."

"I think not," he said, "but you are a prisoner. Like I am a prisoner."

"Are prisoners allowed to stand outside and talk to townspeople?" I asked, hoping to end a conversation that was becoming more and more uncomfortable for me.

He shrugged. "I'll tell them I'll quit painting. Without me, the others will not know what to do. Ciao!" He turned and was gone.

I worked in the kitchen again that day. Mama Peterman didn't mind serving the prisoners, and they were quietly respectful in her presence. I heard no calls of Paulo's name.

"Bell? You're going to the church again today? You've gone every day this week. Even Father Krueger doesn't expect that much from us." Mama, like all the others, was beginning to be slightly scornful of the Italians, perhaps because she had not found them as grateful as she wanted. "Fascists," she would spit, but when I once asked her what that meant, she simply turned a frozen stare on me. Fascists, I gathered, were bad, worse than Germans, but I never spoke of it aloud.

I shrugged in answer to her questions, being deliberately casual so she didn't guess my reason for serving the prisoners so often. "I have nothing else to do except care for Elsa, and she is happy with you."

Elsa indeed was eating a huge, gooey pecan roll and barely noticed when I left the house. As I walked away, I heard her ask plaintively, "Another one, Oma?" The child would be fat as a piglet when her father came home.

When her father came home! The words echoed in my mind, because I didn't want to hear them. Paulo had waited for me every day since our first meeting, and that first uncomfortable conversation had been replaced by long quiet talks. I discovered that he had learned English at school, he had read Zane Grey's novels and Nathaniel Hawthorne's *Scarlet Letter* and liked the former but was indignant over the latter— "To think of someone treating a woman that way, because of love!" he exclaimed. He told me he had a wife and two children at home, and he had volunteered to decorate the church because he missed women.

I laughed. "I thought you were hungry."

"Oh?" His eyebrows rose on his forehead, and he grinned as though caught at mischief. "That, too. But, see? I already get what I came here for. I have the company of the most beautiful woman in all the United States."

"You've hardly met enough to know," I told him, but I blushed in pleasure nonetheless.

"I do not need to," he said. "I know in my heart."

Freddy never spoke of his heart. Sometimes I had wondered if he had one.

Paulo made me laugh, with tales of growing up in Italy—he was a wild young man, sewing more oats than any ten men are entitled to—and he asked with tenderness about my childhood, understood that I was a fish out of water in Umbarger.

"No beans?" he asked once grinning.

"No," I said laughing, "no beans. I miss them."

"Would I like them, these beans?"

"Of course," I said, "they are for hot-blooded people."

"I would like them," he said positively, and we both laughed.

He told me of Fascism and Mussolini. "He tried to take a people with the souls of lovers and turn them into soldiers." He spat. "We are dreamers, not warriors."

"Then why are you still loyal?"

He shrugged. "We are soldiers. We will be called traitors if we are not loyal and, that? It could be very bad."

It was all remote from Umbarger and, at that moment, beyond my grasp. We didn't talk of Fascism any more.

Once when Paulo and I stood talking in the shadow of the church—around to the side where we were slightly hidden from public view, but only slightly—Jimmy Dowling, the long, lanky guard who drove them to and from the camp came strolling toward us.

"Paulo?" he asked almost hesitantly, "You know the rules."

Paulo shrugged. "And you know the price, my friend," he said.

Jimmy frowned uncertainly, but he turned away, muttering over his shoulder, "Don't be too long."

"I will give him cigarettes." Paulo said, laughing. "I have more than he does. I'm better at barter."

After that, Jimmy deliberately kept himself in the dining hall when Paulo and I met. All these years later, I am sure he was not the only one who watched our daily meetings, but no one said a thing. Perhaps they were embarrassed for me, or for Mama and Papa Peterman . . . and maybe some of the women were jealous. But even Mama never said more than, "You are devoted to God's work, Bell."

And I'd reply, "It is to help present a gift to God."

On the days that Mama served food, I marched past Paulo without stopping, though he always bowed in our direction, and said "Good morning, signoras."

Had Mama looked at him, she would have seen the laughter of a good joke in his eyes. She might not have recognized it, but I would. I didn't dare look.

The work progressed—oil murals of the Visitation, the Annunciation, and the Assumption of Mary into Heaven, a carving of the Last Supper, and a relief trim in a pattern of wheat and grapes that Paulo solemnly informed me was "after DaVinci."

The third week that the prisoners were amongst us, Paulo boldly took me into the sanctuary to view the work. The figures were blocked in for the painting of the Assumption of Mary—it was, Paulo told me loftily, oil on canvas, and I replied with equal loftiness that I knew that much. The carving of the Last Supper was rough and jagged, and it was difficult to discern the individual figures. But the murals! Drawn in behind the blocked, one-dimensional figures showing the Visitation and the Annunciation were spread scenes of the Panhandle—green pastures and tiny clusters of buildings dwarfed by the landscape.

"You have drawn Umbarger," I cried in amazement.

"It is your church. It should not have scenes of Italy," he said, "even though God is more at home there."

I opened my mouth to reply in indignation, and then gave it up for laughter.

He kissed me the fourth week. We had been meeting almost daily for three weeks, and we had kept arm's distance between us as though we knew what would happen once that barrier was broken. This day as I turned to go toward the kitchen, he laid a hand on my arm, turned me in slow motion to face him, and then bent to kiss me. It was a gentle kiss, like a promise, almost without passion behind it.

"That," he said, "is a beginning. Unfortunately for us, there will never be an ending."

Suddenly wanting was nearly enough to undo me. For a moment my knees went weak, and Paulo had to put out a hand to steady me.

"Thank you," he said softly. "You have given me a great compliment . . . and a great gift."

Freddy wrote that he expected to be home within a month. Mama and Papa were happier than they'd been since he left, she planning the foods she'd cook for him—sauerbraten and kolaches and stuffed cabbage—and he outlining endless hunting trips, farm work they would share. For both, life seemed about to begin again.

Elsa was as excited as her grandparents, drawing countless pictures for her father and begging until Mama Peterman let her use precious thumbtacks to put them up throughout the house.

"Your husband is coming home," Mama said at least once a day. "It is good. You are happy?"

"I am very happy," I said, but I knew she expected cartwheels, and I couldn't give her that much enthusiasm.

"He is coming home," Paulo said. "I can tell by your walk."

"My walk?" I laughed a little to disguise my nervousness. "No, you can't."

"Yes, I can. He is coming home, and you are not happy."

"It is your fault," I said, my boldness now almost as great as his. "You have made me happy."

"You would trade one cold meeting a day for the warmth of a husband in your bed?" He was grinning, but he was not joking.

"Yes," I whispered, "I would."

"So would I," he answered, his whisper as low as mine.

I rushed away before we could talk more.

"We will be through well before your Freddy comes home," he told me days later. "The work is almost done."

"And then?"

He shrugged, that gesture I had begun to think was his alone. "We will be prisoners again. I will draw pictures of the camp, pictures of the church, pictures of you . . . ."

"Will I see you?"

All laughter was gone, and he looked at me with that same penetratingly dark look that had first captivated me. "No," he said slowly, "but I shall always see you in my mind."

I wanted to cling to him, to spirit the both of us away to some far island. Instead, I managed a slight smile and a wobbly walk to the kitchen, resisting the urge to turn and look at him. Through my back, his gaze almost burned through me.

Father Krueger was in the kitchen that day, happily marking

the progress of the decoration of his church. "They've been here thirty-eight days," he said, "and they'll finish in another two or three. Seven men have done the work of an army, seven out of eight hundred prisoners. The Lord works in mysterious ways ."

That he does, I thought, wondering why, out of eight hundred men, Paulo had ended up where I could meet him. Why had the Lord not been content to leave him in the camp at Hereford, safely away from Umbarger and my discontent?

They actually worked forty-one days. On the last day, Paulo waited for me as usual . . . only there was a difference. "This is the day," he said, his voice revealing neither sadness nor joy. "I want you to have this." His hand pressed something into mine, and when I looked I saw a small silver crucifix, intricately carved and beautifully detailed.

"It was my mother's," he said. "I have carried it for luck. Now I have no need for more luck."

"Paulo . . . ."

"Shhh. You must not say it. I have memories to last a lifetime." Then he grinned, that impish grin I'd come to know. "But here, bend down. I have scissors."

"Scissors?" Alarm must have shown in my voice.

"A lock of your hair," he laughed. "I want to carry it with me."

And so I bent down, and he cut a curl from the back of my head. "There," he said. "Freddy will never miss it."

"I . . . I . . . ."

"Don't say anything," he said, bending to kiss me softly. "And don't say goodbye."

Freddy came home one week to the day later. Three years in the army had toughened him, made of him the man he was not before. He stood tall, straight and self-assured, but when he bent to kiss me it was still with a formal correctness and with none of the tenderness of Paulo. I made that comparison once, with that first kiss, and then forbad myself ever to make it again.

Elsa flew into her daddy's arms, and Mama and Papa draped themselves about him with such joy that my hesitancy was not even noticed. Freddy took it for appropriate wifely reticence.

That night, as I brushed my hair its hundred strokes and Freddy wandered about the bedroom in his dressing gown—both of us as ill at ease as newlyweds—he wandered to my jewelry box and picked up Paulo's cross.

"This new?"

"My mother sent it," I said and never once worried about the lie. It wouldn't dawn on Freddy that my mother had never in her life had such a nice piece . . . and wouldn't have sent it to me if she had.

"It's old. Looks valuable. Where'd she get it?"

"I've no idea. Pretty, isn't it?"

"Yes," he said and threw it carelessly down into the box again.

Freddy and I have had four children, all except Elsa as blonde as their father. Freddy is a successful farmer, a solid citizen of Umbarger and, having enlarged his world, well-known in Hereford and Amarillo. No longer an outsider, I still work for the greater glory of God at the church—and I even miss Mama Peterman, who has passed on to her reward. But Freddy says my homemade sauerkraut is almost as good as hers, and then I am content. It has been a good life, and I no longer feel the itch of dissatisfaction that plagued me during the war. But every once in a while Freddy finds me sitting, staring out the window, that silver cross in my hand.

"Praying?" he'll ask.

"Yes," I'll respond, "praying." And I am.

I've told no one about Paulo, not even Elsa who is heart of my heart. But once, years ago, I confessed to Father Krueger in the privacy of the confessional, and he asked, "Do you wish to run away and find him?"

"No," I said slowly, "he is the reason I do not need to run away.

Dear John

I remember yet writing that letter, beginning with those words. I was eighteen, and it was 1943. John Allen Taylor was somewhere in Europe fighting the Germans with a tank division. Oh, I knew it was his duty to his country and he had no choice—he was drafted—but I was young, and I wanted love right then.

So I wrote, "Dear John Allen," and thought about the irony that his name really was John and I was writing one of those most hated "dear john" letters. "I've met someone else. It is difficult to tell you this, for you've meant a great deal to me, and you always will. I will of course pray for your safety and for a quick end to this awful war. I wish you well in life." I remember pausing over that last phrase and then deciding it set just the right tone. Then I puzzled about how to sign it. "Love," certainly wasn't right. "Your friend" sounded too distant, too cold. Finally, I settled on "Fondly, JoBeth."

And then, before I could change my mind, I walked straight to the post box on the corner and mailed the letter, listening to the satisfying whoosh as the letter slipped through the slot and landed with whatever other mail was in the box. I fairly floated home.

I really had met someone else—a dashingly handsome man named Thomas, some eight years my senior. He didn't have two names like every boy I knew in Ben Wheeler, Texas. Just plain Thomas. In fact, I knew him for almost a month before I knew his last name—it was foreign, Piarski. For years afterward, he considered changing his name to Parsons, because he thought he'd get along better in business if he weren't "foreign."

Thomas had come to town to be a teller in the bank where I was secretary to the bank president. I suppose I ought to mention that the president was my father, Willis Coleman, but I generally didn't dwell on the fact that I worked for Daddy. He made me work harder than he did any other employees, so I didn't see any advantage in it. Daddy's bank was small, but he had decided he need a second teller and put a sign in the window. Well, there weren't many people in Ben Wheeler who could count money accurately, so there weren't many candidates. Thomas said he just happened to be driving through—you had to work hard at happening to drive through Ben

Wheeler, because it was really off the beaten path—and at first Daddy called him a godsend. Later, Daddy privately called him Polacki, which I didn't think was nice at all.

Thomas told me bad knees made him 4-F, and I didn't even think of the contradiction when he whirled me about the dance floor. "I want to serve my country," he said earnestly, "but these knees...." He shook his head woefully. "They just aren't up to marching and carrying a heavy load." He looked pensive. "I admire those men who are fighting. We've got to do everything we can to support them."

I was dazzled, and now, all those years later, I know that I was dazzled by the idea of someone who was not from Ben Wheeler, who was not going to settle down and live out his life in a town so small it had only a farm-to-market road for a main street and not even one stoplight. Thomas Piarski was moving on, and I wanted to go with him. I wanted to go to Dallas, maybe even Houston, and see the world. And deep down I was afraid that John Allen, on the other hand, who grew up in Ben Wheeler, would come back to East Texas to settle and do who knows what? Probably work in the local mechanic's garage, because John Allen had always loved automobiles.

Daddy began to frown on my seeing Thomas. He'd quiz him about where we were going, what time I'd be home, and he'd warn him not to keep me out too late. I had to be at work or in church the next morning, Daddy would say, shaking his finger. Of course, parental opposition just made Thomas all the more alluring. And the next morning, I'd say to indignantly to Daddy, "That's embarrassing. I'm eighteen years old!"

"And he's twenty-six and has been around the world," Daddy replied, lowering his newspaper to stare at me.

I was tempted to reply that Thomas had never been around the world, not understanding what Daddy meant, but I just flounced out of the kitchen. I thought Daddy was overprotective (a word we didn't use in those days) because I was his only child, and it had been only him and me since Mama died when I was twelve. He didn't want me ever to marry, I told myself, and leave him.

Thomas' kisses made him pretty alluring, too. At the door, when he said goodnight, John Allen kissed me once, a mushy, proper, and gentlemanly kiss. Thomas' kisses were hard and demanding, and his tongue did the most amazing things. He'd turn his attention from my mouth to my ears and neck until I shivered with—I didn't know what at the time. And his hands roamed my body, not like John Allen, who always kept his hands properly on my shoulders when he kissed me goodnight. And Thomas could draw kissing out until it took up the whole evening. We didn't much go to the local movie theater.

Needless to say, I was almost immediately madly in love. And within three months, Thomas asked me to marry him. Well, what he actually said was, "I guess I'm going to have to marry you." Later, I'd ponder that comment and reconsider its meaning. At the time I thought he meant I was irresistible.

Over Daddy's objections, we married in the tiny Baptist church in Ben Wheeler. Thomas didn't seem to belong to any particular church and said he didn't mind if the justice of the peace married us, but I wanted a proper wedding. I was entitled to the fancy white dress, although of late temptation had made it hard to keep the importance of being a virgin bride in mind.

Daddy acted out his part and gave me away, and my Aunt Nelda helped me plan the wedding and the small reception—cake and punch in the church Fellowship Hall. And then Thomas and I were off to Tyler, the nearest city, for a three-day honeymoon. Daddy wouldn't give either of us more time off.

We settled down to housekeeping in a little brick house that Daddy owned in town. I still worked at the bank, but I loved coming home at night to fix dinner for Thomas, and on weekends I cleaned house and did the washing and ironing and felt very domestic. Thomas mowed the lawn and generally sat and drank a beer or two while I was cooking. We were blissfully happy.

Our first child, Jane Ellen, was born in Ben Wheeler. "Why'd you give her two names?" Thomas asked.

"All East Texas children have two names," I said, forgetting that it was his single name that attracted me to him.

He shrugged it off.

I stayed home with Jane Ellen, and although Daddy came by to see her, I didn't much keep up with what was going on at the bank. So I was surprised one day when Thomas announced at supper,

"We're moving." Jane Ellen was not quite a year old.

"Moving?" I echoed. "Did you find a bigger house?" We were in a two-bedroom, one-bath, and it would be crowded when the baby I was expecting arrived.

Impatiently he got up from the table. "Moving away from this one-horse town," he exploded. "I've had enough. A man can't get ahead here. Nobody appreciates ambition. They just want to do things the way they've always done them, not move ahead. I need to find a place where I have some chance for advancement."

My heart sank. He and Daddy had argued, I just knew it. But I said nothing. And like a dutiful wife, I followed my husband, this time to Winnsboro, where he was general manager of a feed and grain supply store.

Our second child, Alice Marie, was born in Winnsboro, but we were in Tyler when Joyce Ann arrived. Thomas exploded! "Another girl. Can you produce anything but girls? I need a son to play baseball with and go fishing and do men stuff." I didn't point out that Thomas never did any of those things himself, so why would I expect that he would do them with a son. And even I knew, from high school biology, that the female did not determine the sex of the baby. By then, I wasn't finding Thomas' kisses quite as irresistible, and I surely did not want another baby. Three in six years were enough, thank you.

Besides, we could barely afford to feed and clothe the three we had. Thomas was now managing a shoe store, one of those with the x-ray machine so that you could see how your feet fit in a shoe and whether or not your toes were cramped. We'd left Winnsboro because the owner's son was taking advantage. "Doesn't do a lick of work but takes all the credit and earns twice what I do," Thomas said angrily. "And he gives things away to his friends." When I suggested talking to the owner, Thomas said he tried but "the old man" wouldn't listen.

Daddy came to visit us occasionally, because he wanted his grandchildren to know him and he wanted to know them. They adored him, for he told them stories and played games with them and did all the things that Thomas never did—or that my father had never done with me. He always came when the newest baby was baptized, and I always saw to it that we belonged to the Baptist church in whatever city we lived in. I attended faithfully on Sundays and took the children to Sunday school, but Thomas usually had other things to do.

On his visits, Daddy subtly kept me informed of John Allen and where he was. First it was, "John Allen's back from the war. Got a bit of a limp from shrapnel, but nothing major. Looks fine and sends his best to you."

I murmured, "Give him my regards. What's he doing to do?"

Daddy shrugged. "He's only been home two weeks. I think he needs time."

Next visit it was, "John Allen's gone off to Dallas. Working for a big car dealer over there, I understand."

Now, that I could understand. Feed store, shoe store, car dealer—it was all the same.

"Understand he's going to marry someone over there, a girl with money."

"Give him my best wishes," I said. I couldn't imagine having more money than what it took to get by day-to-day.

From Tyler, we went to Marshall, farther east, and a newspaper, where Thomas tried his hand at being the business manager. It wasn't too long before the books were a hopeless mess, and we moved on. That was the pattern of our marriage. Thomas bounced from job to job and town to town always because he wasn't properly appreciated, couldn't get ahead because of the boss, always someone else's fault.

Our fourth and last baby, John Paul, was born in Kaufman, where Thomas managed Zaby's barbecue and catering for several years. I thought we had settled down, but new owners took over the restaurant and Thomas disagreed with their religious philosophy, which they displayed at every chance on the walls of the restaurant, the menu, even placards on the table. I was taught that we are called upon to witness, so I thought such displays were their right and a good thing to do, but I never said that to Thomas.

We moved to Canton, which is only twelve miles from Ben Wheeler and put me closer to Daddy, who was now failing in health. I suggested we bring him to live with us, but Thomas didn't like that idea, so I went two or three times a week to Ben Wheeler while the children were in school. And sometimes on weekends I took them with me. Thomas was working for the Canton Chamber of Commerce, which meant he was especially busy on First Monday weekends, when the town overflowed with sellers and buyers of everything from antiques to dogs and horses. The children and I usually escaped to see Daddy on those weekends.

Daddy's failing health turned out to be cancer, and I lost him at a relatively young age—for both of us. I was thirty-three, and he, fifty-nine. Toward the end, he was in a hospital in Canton, and I spent long hours by his bedside. We had good long talks, and he was honest with me.

"I didn't want you to marry him," he said one day, almost out of the blue. "I thought all along he was taking money from the bank. Not a lot, just a little bit here and there. I don't trust him, and now I'm leaving you in his hands."

I had no idea what to say. I knew they didn't like each other, but I had never known why. And now, after fifteen years of marriage to Thomas, sad to say, I believed my father, though I could hear Thomas' denials ringing in my ears.

"Daddy," I whispered, "I'll be fine. Thomas is good to me, and I love him." Well, it was sort of true.

"It's not such a sin these days to divorce," Daddy said. "I'll leave you enough money that you could get by."

I shook my head. "No, Daddy, leave your money in a trust fund for the children's education." Without even thinking about it, I knew I wanted the money secure, where Thomas couldn't touch it. And that's just what Daddy did. But what I couldn't say was that though life with Thomas was often difficult and uncertain, I didn't have the nerve to leave and strike out on my own. I had chosen my future, and I'd stick with it.

Daddy took the conversation in another direction. "You hear about John Allen? He owns the biggest Chevrolet dealership in Dallas. Seems he worked hard, saved his money, and bought it from the owner."

I let my mind play with that for a minute or two and then asked, "What about his wife? The rich one?"

"His mother says they're happy, have two sons, live in a big house in Highland Park—that's the wealthy city within the Dallas city limits."

"Bet he doesn't call himself John Allen anymore but just plain John," I said.

Daddy chuckled, a rare sound from him these days. "No, I 'spect you're right."

Those days Daddy and I were closer than we'd been since before I went to high school, and I treasure them. He died a few weeks after that conversation, and I buried him in the cemetery at Ben Wheeler, next to Mama. As the minister spoke comforting words and I threw the first handful of dirt on the coffin, I couldn't help but think that there went the one man on earth that I knew would take care of me. Then I turned back to Thomas and held his hand tightly.

Jane Ellen and Alice Marie finished high school in Canton, and when their father announced we were moving to Mineola and an automobile dealership—oh, cruel irony!—they elected to stay in Canton as roommates. Jane Ellen worked in a doctor's office, and Alice Marie at the public library. Within two or three years, both were married and raising families—Daddy's trust fund for their education became a fund for their children.

We lived in several more towns—Jacksonville, Athens, and Longview—with Thomas, now firmly into middle age, always looking for a place where "a man can get ahead." He never did play baseball or go fishing with John Paul, but my son did those things with the Boy Scouts and grew up to be a fine, tall, straight young man. I wished Daddy could have seen all my children as young adults.

I lost Thomas in 1985 when he was sixty-eight. A heart attack. By then we were back in Canton, close to the girls, and we buried him in the Canton cemetery. I gave up the rent house we'd been living in and went to a small cottage behind Jane Ellen's home. Joyce Ann was off in Dallas in school, and John Paul had joined the U. S. Army (over my protests). I began a new life, one not at all unpleasant. Yes, I missed Thomas—he had been part and parcel of my life for over forty years, and you don't break that habit quickly or easily, but I was content.

I am nearing eighty now, and Jane Ellen tells me she's taking me for a "fling" in Dallas for my birthday. We'd stay at the ritziest hotel, the Adolphus, where we'd have "high tea" one afternoon.

I suspected it was not iced tea, and I was right. Three kinds of tea—one of them green, which tasted like medicine to me, but one with spices and citrus that was really good. And we had tiny sandwiches of cucumbers and egg salad and things like that—I thought of what Thomas would have said if I'd served them to him. And then we were served these hard little rolls that seemed tasteless to me.

"Mom," Jane Ellen said, "they're scones. Everyone eats them these days."

"Not me," I said, putting one back on my plate after one bite.

Finally we had that sweet tea I liked with little chocolate cakes—now that was good.

"Mom, I have a surprise for you."

"Surprise? Jane Ellen, this is all the treat I need. You don't have to do more."

"I talked to John Allen Taylor yesterday. He wants to see you while you're in Dallas, so we're meeting him for dinner tonight."

Him? What about his wife? For a moment, my heart leapt. But, cautiously, I said "Is his wife joining us?"

"Yes. We're having dinner with them here at the hotel, at his invitation."

Well, I was a nervous bowl of jelly all the rest of the afternoon. What would I say sixty-some years later to the man to whom I'd written a "dear john" letter? And him a huge success in Dallas, living out as it were my young dreams.

John Allen Taylor and his wife strolled into the lobby of the Adolphus with a familiarity that told me, unlike mine, this was not their first visit there. I glanced briefly at his wife—tall and not stooped with age, silver hair that had recently been to the salon, and a silk pantsuit. I'd worn my best black pants and bright, quilted print jacket Jane Ellen had chosen for me, but I felt dowdy. Provincial.

But it was John Allen who riveted my attention. I remember a slim, undeveloped youth, and toward me came a tall man, broad-shouldered, erect and confident. Military service and business success—both things Thomas never had, but I had promised myself not to make that comparison, even in my mind—had brought him a graceful maturity.

Holding out both arms, he boomed, "JoBeth! Did you know you saved my life?"

Startled, I stopped but John Allen came forward and wrapped

me in an embrace. "I've wanted to do that for sixty years!" he said. "I've told Elizabeth all about it"—he smiled at his wife who smiled back and nodded in agreement—"how you took a bullet for me. Your letter, that last one you wrote me, was folded and taped to the turret of my armored vehicle, along with your picture. A bullet punctured both and would have killed me if I hadn't dropped down from the turret—you slowed the shot just long enough." He shrugged, and his eyes danced in amusement. "If it weren't for you, I wouldn't have had the wonderful life I've had."

In more ways than one, I thought—yes, probably with just a trace of bitterness.

Dinner was pleasant. There were no prices on the menu, so I was at a loss for ordering, not wanting to take advantage, and settled for a chicken dish that I figured would be reasonable. Elizabeth Taylor had lobster, so I guess I should have known cost was no problem. Jane Ellen later told me that only the host's menu had prices—a sign of gracious living, but I'd never heard of such.

We traded news of children—their sons were a lawyer and a doctor—and of our lives, all polite chitchat, for we didn't have much in common. They traveled frequently, sometimes to places I'd never heard of, but then I'd lived in towns Elizabeth had never heard of. John Allen—his wife called him John—and I exchanged stories of Ben Wheeler and our families, lamenting that today the town, never prosperous, had fallen on hard times. By dessert—baked Alaska, another surprise for me!—it was hard to carry on the conversation. We parted shortly thereafter, all expressing our pleasure at the reunion, and Jane Ellen and me being overly grateful for the lovely dinner. But there was no mention of keeping in touch or meeting again. We lived in different worlds.

Changing into our nightclothes that night, Jane Ellen softly asked, "Mom, do you ever think about what life might have been like if you hadn't written that letter?"

"It's no good thinking that, Jane Ellen. John Allen's life might have been different too, if I hadn't written the letter. No, life works out the way it was meant to—and I was meant to write that letter."

As we drifted off to sleep, I whispered, "Jane Ellen, thank you for a wonderful birthday. I've loved it, but I sure will be glad to get back to Canton tomorrow."

The Death of Rastus Reynolds

For years, folks kept seeing Rastus Reynolds in Mexico. Lyle Gooding swore he saw him on a plaza in Monterrey, feeding the pigeons. Lyle called to him, but Rastus never looked up from the pigeons. And Mary Helen Johnson saw him in a cantina in Nuevo Laredo, though I always did want to ask her what she was doing in a border-town cantina. She said he had two Mexican women on his arms—"dark-eyed and voluptuous but not young things," was how she described them—and looked puffed up like an old tomcat. And once Brother Manfred of the Cleveland Hill Baptist Church said he saw him at a bullfight. I really wanted to ask Brother Manfred what he was doing at a bullfight, but I figured that would be impertinent.

But, you see, when all these folks saw Rastus, he was dead. And not a one of them—not Lyle, not Mary Helen, not even Brother Manfred—ever talked to him, so they couldn't ask him about his death and resurrection. And they couldn't even prove they'd seen him, but they swore on the Bible that it was the truth. And when a Baptist swears on the Bible, you got to take him serious.

I believed they saw him, because I didn't really believe Rastus was dead. You see, he was what you might call a character in Cleveland Hill. He lived out on the highway, just inside the city limits, in a board-and-batten shack that was probably fifty years old and looked like it might not make it another fifty days. Rastus had one of those junk shops you see along the highway—you know, with the rusting iron bedstead and the copper washtub that's all dented and green but looks like you might could get it pounded back into shape and refinished if Rastus didn't want $25 for it to begin with. He had a birdbath out there for years, with Venus or some such Greek female wearing very little clothes while she poured water from a jug into the birdbath. Must have been one of them re-circulatin' things or else it used a whole heck of a lot of water. Either way, Rastus never could sell it.

But the strangest thing about Rastus' junkyard was his chickens. He kept this rooster and a bunch of hens—no fancy kind, just plain old chickens. If you bought an iron bedstead from him, he'd throw in some fresh eggs. And if you wanted a really fresh fryer, Rastus

167

would part with one of his young chickens. Folks used to go out there to buy them because, you know, ain't nothin' as good as fried chicken from a bird that's just had its neck wrung. But anyways, the city told Rastus he was inside the city limits and having livestock was illegal. He whooped and hollered and carried on something frightful. Hadn't his great-great-grandfather founded this town? And hadn't his grandfather owned the bank, and didn't his own daddy serve as the town's only doctor for years, at considerable cost to himself? Lawyer Warren Biggs, who was sort of the city attorney as if Cleveland Hill had or needed one, shook his head and said it didn't matter: Rastus couldn't keep livestock, and chickens are livestock. He had a week to find a new place to keep them.

All that week no one saw Rastus. He didn't sit out on that lawn chair with the sprung seat in front of his shop watching the cars go by like he usually did. He didn't appear in town at the grocery or the drugstore. Folks began to wonder where he was. The chickens were still there, though. Then, the day the week was up, Lawyer Biggs went out to serve him a warrant, and there was those chickens, all dressed in gingham dresses, with tiny sunbonnets on their heads. The rooster, he had on a black jacket with a white front—looked like a tuxedo.

"These are my pets," Rastus announced, daring Lawyer Biggs to contradict him.

The chickens stayed, and after a while, when the dresses and the tuxedo wore out, the chickens went naked again, and nobody ever said nothin' about Rastus keeping livestock.

Rumor was that Rastus had a lot of money stashed away, though I knew for a fact, being the security guard of the town's bank, that he didn't have it in the Cleveland Hills Savings and Loan Company. Mary Ruth Johnson, the cashier, told me on the q.t. that Rastus didn't have a dime in his savings-and-loan account. Everyone knew he came from one of Cleveland Hill's old families. The Reynolds had been plantation owners in East Texas back before the Civil War, and they managed to hold on to their land and their fortune through the generations right down to Rastus. He was the one let it all go to—well, you know, in a hand basket.

After his parents died, he let that big old two-story white house out on the edge of town get in such poor repair that finally the county sold it for taxes. That was when he moved into his junk shop. But everyone believed he still had his granddaddy's money, probably hidden under his mattress or in a coffee can in his refrigerator. 'Course he didn't spend none of it if he could help it. Rastus would wait for you outside Kroger's and when you had your hands full of groceries your wife made you carry, he'd sidle up and ask in a whiny tone, "You got a smoke?" Or if you were in the drugstore drinkin' coffee, he'd join you real companionable like, order a cup of coffee, and then just before the check came remember that he was late to meet somebody.

Probably he was late to meet one of his wives. Rastus had three. Only man I ever heard of who had three wives who each knew about the others and didn't seem to care. None of them lived in Cleveland Hill. Rastus had them scattered around in about a thirty-mile radius.

There was Lucille, who lived off toward Liberty and ran a beauty shop in her home, though I thought if her own frizzy hair was any indication of what she did for her customers, she might as well hang out the closed sign.

Marjorie lived on the highway to Humble, but she lived the closest and worked in Cleveland Hills at the drugstore. Maybe that's why Rastus drank so much coffee there. She was a pretty thing, kind of quiet, with big brown eyes, and when Rastus was there, those eyes would get a kind of puzzled look in them, as if she didn't know what to make of him.

And finally there was Dora, who had a house near Conroe. I mean I always thought she had a "house"—that is, I didn't think Rastus was the only man who visited her, though he may well have been the only one to think he was married to her. Dora had dark red hair—the henna kind—and was big-chested ("voluptuous" to use Mary Helen's word) and she wore her clothes skin tight. Mary Helen called her "one of those women."

But not a one of his wives lived at that junk shop with him. I guess he just sort of visited them from time to time—what do they call that? Convivial visits? My own theory was that each of them women was probably glad Rastus had someplace else to go so she didn't have to put up with him for more than a brief visit. Now if you believe the local gossip, the reason they put up with him at all was all that secret money he had. Lord knows, he must have had money if he was paying rent on three houses.

Oh, Rastus was a good enough fellow, if you could just sort of howdy with him and then move on. If you got cornered talkin', he'd start in on how mean folks in Cleveland Hill were to him, and pretty soon he'd work himself into "and my grandfather and father pillars of the community." He must've recognized he wasn't no pillar himself. But he never acted like he liked the town or the people.

So when he up and moved to Mexico suddenly one day—just left all his wives and that Venus in his junkyard still pouring water and those chickens pecking around—we thought he'd finally got fed up enough to go somewhere else. But we were all curious. Folks began to ask Marjorie about him, because she was the closest and easiest to ask, but she'd just shrug and tell us we knew as much as she did. I heard Brother Manfred say that Dora told him Rastus had gone on a vacation—but I didn't ask Brother Manfred what he was doing visiting Dora. Lucille's customers didn't get much more from her. "Oh," she'd say, waving a comb in the air, "he'll be back. You know what they say about a bad penny."

Weeks passed and he didn't come home. "Maybe he's found himself another wife in Mexico," Al Procter joked. "You know, them . . . ." I cut him off with a dirty look, because I don't cotton to jokes about other races. Brother Manfred's theory was that Rastus had lost all his money in Juarez, never got farther into Mexico, and couldn't afford to come home. Finally, we all kind of settled in and forgot about Rastus.

But then there came that letter—a real pitiful letter, especially seeing as how it came from a man who never had cared much about Cleveland Hill. Why Rastus wrote to Brother Manfred, I'll never know, but that's what he did.

Dear Brother Manfred,
I have come on hard times and wisht I was back in Cleveland Hill, where folks always treated me so kind. I was beat bad by some Mexican thugs who were after my money and took every penny I had before they left me to die and kicked me in the head to make sure I was dead. I lay there real still and played possum, and after a few more kicks at carefully chosen parts of my anatomy, they went on and left me on this dirt road.

I laid there for days I thought, but later I found out it was about six hours. I tell you that's longer than I want to be wondering if I'm gonna' live or die. I couldn't move because of my broken leg, and my head hurt awful from that kick.

Well, this woman come along in the dark of the night. Her name's Isobella, and she's real good to me. She brought back a little wagon that a goat pulled, piled me into it, and took me to her hacienda—only it isn't no hacienda. Just a one-room adobe house. But she's been takin' real good care of me, and she says I'm gonna be just fine.

You can bet as soon as I'm healed, I'm coming back to Cleveland Hill where I have friends. Meantime, would you please tell Marjorie and Lucille and Dora what has happened. But don't tell them about Isobella.

Your friend
Erastus P. Reynolds

Brother Manfred practically posted that letter on a billboard. Well, not really, but he did go to the newspaper with it, and they printed an article about this terrible tragedy that befell Rastus. And Brother Manfred preached on it Sunday morning. Since most everybody in Cleveland Hill went to the Baptist church, word got around pretty quick. We all prayed for Rastus and wrung our hands and said how awful it was and what a blessing that he'd be safely home soon.

But then Brother Manfred got a letter from Isobella. Now Rastus made her out to be a poor peasant woman, but she wrote a fine hand. I saw the letter, because Brother Manfred showed it to me, and her handwriting was full of swirls and loops, not that plain old Palmer stuff we learned in school.

I regret to inform you that Erastus P. Reynolds passed from this earth into the hands of his Lord on Friday, the eighth of July, 19 and 52. He had been in great pain, and though I mourn his passing, I know it was a blessing. His last words were for his family and friends in Cleveland Hill, and he begged that you all remember him kindly. He was buried in Cholula, Mexico. Should his family wish to visit the gravesite, I would be honored to take them.   Isobella de Vaca

Brother Manfred was so overcome he held a memorial service one weekday—wouldn't do to detract from Sunday's doing—and most of the town came to mourn Rastus. Strange, none of his wives were present. I think they felt like I did—something was rotten in the state of Mexico.

No one ever went to visit the gravesite, but those sightings in Mexico began shortly after that letter was received. It got so bad, especially after Brother Manfred's report that folks were making up excuses to go to Mexico when all they really wanted was to look for Rastus.

Not me. I wasn't gonna' have no part of that foolishness. I knew Rastus too well. He wasn't dead. He was down there in Mexico frolicking with Isobella—I bet she had money—and he had forgot all about Venus and the chickens and Marjorie and Lucille and Dora.

But one time I was in Mexico on other business—okay, it was a vacation in San Miguel, where my wife had wanted to go for years and I'd always put her off, but when I retired I didn't have any more excuses. So there we were, going in those cathedrals, eating at the Mexican version of trendy restaurants, gawkin' at all the tourists and Americans who stroll around San Miguel. And we're in a sidewalk café, when who comes walking toward me but Rastus.

"Rastus!" I called out.

This man never looked at me. He had his hair in a ponytail—now that wasn't unusual for Americans in Mexico, but it was a new twist for Rastus—and he was holdin' hands with this large woman—I think ample is the term—who had black hair streaked with grey and a . . . well, a patrician face, if I know what that is.

"Isobella," I murmured.

"What'd you say?" my wife asked.

The woman turned and looked at me and—I swear this is true—she winked.

When I got back to Cleveland Hill, I had me a little talk with Brother Manfred, told him he ought to write this Isobella and ask for a picture of Rastus' gravesite and while he was at it he should get a picture of Isobella.

Rastus Reynolds ain't dead. He's down there in Mexico laughing at all of us, especially Marjorie who got to take care of the chickens.

Wildflower Wreath

The newspaper photo showed a beefy-faced man, his jowls heavy, his eyes puffy and—yes, she had to admit it—dead. They were the eyes of a man who found no joy in life, nothing to live for, a man who had lived hard and, at least of late, hadn't much enjoyed it. Cynthia Hunt wouldn't have recognized him, but the headline on the obituary informed her that Thomas G. Johnson had died of a massive heart attack at the age of sixty-eight. He was to be buried on his Texas ranch in three days.

She stared long and hard at the photo, looking for some sign of the man she had known. Then, deliberately, she crossed the room to a small desk, opened a tiny drawer above the writing surface, and pulled out a battered and worn photo.

This man was young, handsome, full of life. His eyes smiled at the photographer—and at the world—full of excitement and the wonder of days to come. On his shoulders sat a young girl, no more than three, her dark hair hanging thick and straight to her shoulders, her face crumpled into laughter. With one hand, the man reached up and held the girl securely in her precarious seat. Both of her hands were wrapped familiarly—and lovingly—around his ears, as though she was using them for handles to balance herself.

She sat staring at the photo, fingering it gently, as the sun went down. The room grew dark, its whitewashed walls and beamed ceiling reflecting first the red of sunset and then the gray of dusk. Through the window, across from the couch where she sat, Pike's Peak turned black with night and lights began to shine in the homes scattered in the foothills above Colorado Springs. Still, she sat unmoving.

"Cindy? You home?" Jon's voice cut through the darkness, its questioning tone bringing her back to the present.

"In here," she said softly. Then, when he had joined her and given her a peck of a kiss, she held out the newspaper clipping. "He's dead."

He took it from her gently and read it slowly. "Your father," he

173

said, but there was no question in his voice. He knew the answer.

Her head was bowed, as though she didn't want to look at him. These days her hair no longer hung straight and thick about her face but was drawn back, fashionably, into a chignon. She hadn't changed from the day, and her grey pinstriped suit, its tailored lines softened by the ruffles of an ecru blouse, was crisp and efficient, the perfect outfit for a lawyer. "The classic upwardly mobile outfit," she had laughed when she bought it.

"Doesn't look anything like the picture you've shown me," he said, still holding the newspaper. He was as blonde as she was dark, as tall as she was petite, and he was dressed in jeans and a sweatshirt. As a veterinarian, he had no need of upwardly mobile clothes.

"No. He changed. I . . . don't know why." She held out the worn photograph, and he took it, staring first at one and then at the other.

"What do you want to do . . . I mean, what can you do?"

"Services will be held on the Johnson ranch," she read. Then, "I'm going to the services." Her eyes were fixed on the mountains out the window.

He wanted to tell her what she already knew—services on the ranch would be private, the family would not want her present—if they knew who she was. If they didn't know, this was not the time to tell them. Instead, he said simply, "I don't think I'd do that."

"I have to . . . I loved him once, and he loved me . . . and he loved my mother."

He wanted to remind her that now her mother and father were both dead, and if she went to the funeral, it would be only for herself. But instead he said, "I'll drive you."

"No. I have to go alone."

She left early the next morning, pointing her Lexus toward Amarillo and the prairies of North Texas. After he'd kissed her goodbye and watched as the car disappeared around the bend in the mesa road, he went back in the house and discovered that she'd taken the worn photograph and her beaded suede tribal dress.

By time the sun was up, she was halfway to Raton. The mountains, now bathed in golden morning light, watched her as she sped down the highway that edged along between the plains and the mountains. By noon, she was in Clayton. In Texline—at last in Texas —she stopped at McDonald's for a salad and iced tea, and by four o'clock she was in Amarillo. If she pushed on, she could spend the night in Henrietta, though it would be late when she arrived. She had no idea whether the town had a decent motel. She stayed in Amarillo, at the Holiday Inn, eating in the dining room and spending the evening staring blankly at the television set while her mind whirled. What would she do when she got to Henrietta?

Next morning, she was up early, on the road, and in Henrietta well before noon. She found a Days Inn with a spacious, clean and absolutely nondescript room. The drapes and bedspread suggested someone had gotten carried away with Santa Fe motifs, but the carpet was an inappropriate rosy beige and the walls were without pictures of any kind.

Cynthia flipped on the television to bring some life into the room and studied the local newspaper she'd bought at the reception desk. Services for Thomas G. Johnson, "respected local rancher and horseman," would be at two P.M. tomorrow at the family ranch; Walker Funeral Home was in charge of arrangements.

"Well, Walker Funeral Home," she said aloud to the empty room, "here I come, ready or not."

Thirty minutes later, she was showered and changed into a two-piece navy blue outfit with a broad white collar. The jacket hung well below her hips, and the skirt ended well above her knees. Swinging a small navy shoulder bag, she was very aware that she was stylishly out of place in this small Texas town. When she stopped at the motel office to ask directions, the clerk—a dumpy, middle-aged man—could hardly speak for staring at her. Cynthia smiled triumphantly at him as she turned to leave.

The funeral home, some two miles from the motel, was a new building which tried to be early American, with white columns and white wooden trim around red bricks, but ended being merely new and tasteless. Inside, it smelled of flowers. Muzak played softly but insistently.

"May I help you?" The receptionist had steel-gray hair, with lots of blue tint in it, and an automatic smile.

"I . . . I'm with Mr. Johnson's family," she said, with barely perceptible hesitation.

The eyebrows went up immediately, and the automatic smile vanished. "Mr. Johnson? Just a moment, and I'll call Mr. Walker."

If she had expected a small and gentle man with a permanent look of compassion painted on his face, Cynthia was surprised by Mr. Walker. He was young—younger than she, maybe thirty—tall, and brusque.

"I'm afraid there's some misunderstanding," he said, after offering his hand for a brief but firm handshake. "I'm acquainted with Mr. Johnson's family, and they're all already accounted for."

Cynthia cocked her head to one side—a habit Jon had been trying unsuccessfully to break because it was, he said, too coy— and looked at this self-assured young man. Then, taking a deep breath, she said, "I'm his daughter."

"Preposterous."

"I could show you a picture . . . but I really don't need to prove this to you." She wasn't sure what it was she had to say to this young man, except that she expected to be counted as family at the funeral.

"No," he agreed, "I don't suppose you do need to prove it to me. But if it's inheritance you have in mind, you'll have to prove it to the Johnsons' lawyer."

Inheritance? The thought struck her as funny, and without meaning to, she filled that silent reception room with deep, rich laughter. "Inheritance?" She laughed again, until he looked totally discomfited.

But his next words startled her. "You're Indian, aren't you?"

She drew herself up. "Kiowa." Then, scornfully, she added, "A breed. My father was white, as I told you."

"Tom Johnson? Impossible!"

"Not impossible. My mother could testify, but she's been dead six years." Her voice, which had shown a hard edge to it, began to soften, "I can testify . . . he was part of my early childhood. I have the picture." But she held her hand firm on the clasp of her bag. She had no need to tell this man.

Suddenly, he was smooth and courtly. "Won't you sit down here, just for a moment? I have something to attend to, and then I'll be right back to finish this discussion."

He nearly planted her in an overstuffed chair, across the huge room from the receptionist, and then, without a backward glance, he strode around a corner and down the hall. The receptionist stared unblinkingly at Cynthia, who smiled back vaguely and wondered what her next move would be. The ringing of a phone solved her dilemma—the receptionist turned to answer it, and Cynthia rose cat-like to follow Mr. Walker.

She walked softly down a long, carpeted hall, past several closed doors. She slowed as she approached an open door.

"No, I am *not* making this up!" Walker's voice was indignant. "I tell you there's an Indian woman here says she's Tom Johnson's daughter. . . . How do I know what she wants? To grieve for him, I guess. Maybe she'll whack her fingers off at the knuckles." He gave a nervous laugh.

Cynthia stiffened, then walked deliberately to the open door. "No, Mr. Walker, I won't 'whack' my fingers off, not even my hair, though my mother might well have done so were she alive today."

Back in her motel room, she flung herself on the bed, her breath still coming in gasps of anger, the tears she held back stinging at her eyes. Gradually she calmed, and soon she slept, to awaken only when the phone rang.

"You haven't called!" Jon was almost accusing. "I . . . well, I knew you were all right, but still . . . ."

"I'm fine," she said, her voice still thick with sleep.

"Have you seen the family?"

"No. The funeral director and the lawyer. He thinks I want Tom Johnson's money."

"I was afraid this would happen. Shall I fly down there?"

She laughed. "To where? Amarillo? It's still four hours by car. So's Dallas. No, I'll be fine. I just have to puzzle it out."

It was his turn to chuckle. "I have faith in you. Call me tomorrow?"

"Yes. The funeral's in the afternoon. I'll call after that."

As she splashed water on her face, touched up her light makeup, and brushed her hair, she was tempted to leave tonight. Why cause difficulty? If her visit was going to alarm a grieving family, why not just leave? Her father would never know . . . and besides, he'd left her years ago. But she had come to bid him farewell, finally, and she would stay to do that.

An inheritance? The insult hit home again, causing a flush to creep up from her neck to her cheeks. It wouldn't be impossible, she thought idly, to document her relationship, to establish a right to an inheritance. Jon would have the money to raise the horses he'd always wanted to, and they could build that house in the foothills . . . . If the Johnson family thought her appearance at the funeral was trouble, she could show them something much worse.

She ate dinner in the cafe next to the motel, sitting in a cracked vinyl booth before a chipped Formica table. The chicken was tough, the salad tired, the coffee strong enough to keep her awake the rest of the night. When the waitress brought her food, she'd asked, "Which way to the Johnson ranch?"

The waitress was grandmotherly—overweight and frazzled looking, with streaked gray hair and a shapeless calico dress but a kindly expression on her face. "Now why would you want to go out there, hon? That's private property, so they tell me." She turned and left quickly before Cynthia could pursue the conversation.

She was staring out the window as she chewed rhythmically on the chicken, hoping that persistence would soften it, and she didn't see the man until he had slid into the seat opposite her.

"Mind?" He wore a leather bomber jacket that hung open enough to reveal a sheriff's badge pinned to his khaki shirt. He was older than he seemed from a distance, with steel gray hair and blue eyes that couldn't hide his amusement.

Probably, Cynthia thought, he's my father's best friend, come to warn me off, though she didn't know why he would be laughing at that. She nodded her head, and he relaxed a little in the booth.

"I'm Sheriff John Benson. The Johnson family lawyer told me you were out here. Told me to look you up and order you out of town."

She opened her mouth to answer, but he held up a hand in the traditional peace sign. "Told him I couldn't do that. Didn't have no legal reason, and I doubted you'd give me one. Now I've met you, I know you won't."

"Thanks."

"I can tell you how to get out to the ranch, 'course like Betty told you, it's private property. My advice is not to do it."

"I need to say goodbye to him, and I want to see where he lived. I want to try to understand about him . . . and why he left me."

"Don't think the answer's out there on that ranch," he said. "Think the truth is that answer's gone to the grave with Tom, and won't none of us know. Question is how important it is to you? Enough to cause a real fuss? To hurt some people that maybe don't need to be hurt? Like his wife and three children."

"Are they good people?"

"Good as most, maybe a little better than lots that have as much money as they do. She's a third wife. First two didn't work out. Guess with your mama that makes four . . . and who knows how many else. No, they're all right. But they won't welcome you. You'll make them afraid, and greedy. You'll bring out the worst in them."

"Was he a good man?" Suddenly it was the question she had come to ask.

"He was, and he wasn't. He was a fine cattleman, knew cattle and horses like few men do . . . but he had other interests. He gambled, and he was what you'd call a womanizer, I guess. He drank some—more than that, in truth—and he gambled more than a little." He looked straight at her, blue eyes unblinking as he delivered what he saw as necessary truth.

"Why are you telling me this?"

"'Cause I think the truth is what you come a long way to find, and you're entitled."

"My father," she said slowly, "was an honest, decent man, a kind and loving man."

"'Spect he was. But this Tom Johnson who died, he wasn't your father. Not any more."

"What changed him?"

Betty brought more of the awful coffee, which Sheriff Benson drank unconsciously. Cynthia held up her water glass to ask for a refill.

"Money, age, disappointment, who knows. But you lost him a long time ago, and I 'spect you already done your grieving."

They sat in silence for a long time, though Benson's gaze never left her face. Cynthia looked out the window, then at him, and suddenly she began to laugh aloud.

"Where were you thirty years ago when I needed you?" she demanded.

"Right here in Henrietta, keeping the peace." He grinned as he got up and left. At the door of the restaurant he turned around and gave her a mock salute.

Smiling, Cynthia returned the gesture. Then she motioned to Betty for another cup of coffee. It would be a long night.

Thomas G. Johnson was buried in a private ceremony on his ranch the next day. Only the immediate family and a few close friends were assembled. The grave site was surrounded with floral tributes, some tasteful, many garish. Among them, though, was a simple bouquet of prairie wildflowers, blooms of blue and gold interspersed with feather-like prairie grasses. And carefully pinned to the tallest blossom was a worn and tattered photograph of a laughing young man holding a young girl on his shoulders.

The Reunion

Women lowered their eyes and clutched their children more tightly by the hand when they walked past her on the street. Men tipped their hats and greeted her politely, but she saw the frank curiosity in some eyes, the open longing in others.

Once, when she was sitting on the verandah of her house on Fourth Street, a man walked by with his son, who looked to be about six and was wearing cowboy boots and jeans, just like his daddy. The two shared the same carefully cultivated bowlegged way of walking. When the father, now directly in front of her, tipped his Stetson and said, "Mornin', Miz Parker," he gave the boy a jab in the shoulder. The boy looked at her shyly and muttered, "Mornin'."

She smiled at both of them, returned their greeting and watched them walk on down the street. They were less than half a block away when she saw the father lean over and whisper in the boy's ear. The boy looked up at his father, puzzled. Then the father leaned down and gave a longer explanation, and the boy turned to look again in her direction. Seeing her watching him, he quickly turned away again, shoved his hands in his tiny pockets, and swaggered off down the street.

She could hear their conversation in her mind:

Father: Son, you know who that was?

Boy: No, sir.

Father: That's Eunice Parker, and you got to always be polite to her.

Son: You told me I got to be polite to everyone.

Father: But Miz Parker, she's special. Her real name is Etta Place, and she was the Sundance Kid's girlfriend.

Boy: Who's that?

Father: The Sundance Kid? Why, him and Butch Cassidy were the most famous outlaws ever in the Old West, robbing trains and banks and no one could catch them. No sir, not a sheriff or a posse or even that Pinkerton detective that trailed them.

Boy: Was she an outlaw?

Father: I suppose she was. She rode with them on those robberies,

181

and she followed them when they went to South America. Yes, son, I suppose she was an outlaw once. But she's respectable now, and you got to be polite to her. It's sort of an honor that she lives right here in Fort Worth, Texas.

Boy: Yes, sir.

A respectable outlaw, she mused. What a way to be known!

But Eunice Parker was respectable. It was 1934, in the midst of the Great Depression, and she ran a clean and proper boardinghouse in Fort Worth, with four boarders—two men who were drummers and gone a lot, selling their wares across Texas, a schoolteacher with owlish glasses who spoke little at meals and spent his entire life, out of school, holed up in his room, preparing his lessons, one presumed. And then there was Mrs. Foster, a widow old beyond her fifty-some years, who spent her time crocheting afghan squares. Eunice thought she must have made enough squares for twenty afghans, but she never saw Mrs. Foster piece them together.

If Eunice Parker was Etta Place and had an ill-gotten fortune hidden away somewhere, it wasn't obvious from her house or her life. Inez Jones, a black woman, kept the boardinghouse clean, changed the linen, and sometimes served as the parlor maid by answering the door and turning away door-to-door salesmen, undesirable people who wanted to rent a room, and men who were just curious. Eunice herself cooked breakfast and supper for her tenants; they got their midday meal on their own. Even that fueled the rumors, for hadn't Etta Place cooked for the Hole-in-the-Wall Gang?

Miz Parker attended church regularly, gave generously to charity, and had lavish treats for the children on Halloween, though few parents allowed their offspring to knock on her door. She drove about town in an old Ford kept immaculately clean by Andrew Wilson, a black man who tended the lawn around her house and saw to her car. She had a good relationship with her banker—he considered her one of his more reliable clients—and a charge account at the grocery. She was, indeed, a model citizen, although no one knew, beyond that persistent rumor, where she came from or why she was in Fort Worth.

Eunice had a few friends but very few. Sometimes she sat on

the verandah with Mrs. Foster and listened as the old woman talked, her crochet hook flying in and out of the latest square. Eunice wondered if she would sometime forget herself and keep going until a square was big enough to be a coverlet in itself.

"I bet you could tell us a lot of stories," the older woman said. (Actually, she wasn't that much older than Eunice, but she looked and acted of another generation.) "I hear rumors at church about you, and from what I hear you have some grand and exciting adventures to tell."

"I've had some grand and exciting adventures," Eunice admitted, "but I don't exactly want to tell them. Thinking about the past makes me sad."

"Well, now, dearie, ain't that true for all of us. Thinking about my dear Albert makes me sad, but gone is gone, and I have to accept that. Don't mean I won't talk about the good times we had together. Did I ever tell you about the day Fort Worth burned? Watched it together, we did. Went right down there to the South Side and stood so close we could feel the heat of the flames."

Eunice thought that sounded foolish, but she didn't say so. Neither did she ask for the story of the day Fort Worth burned. She knew it would be forthcoming.

"Nineteen-hundred-and-nine, it was. And we was married, with a family. But we took those babies and went right down there, just like the young folks did. It was the most exciting thing I ever saw. Burned Broadway Baptist Church, the Presbyterian church, a whole lot of railroad cars, and some businesses and lots of houses. One fireman even died—I forget his name. Newman or something. And you know, standing there right as plain as God, there was one of them fancy no-good ladies from Hell's Half Acre." The minute the words were out of her mouth, Mrs. Foster regretted them. After all, Eunice Parker had practically been the same as those "fancy ladies." She clasped a hand over her mouth and said, "Oh, my dear, I am sorry. I didn't mean nothin'. . . ."

But then the woman would be right back to the subject of Eunice's stories that she could tell, if only she would. "You ever been to South America?" she asked one afternoon.

Eunice smiled at her lack of subtlety. "Yes," she said, "I've been there."

"Heard there was a gunfight down there, twenty-some years ago or more, and two Americans were killed by the local police. But no one knows for sure who the two were."

Eunice considered her reply carefully. Most people assumed the two were Butch Cassidy and the Sundance Kid, but rumors flew that Cassidy had survived, that it was Kid Curry who died with Sundance. Eunice herself believed that and wondered often about Butch—where was he? Would he come looking for her? Sometimes she was convinced he was dead, simply because he hadn't found her. Other times, her imagination took off in flights as her mind's eye saw him somewhere with a new identity, perhaps a respectable businessman, even a banker. The thought made her smile.

"I always heard they were two outlaws, wanted both here and in South America," she told Mrs. Foster.

The other woman sniffed. "Just thought, havin' been there and all, you might know a little more about it."

"Strange you should ask," Eunice said and rose to go into the house.

Eunice Parker sometimes tired of Mrs. Foster. She liked Freddy Wisenhut a lot better. He was the policeman who patrolled the bluff area on foot, overlooking the Trinity River, where Eunice's boardinghouse was located. He'd stop of an evening on his rounds because he knew Miz Parker would give him coffee and pie, if there was any left over.

"How's it goin', Miz Parker?" he'd ask as he forked a mouthful of apple pie. "People treatin' you okay?"

"Sure, Freddy, folks are nice to me." *Just distant and cautious,* she thought.

"You don't have friends, like my wife does. She's always got a gaggle of women to talk to and play bridge with and all that. Keeps her from gettin' lonely while I'm working. Somctimcs I worry about you. Ain't you lonely?"

She laughed aloud. "Freddy, I don't want a gaggle of women about me. And no, I'm not lonely."

"Got memories to keep you company, I 'spect," he'd say.

"Yes," Eunice said, "I do."

And Freddy didn't push it any further, the way Mrs. Foster would have.

Freddy and Mrs. Foster and all the others, even Pastor Robinson at First Methodist, wanted her to confess and tell the truth about her identity, titillate them with stories of the old days with Butch Cassidy and the Sundance Kid and the Hole-in-the-Wall Gang. Eunice Parker wasn't about to do that. She kept her counsel, and she wondered about Butch Cassidy, who and where he was now.

Bill Phillips sat in his office in the Phillips Manufacturing Company in the Spokane, Washington. He stared for a long time at the framed picture of his wife, Gertrude, and their adopted son, Billy Dick, that sat on his desk. Gertrude had tried, God bless her, but she couldn't keep up with him in any way. There was the time during Prohibition when she'd poured all that raspberry wine down the sink, during a party. "It's against the law," she said indignantly, when the hostess of the party complained loud and long, wanting Bill to do something to right this terrible wrong that could not be righted. Etta, he thought, was never bothered by what was against the law. And Gertrude had long since banished him from the marriage bed—"no children ever going to come of it, so there's no need," she had said. *No need?*

Gertrude was always trying to get him to church, when he wasn't at all sure the Lord would welcome him. "It's your duty as a parent," she shrilled, and he shrugged, remembering long rides in the mountains with Etta, when she talked about feeling the spirit of the Lord in the trees and mountain meadows.

"If you made more money with that company, we could send Billy Dick to private school," Gertrude said too often. "You should ask Riblet Tramways for more money for the metal you sell to them."

Etta never worried about money. When they had it, she loved spending it, loved the clothes Sundance bought her, the fancy dinner at the Brown Hotel in Denver; when they didn't have it, she knuckled down, cooked from her garden, and wore Sundance's old shirts.

Bill Phillips knew this wasn't how it should've turned out. He remembered days at Hole-in-the-Wall, when it was the three of them—Butch, Sundance and Etta—against the world. They'd laughed and played and drank and had snowball fights. Sometimes he was jealous of Sundance, but most times he snuck off to see Mary in Caspar. Even then, he carried the image of Etta with him. And now, all these years later, she wouldn't let him go. Etta, with her dark good looks, her frank enjoyment of everything from a neighborhood Thanksgiving supper to a bank robbery, her willingness to be "game," no matter what it cost her in discomfort.

"How did it turn out this way?" he asked himself, a question not new to him.

Suddenly he turned the picture of Gertrude and Billy Dick face down on his desk, rose and went to the door, locking it securely from the inside. Back at his desk, he reached into the center drawer and fumbled for the locked, hidden compartment. Twisting the key to release its contents, he pulled out several papers and a photograph. He unfolded a large, yellowing sheet of paper. Smoothing it with one hand, he read the words: "Reward. Hole in the Wall Gang. Butch Cassidy and the Sundance Kid." He didn't bother with the small type. He knew by heart that they had only offered $500, and he had considered it at the time an insult. Now, no one would pay fifty cents for the capture of Butch Cassidy. All interest in the Hole-in-the-Wall Gang had died out, since everyone assumed Butch and Sundance had died in a shootout in Bolivia.

He stared next at the photograph. It showed a man and a woman in their late twenties, perhaps early thirties. Clearly the man was not Phillips—he was slimmer, shorter, and looked to be fairer in complexion, though photography of the day made that hard to determine. The woman, though, was strikingly beautiful, her dark hair fixed in a roll around her face, her expression serious but ever so gentle. She wore a dark dress with a splash of lace bursting from the front—Butch knew that lace trimming had a name, because Etta had tried to teach it to him, but he never could remember. Pinned on the dress was a lapel watch. Phillips sighed, remembering how important that watch had been to her. He'd bought it for her, when Sundance had spent all his money on a diamond tiepin for himself. Damned selfish Sundance, with that beautiful woman on his arm!

Finally he smoothed out a letter on Pinkerton Detective Agency letterhead. The irony of going to Pinkerton for help pleased him. The letter was dated February 1934, long after Pinkerton's had given up the search for Butch Cassidy. Now the detective assigned to "the Phillips case" wrote that he had located a woman in Fort Worth, Texas, who was probably Etta Place.

Long ago his love for Etta had necessarily come second to his loyalty to the Sundance Kid, and the love had remained hidden. But since Sundance died in that shootout in Bolivia, Phillips, as he called himself, had dreamed of finding Etta. He'd even gone to some of the places they'd been—Hole-in-the-Wall, though he knew better than to expect her to be at that isolated cabin by herself. And San Antonio, where he and Sundance had first met her—but Fannie Porter's sporting house was closed and shuttered, the neighborhood on San Saba Street now respectable. He thought about the Brown Hotel in Denver, which she'd loved, but he doubted she'd be there. In the old days, he would have known how to find her himself, but now he'd had to turn to Pinkerton's. And they'd done the job for him.

He knew he was going to Fort Worth. When Riblet Tramways wanted to send him to Bolivia—Bolivia, for God's sake, of all places!—he had refused to go. Now he'd just tell Gertrude he had to travel to South America for the company. He'd drive to Fort Worth so no railway ticket could be traced—old habits of caution die hard.

He arrived in Fort Worth on a Thursday afternoon in June. It was hot, as Texas June afternoons always are, and Eunice had closed the house against the fierce sun, hoping to retain any morning coolness the house might have captured. When she heard a car drive up, she pulled aside the drape, ever so slightly, and saw a grand and fancy Ford at the curb, dark black, of course, but polished to a sheen. The iron gate at the street squeaked open, and she watched him mount the stairs, a large but still graceful man with a round face, almost as baby-like as it had been in youth, though now he was well into his sixties or even beyond. He was wearing a suit, crumpled by the heat, and he looked uncomfortable but determined. Letting the curtain fabric drop, she called Inez.

"Answer the door, please. I'll be in the parlor, and I'll see our visitor."

Within minutes, Inez announced a Mr. Phillips from Spokane, and Eunice asked her to show him in. Mr. Phillips from Spokane, she repeated to herself with amusement. When he came into the parlor, she stood at the mantel, her back to him.

"Etta?" His voice had a hopeful, soft quality, and she felt sorry for him.

But when she turned to face him, she said, "You didn't die in

Bolivia." It was almost an accusation.

He stared at her. At length, he said, "You're not Etta." And his voice was strong with accusation and, at the same time, weakened with disappointment.

"Why do you say that?" she asked curiously.

"Your hair, it's gray. And your movements . . . they're just not Etta. And your eyes . . . I don't know, but you don't look . . . you're not Etta, are you?" He was almost pleading with her to confirm his worst suspicion.

"I'm Eunice Parker," She said it flatly, definitively. After a moment, she spoke again, "But you know, Etta would probably have gray hair by now. You do. And she might be wearing glasses like I am." She took wicked delight in pointing these things out to him.

"But . . . ." He sank down on the sofa, rolling his hat in his hands.

"What took you so long to find me?" she asked.

"I didn't know where to turn," he said, raising his hands helplessly. "I done research, and I heard all these rumors, and Pinkerton's, they reported to me. . . ."

"Pinkerton's?" she echoed in disbelief. "Why would you go to the people who haunted you to the ends of the earth?" She couldn't believe that he couldn't have found her himself.

He shrugged. "Nobody cares any more about Hole-in-the-Wall. There's no reward. And I tried, but I couldn't find . . . " he hesitated, "couldn't find Etta myself."

She waited, offering neither sympathy nor encouragement.

"It made sense to me," he went on, "that Etta was living in Fort Worth and running a boardinghouse." He gave her a smile, an ironic grin. "Not a house, but a boardinghouse. And . . . and I came to find her." He paused a minute. "I remembered how you . . . I mean, how . . . "

She wanted to go to him, to take his hands in hers and tell him how sorry she was. But she stood, stick-like, in front of the mantel. Instead, she spoke crisply. "Etta died. In Denver. Of appendicitis. Shortly after she came back from Bolivia."

"She did make it back?"

Eunice nodded.

"Appendicitis?"

"It wasn't diagnosed in time for surgery. That was more than twenty years ago. Still, it shouldn't have happened. I don't think she went to the doctor in time."

"Maybe she was afraid to," he speculated. Then he slammed his clenched fist into his other hand. "I . . . I needed to see her."

"I'm sorry," and she really was. "May I get you some lemonade?" It was, she knew, an inane offer.

He didn't want lemonade—he wanted to belt back a drink and cry out to the gods about unfairness. But he said, "Yes. Yes, that would be good. Thank you."

After Inez had served the lemonade and pulled the pocket doors discreetly shut, he looked at Eunice. She had by now taken a seat opposite him.

"Why?"

"Why what?"

"Why do you pretend to be Etta?"

She shrugged. "I don't really. I'm Eunice Parker, which is really my name. But I was a nurse in Denver when she died . . . and she confided in me. It was as though she wanted at the last to tell her life story, to set the record straight, and she wanted to live on in history. I listened, and I took notes in my brain of what she was telling me. I can tell you about the hold-ups at Montpelier and Belle Fourche and Castle Gate. And when she died, I kind of took her identity. Maybe the way to say it is I identified with her. And I guess in Denver I talked about the Hole-in-the-Wall Gang so much that people suspected I was her. I didn't ever correct them."

"Why Fort Worth?" His voice was strangled, as though he was finding speech difficult.

"Sundance brought her here once and promised her a big house here. She loved this city."

"And why do people here think you're Etta?"

She shrugged. "Rumors spread from Denver to Fort Worth."

"And to Washington," he said bitterly. "Why would you let people think that about you?"

She laughed aloud then, the first sign of real emotion he'd seen from her. "That I was Etta Place? That's so simple I can't believe you don't see it. Etta Place is probably the most fascinating woman of the West—everyone wonders what happened to her, why she rode with you, where she came from. She's fascinating because there are so many mysteries about her. Me? I was Eunice Parker, nurse, dull, nobody. Never married, never had a lover. As Eunice Parker who used to be Etta Place, I have all those things, at least in people's imaginations. And I get lots of attention."

"And you fooled me," he said, his tone was still bitter.

"Are you going to tell?" she asked.

"Are you going to tell that Butch Cassidy came to visit you?" he countered.

She wouldn't have to tell. Mrs. Foster and Freddy Wisenhut would assume, and the word would be spread. Eunice Parker's reputation in Fort Worth would go up one more notch.

Before Bill Phillips was even at the end of the block, Eunice Parker was brushing the gray powder out of her hair. She threw the glasses in a wastebasket.

Less than six months later Eunice Parker's boardinghouse went up in flames late one evening. The boarders, including the talkative Mrs. Foster, escaped, but Eunice perished. Fire officials speculated that she had been smoking in bed and had fallen asleep, and gossips in town whispered that it was typical of "her kind" to be smoking in bed.

Pinkerton's reported the death to Phillips, although he was no longer a client. It was, they said, a professional courtesy they extended. For the rest of his life—and it was neither long nor satisfactory—Phillips wondered about the identity of the woman he'd visited in Fort Worth. A nagging doubt bothered him—could she really have been Etta?

The Sign of the Cross

It was a huge banner, an outrageous display of bigotry. Black letters, so crudely drawn they looked to be made by a child and not a good student at that, were splashed across a cloth banner that was at least three feet tall and hung clear across the street, about ten feet high, from light pole to light pole on the south side of the courthouse square, easily read by all who drove around the square. "Pope-loving Jews get out of town before sunset!"

Behind it the Davidson County courthouse, a Victorian limestone building of three floors and tall turrets, stood in contrasting majesty, surveying the small West Texas town over which it held dominion. Residents claimed the Davidson courthouse outshone that limestone bit of grandeur in Fort Worth, some sixty miles to the northwest.

Davidson Chief of Police Jim Lee read the sign at seven that morning when he headed for his office in the courthouse basement. He was tall—well over six feet—and a solidly built man who tended to take big strides, though he seemed to roll a bit when he walked, perhaps a habit from his days in the navy during the Korean War, still not too distant in the fall of 1959. The sign stopped him cold. He ran a hand through his dark hair and muttered, "What damn fool . . . ?" Mentally he made a note to send deputies out to remove the offending banner. It would require ladders and at least two men to keep it from crashing onto pedestrians and cars below.

Glancing up at the turrets above him, Lee thought the round windows looked like eyes peering in disapproval at the banner. With a disgusted shake of his head, he jogged down the steps of a side entrance to the building, greeted Dorothy, the office secretary, with a grumpy, "Mornin'." It wasn't a good start to the day.

"Morning, yourself," she said tartly. "Old Man Gibbons says someone's been after his cows again, one of 'em's missing, and Mrs. Albertson is sure she saw a prowler in her flower bed last night."

"Why didn't she call last night, then? Jones could have taken care of it."

Dorothy and the police chief exchanged knowing looks. Jones never took care of anything he didn't have to.

"Worst thing," Dorothy went on, "is that the mayor is up in arms about speeding around the courthouse square. Wants to talk to you immediately, wants to set up more patrols, make a big splash, if you ask me. But you better call him."

The chief wanted to ask why the mayor didn't get a life, but he went into his office and dialed the phone. The call distracted him, and it would be noon before he asked two of his deputies to take down the blasted banner, roll it up, and put it in his office if he needed it for evidence.

By noon, most people in Davidson had seen the sign—or heard about it.

Sarah Corbin saw the sign much earlier, on her way to Davidson High. She stopped to study it carefully, her heart pounding as the meaning sank in. Her hands shook on the steering wheel, and for a minute she thought she might pass out, though she had never fainted in her life. "To hell with school," she muttered and whipped the Corbin family's aging Pontiac around the square to park it in front of the office of the *Davidson Daily News*. She put the parking brake on, ignored the parking meter, and pushed open the door of the newspaper office.

The newspaper's store-front building was as familiar to her as her own home. The plate glass was covered by Venetian blinds, but the day's front page was always posted on the two windows that flanked a glass door. Once through the door, she faced a chest-high counter on which were subscription blanks, advertising orders, the day's paper, and two ashtrays filled with cigarette butts. Behind the counter were six scarred wooden desks where the reporters, including Cynthia, the so-called society reporter, and Julia, the paper's bookkeeper, held forth. As always there was a phone ringing. She heard Barney Withers answer it with a bored, "Davidson Daily." His expression never changed, so she figured it wasn't the story of the year.

Glass windows without the dusty blinds looked from the office space into the larger rear area of the building which housed the printing presses. Sarah drew a deep breath and smelled the tangy, oily odor of fresh ink. Even early in the morning, the presses were clacking, printing the advertising sections of tomorrow morning's paper. Old Man Smith—no one ever called him anything else!—was picking type out of a box to set a headline, his green eye-shade pulled so low on his forehead that she wondered that he could see. She knew without looking that his fingers were stained with a black that would never come off. The old man always called her "Missy" and wanted to teach her to set type, but so far she'd not been interested.

She pushed through the swinging door in the counter, waved casually at Barney and Julia—everyone else was apparently out for morning coffee—and walked unannounced into her father's office. He was pounding on his old Olympia typewriter, his back to the door. At eight o'clock on a hot Texas September morning, he wore a suit coat, and she knew when he turned to face her she'd see a fresh white shirt and a conservative, small-print, red-and-blue tie. His thinning brown hair was neatly combed away from his face, and she could see the wire ends of the frames of his glasses.

Any other day, Sarah would have viewed him with affectionate humor. Today her voice burst out shrill and frightened. "Dad!"

Turning in surprise, Jacob Corbin said mildly, "Sarah? Why aren't you in school?"

"I . . . I had to come see you," she said, closing the door behind her and almost letting it slam. The office afforded little enough privacy, for it too had windows with no coverings that looked out on the reporters' area in one direction and the printing presses in another. Still, the closed door would keep others from hearing every word of what she had to say.

"Did you see the banner?" she demanded, trying to keep her voice calm.

His puzzlement was genuine. "Banner? What banner?"

"Over the square. Let me tell you what it says." She repeated the message word for word. Then, "It's that editorial you wrote, Dad. And you're the only Jew in town . . . except me. You've got to go. Please, please tell me you will."

The combination of love and fear in Sarah's voice was hard for Jacob Corbin to resist. He reached for his pipe and spent a long time getting it lit, giving himself time to think. He studied his daughter, taking in the blue jeans, the white shirt and the blonde pony tail which she wore low on her neck instead of pulled tight at the back of her head like most high-school girls. All the time, he was thinking, *I won't tell her about the soap message on the office front windows this morning—"Leave town now, Kike Pope-lover."* Aloud he finally said, "No. I didn't see it. And no, I won't go anywhere."

She grinned in spite of herself. "You did see it . . . or you know about it. You've got to go, Dad. You can't put Mom and me at risk like this, let alone yourself. We'll all go to Aunt Ruby's farm at Decatur. That's far enough away." The fear returned to her voice by the end of the sentence.

He smiled gently. "I guess it is. It's almost a hundred miles. Sarah, if your mother wants to go, the two of you may. But I'm staying here."

"Why?" Her voice trembled. Why would he stay here and risk violence to himself, his newspaper, his home?

"That sign doesn't mean anything," he said, his voice filling with scorn. "It's just some coward who won't speak out. And even if I thought there was danger, I wouldn't leave. As a newspaperman, I have to stand by what I've written."

What he had written was a strong condemnation of the Baptist churches, including the church in Davidson, that in the enlightened year of 1959 were warning—no ordering—members to vote against John Kennedy for president of the United States because he was a Catholic. The Baptist position was that the Pope would rule the country if Kennedy was elected and the forces of sin and evil would take over. Besides, Catholicism was a danger to the souls of men.

"I can't go back on my belief that the church and politics *must* be separate," Jacob Corbin said, shrugging. "It's in the Constitution, you know." He looked at Sarah as she stood before him, her hands on her hips, demanding an explanation. "And I don't think that banner you're talking about is serious."

"It looks like a slow fourth-grader wrote it,'" she said, almost a non sequitur. She was fighting for time because she didn't want to tell him that she knew it was indeed serious, that she knew who'd written the sign.

Two nights earlier, when she'd sat in Tom Kittredge's car on a country road outside town, she'd let him put his hand in her blouse, on her breast. As he flicked at her nipple and tried to arouse her enough to let him put his hands elsewhere, he whispered brags into her ear.

"Something big's gonna' happen," he said, his voice low, deep and heavy. "We're gonna' scare us some pope-lovin' commies."

An alarm had gone off in her head. "Like who?" she asked, panting to fake an arousal that she might have felt a moment earlier but that now had been driven away by sudden instinct.

"You know," he whispered, kissing her neck and then blowing in her ear, "them fools that think Kennedy won't turn this country over to the Pope right after he takes the oath of office." One hand still planted firmly on her breast, he let the fingers of the other hand move downward until they were stopped by the waist of her skirt. Tom was undaunted. His reached for the hem of her skirt, whispering, "Come on, let me show you how good it feels." The skirt was long and full, and he had trouble fumbling around in its many folds.

She pushed the hand sharply away and pulled back from him so forcibly that the hand in her blouse slid out almost involuntarily. "No. Take me home."

Tom Kittredge was no small young man, and Sarah knew that if he wanted to force himself on her, he could. She had been flattered—no, ecstatic—that the six-foot fullback had shown an interest in her, but on this, their third date, the thought had earlier flickered through her mind that she didn't like him at all. She had quickly squelched that thought. Every girl at Davidson High wanted to go out with Tom Kittredge, and Sarah Corbin liked basking in his popularity. She wanted to be Tom Kittredge's girl. What she hadn't realized—and was just now thinking about—was what that position might cost her.

He tried one more time, taking her face in his hands and kissing her hard, his tongue exploring her unresponsive mouth. Then, disgusted, he pulled away and lit a cigarette. "Okay, Miss Goody Two-Shoes. It's your daddy we're after. He shouldn't have wrote what he did in the newspaper. He's a kike, an outsider in Davidson, and he ought to be careful."

She swallowed quickly, afraid that whatever she said might turn him violent. She wanted to yell at him, to tell him never never to use the word "kike," tell him that her father was the best person she'd ever known and made him look like cowshit, tell him that he himself *was* cowshit. She even wanted to correct him and tell him it was "written," not "wrote." But she said none of that.

Instead, she said, "In an editorial a publisher can say anything he wants. It's clearly his opinion, not fact."

"Well, his opinion's wrong," Tom said, blowing smoke directly into her face. "Folks around Davidson have put up with his ideas long enough. You'd better tell him that."

Sarah knew only too well what he meant. Her father did not fit into Davidson, a West Texas town of some ten thousand souls, many of them farmers who'd had little schooling. He was a northerner and a Jew. He'd come south from Chicago to Southern Methodist University only because it was the only school that offered him a baseball scholarship. For the first two years most things Texan disgusted him, from the barbecue to the braggadocio, and he swore he'd hightail it back to Illinois as soon as he had that B.A. in journalism in hand.

But then, in his junior year, he met Elsie Thompson, whose father ran the daily newspaper in Davidson, and who herself declared that she could never live outside Texas.

"I have to . . . well, I have to live among the people I've known all my life," she explained in a gentle voice with just a touch of West Texas about it. "And my parents . . . I couldn't leave them and go *north.*" The emphasis on the last word indicated that it was at least as foreign as China and perhaps more so. His Judaism didn't trouble her one bit, though it gave her father tremors when he woke in the early morning hours and realized what his daughter was about to commit to.

"He'll go to church, won't he?" he'd asked her at one point.

"Of course he will," she said with the confidence of the young and naïve. But she was right. He'd attended the Methodist Church with her every Sunday for years, although he vowed he'd never go to the Baptist.

There had been no hand in the blouse, no clumsy attempts to reach under her skirt. It was, after all, 1937 and Elsie Thompson was a good Baptist. But Jacob Corbin was enchanted with this young woman, the first who'd ever kissed him full on the mouth (he blushed to admit that at the age of twenty-one, but it was true).

"We'll live in Davidson," he said. "I'm a journalism major.

Maybe your father will let me work on his paper."

"Oh," she said happily, "I know he will."

And that was just what happened. They married and moved to Davidson, settled into a small wooden bungalow, and Jacob went to work on the newspaper. In time, an only child, Sarah, was born, and then Elsie's father, old J. B. Thompson, decided he'd had enough and turned the paper over to Jacob, albeit with some misgivings about his Jewish, northern son-in-law's ability to please Davidson's everyday folks. Jacob, Elsie and Sarah moved into a bigger house, Elsie stayed home like a good 1950s housewife, and Sarah began to wend her way through the Davidson public school system, always fretting about what others thought, always anxious to be one of the gang, always a worry to her father who longed to see a spark of individualism in her, a willingness to go her own way in spite of the crowd. Up until now, he'd been disappointed. It didn't make him love her any less fiercely.

Jacob Corbin never lost all his northern ways. One was his staunch loyalty to the Democratic Party which, in Texas at that time, wasn't much of a problem, at least until Kennedy announced for the presidency. But of more trouble was his insistence on a clean white starched shirt every morning and another for dinner that evening when he sat down with his wife and daughter to a linen tablecloth and a full and proper meal, pot roast being his preference. He never rode horses, though he'd ridden English-style as a boy, and he didn't shoot dove or quail. He owned no blue jeans, and he didn't chew. In short, Jacob Corbin failed to adapt to Davidson. He expected the town to accept him as he was, and many did. But there were holdouts.

"Grandpa's unhappy," Sarah said. "He doesn't think you should have written that editorial. Says it's bad for business."

"Your grandfather turned this paper over to me, and he knows that. I won't let him dictate to me any more than I will let that fool who wrote on my windows with soap frighten me." There was no compromise in Jacob Corbin's voice, but as soon as he mentioned the soap, he knew he'd made a mistake.

"What soap?" she demanded, angry now. "Why didn't you tell me?"

He shrugged. "I didn't want to worry you. I really didn't know about the banner."

"What did this one say?"

He shrugged again. "Same sort of thing."

"Daddy, please, please, leave town." She ran to kneel before him and grabbed one of his hands.

He stroked her hair as he had done when she was a small child. "I can't, Sarah. I would do almost anything in this world for you. But I can't compromise my integrity."

She stood before him. "I'm scared. Scared for you, scared for Mom."

"It's not that serious," he said, rising to hug her, oblivious of his watching staff. "Go on, now, and go to school. If you need a note for being late, I'll give it to you."

"No note," she said, hugging him quickly and turning toward the door. He couldn't see the tears in her eyes.

She tried to replace her fear with anger. *I don't understand,* she thought as she jammed the gear shift into first. *I spend a lot of time trying to figure out what to do so people will like me, and he doesn't even think about it, doesn't care what anybody else thinks.*

Classes were changing when Sarah walked into Davidson High, an aging yellow brick building that smelled of mold and years of chalk dust. She hadn't even reached her locker when she heard a deep male voice call out.

"Hey, Corbin! Your old man gonna' leave town 'cause of that banner and the lettering on his window?"

She turned to see Don Travis leaning against the wall, watching her with a cynical smile. She wanted to demand how he knew about the signs, especially the soap on the window which had apparently been washed off before many saw it. If he knew about it, he'd been part of writing it.

But Sarah simply shook her head and pushed past him to her locker.

Travis didn't give up. "He better leave, you know. Somethin' will happen, and it won't be pretty."

Don Travis' only claim to fame was that he was Tom Kittredge's best friend. He hadn't made the football team, he was barely passing his classes, and he had to work at the Dairy Queen because his parents lived a barely-get-by hard-scrabble existence in a shack on three acres on the edge of town. It always puzzled Sarah that Tom was so loyal to Don.

"Shut up, Don," she said angrily.

"I'll tell Tom you talked to me that way." There was almost a whine in his voice, and she wanted to ask, "Don't you ever have a thought of your own?" But once again she bit her tongue to keep silent.

The encounter set the pattern for the day. From three or four of the boys, there were stares, sly jabs such as "Where you goin' tonight, Corbin?" and outright threats: "You better get your pa to listen to us." Confused, Sarah ignored them all, not because she wanted to hold her head high and be better than her tormentors but because she simply didn't know what to say beyond begging them to leave her and her family alone. And she knew enough not to beg. She didn't see Tom Kittredge all day, which was unusual because lately he'd hung around her locker between classes.

She thought even her best friends acted funny at lunch, avoiding her eyes, one even deciding to sit at another table. They must all have seen the sign, but they avoided talking about it. They talked idly of the weather, the new principal, how hard physics was and why girls shouldn't have to take it. Finally conversation ground to a deadly silence.

Sarah was about to pack up her uneaten lunch when Melissa Albright breezed up to the table and blurted out, "Guess who I have a date with tomorrow night? Tom Kittredge! What a heartthrob! I am so excited!" She talked in exclamation points and only too late saw Sarah. "Oooh, Sarah, I am sooo sorry!"

"It's okay," Sarah said, rising from the table. "I decided he's not my type." She wondered if she should warn Melissa and decided against it. All the girls would think it was simply sour grapes. As she walked away, she heard Melissa giggle and say, "How could he not be her type? He's every girl's dream!"

"Nightmare is more like it," Sarah said to herself through clenched teeth.

The rest of the day she felt sure the other students at Davidson High were watching her from lowered lids, carefully measuring her movements. What she didn't feel, even from her friends, was support, and that hurt. "They're probably scared," she told herself, "but then, so am I."

What Sarah Corbin didn't know was that her father had gone to see Jim Lee, whose first response was "Banner? Oh, damn, I forgot to get it taken down. Do it right away."

Jacob Corbin raised a hand face out, asking for the chief to wait a minute. "There's more to it, Jim," he said. And he went on to tell of the soaped message on the newspaper office window. Finally, he said, "My daughter's scared. She seems convinced that something really will happen. I don't think so . . . but I can't ignore her."

Lee stared off into space a moment. "Maybe she knows something we don't, something she's not telling."

"My daughter is completely honest with me," the other man said.

"That's what parents always say, Jacob, and I know Sarah's a good girl. But she may be too scared to tell you everything." He thought again, longer this time, forming a plan in his mind. "Tell you what I want you to do. Go home tonight and tell your girl that I promise—I guarantee—your safety. But I want you to promise me something. If you hear anything unusual, anything that makes you suspicious, go to the back upstairs bedroom of your house and *stay down*. I'll be around."

As he left the office, Jacob Corbin's mind was in a tumult. How could he tell this to his wife and daughter without frightening them to death? That the police chief took it so seriously was proof that the danger was real . . . and that he, Jacob, had been wrong.

Sarah sat stone-faced, playing with uneaten food on her plate, while her father told of his visit with Chief Lee.

Elsie, his wife, waved a vague hand in the air, unconcerned. "Why, I've lived in this town all my life," she said in her soft voice. "Nobody would do anything like that. It's silly."

"No, it's not, Mom," Sarah said tightly.

"Well, I'm not going to hide in the back bedroom," she announced, taking another forkful of black-eyed peas.

"For me, please," Jacob said, and Elsie melted. After nineteen years, the two still adored each other.

Sarah went upstairs to study, wishing her parents would go to their bedroom on the second floor to watch TV instead of sitting in the downstairs study, a TV room surrounded with bookshelves and too many windows. She wanted to tell them not to turn the TV on so high that they couldn't hear noises outside.

She stared at her English book, uncomprehending, and the minutes crept by. Every noise outside startled her, and she went to the window several times, only to stare at a peacefully empty street. Once she made a circuit of the second floor, looking out each window to see if she could find Chief Lee. She couldn't.

Hearing her walking around, her father called up, "You okay, Sarah?"

"I'm fine," she said. Her voice was still tight.

Around eight, she stiffened, knowing that what she heard was trouble. Suddenly cars raced down their quiet street, horns blared, and she could hear shouting, though she couldn't make out the words. "Come upstairs NOW," she shouted to her parents.

They came, Jacob looking steely angry, and Elsie puzzled and flustered. "Into the back bedroom," Jacob said.

The three of them sat on the floor in the back bedroom, huddled together, listening to loud yelling and screeching. Then there was a long silence, so eerie it frightened Sarah all the more. After five minutes, she said, "I'm going to crawl to the front window and look out."

"Sarah . . . ." her father protested.

"I can't just sit here," she said. She walked through the inner hallway upstairs, but once she was in her own bedroom, which fronted on the street, she dropped to her knees and crawled to the window. Peering cautiously over the windowsill, she stared and then let out a soft, "Those bastards!"

Behind her, her father said in a shocked tone, "Sarah!" He moved next to her and peered out. Then he said, "You're right. Those bastards."

Below them, on their front lawn, five figures hooded in white were struggling with a huge wooden cross, trying to get it to stand upright in the grass. The hole they had dug wasn't deep enough, and three had to hold the cross, while the other two dug some more.

Before Jacob Corbin knew what was happening, Sarah was on

her feet, bounding down the stairs, flinging open the front door and striding to the edge of the porch. "Tom Kittredge and Don Travis, you get the hell out of here now!"

Just as her father emerged to stand behind her, the five figures all looked up. The three holding the cross dropped it, and it landed on the foot of one, who let out a great howl. Sarah knew it was Tom Kittredge crying out in pain.

"I hope your foot is broken, you sorry excuse for a person," she screamed. "Take that cross and get out of here NOW!"

They stared at her in disbelief, frozen and uncertain what to do next.

"Let's show that bitch a thing or two," said a voice she didn't recognize. "She can't talk to us like that."

"I dunno'." This was Don Travis, Sarah knew. "I . . . I ain't never hurt a lady."

"She's no lady," retorted the first one. "She's a Jew."

Heart pounding, thoughts racing, Sarah stood her ground and said, "Get on out of here!"

Instead of leaving, they began to advance toward the house in a large pack, as though clinging to each other for security. Two of them carried wooden clubs of some kind; one of them was limping, and Sarah knew it was Tom.

"Sarah," her father said, "let's go inside."

"I will *not* let them scare me," she yelled. "You taught me that."

"Then I'm right behind you," he said. He looked around for some kind of weapon and was about to reach for a heavy pot filled with fading petunias.

From inside, Elsie called in a plaintive voice. "What's goin' on? Are you two all right?"

No, Sarah thought, *we're not. We're scared, and we may be about to get beaten. Where is Chief Lee?*

Just then, a loud, authoritarian voice commanded, "Okay, boys, that's enough. Drop your clubs, and drop to your knees." Lee and patrolman Ritchie Glover rounded the corner of the Corbin house. They were unarmed and walking casually, as though going to a picnic.

Where did they come from? Sarah wondered. She wished they had guns.

The five hooded figures stared. Two started to run, but Lee warned, "Don't do that, boys! I know who you are, and I'll get you, only then evading arrest will be added to the charges. Drop to your knees now."

One chanced it and ran. Deputy Glover chased him and quickly tackled him. The other four dropped to their knees instantly.

After the five were bundled into a van belonging to the police department and the cross was dismantled and thrown into the van, Deputy Glover drove away. Sheriff Lee mounted the steps to the front porch, where the three Corbins stood with their arms around one another.

"Missy," he said, looking at Sarah, "you were pretty brave tonight."

"I was pretty mad," she said, looking down in embarrassment.

"You were foolish," her father said, "but I was very, very proud of you."

"Yeah," Lee said, "you should be. You folks want to leave town for a few days, till things quiet down? I got a feeling what we've got in that van is some of Davidson High's finest, from some of the better families in town. Liable to be a lot of bad feelings. And I don't need you to testify at an indictment or anything. I saw enough myself, got the evidence."

Sarah spoke for her family. "No, we're not leaving. I have school, and Dad has a newspaper to get out. And Mom . . . she has to feed us and keep us together."

Elsie ventured her first timid words. "The Klan? We've never had the Klan in Davidson. That's East Texas, not here."

"No, ma'am," he said. "They were just wannabees. Shows you what can happen when folks stir up bad ideas."

He tipped his hat and descended the stairs. The Corbins watched him go for a minute and then turned to go inside. As he walked away, Lee heard Sarah say, "I'm famished. Is there any meatloaf left?"